PALACE OF MIRRORS

Brett Farrell returns to Palm Beach after ten years as a war correspondent, accompanied by headlines proclaiming "PALM BEACH HEIRESS AWARDED PULITZER PRIZE."

She had achieved the pinnacle of success as the foremost photo-journalist of the decade. And yet upon coming home, Brett felt as if she had somehow assumed the identity of a stranger in an alien land.

The scene was now set and brightly lit, as for a troupe of actors gathered together upon a stage. Elaborately costumed players acting out their parts against a backdrop of green golf courses, Mediterranean fantasy mansions and gleaming white yachts basking in the sunlit blue of shallow summer seas.

Once again, the Palm Beach season had begun.

PALACE OF MIRRORS

CHARLES RIGDON

PaperJacks LTD.

TORONTO   NEW YORK

PaperJacks

PALACE OF MIRRORS

PaperJacks LTD.

330 STEELCASE RD. E., MARKHAM, ONT. L3R 2M1
210 FIFTH AVE., NEW YORK, N.Y. 10010

Donald I. Fine edition published 1987
PaperJacks edition published August 1988

ISBN 0-7701-0863-6
Copyright © 1987 by Charles Rigdon
All rights reserved
Printed in the USA

*This novel is dedicated
to the memory of
William Montalvo*

Obsessed by a fairy tale,
we spend our lives searching
for a magic door and a lost kingdom.
Eugene O'Neill—More Stately Mansions

PROLOGUE

PALM Beach had flourished as the gilded pleasure isle of wealth and privilege for over a quarter a century. It was an island paradise where pastel palazzos nestled among tropical gardens, aquamarine swimming pools and putting-green lawns.

What had once been a wilderness of palm-fringed beaches and dense mangrove swamp was now separated from the Florida coastline by symbolic twin drawbridges that insured the privacy of tycoons, millionaire expatriots and captains of industry—a platinum-plated elite given over to the glorification of looks, style and status, whose lineal and spiritual descendants continued to return each Palm Beach season.

They were all members in good standing of Palm Beach's hedonistic social set—those for whom the name of the game was always instant gratification, be it in the bedrooms or the boutiques. Lithe and ageless men and women for whom there could never be a single wasted moment.

That season in Palm Beach was the ultimate moment of truth for all those who had gathered to celebrate themselves. A flurry of famous names and celebrated faces, playing out their games against a lush and extgravagant backdrop, a backdrop that none of them knew would shatter before the season's end.

At that moment in time, Miami was the axis upon which the

Caribbean world turned, and Palm Beach was the gilded playground just sixty miles to the north that drew all comers.

The tropic islands of the Caribbean had become an arc of crisis, seething with political and racial unrest, while Central America was exploding with revolutions nobody could understand or follow. Good guys were bad and bad guys were good. The vast flow of immigration and illegal drug money sweeping northward from the volatile world of Latin American had introduced a legacy of frenzy and tumult into southern Florida. And even amid the elegant seclusion, Palm Beach itself was no longer immune to the air of spectacle and impending chaos.

That season the outer world intruded at last, and it soon became evident that terror and violence could bloom like malodorous tropical flowers behind the high, vine-covered walls. The pirating of luxury yachts by drug runners was an almost daily occurrence in the Florida Straits, and Fidel Castro had opened his jails and mental asylums to send the scum of revolutionary Cuba washing up on the resort colony's pristine beaches like a malevolent tide. With its palm-fringed estates, gleaming yachts, tropic sun and blue gulf stream, the princely paradise had suddenly become a war zone.

The Palm Beach season had only just begun, and yet there was already something tragic and inevitable written upon the winds. . . .

CHAPTER ONE

BRETT knew she was dreaming, but it still seemed so real.

Once again she heard the monstrous roar of the crowds rushing headlong through the streets opf Teheran. The shrill crying of veiled women, and the staccato burst of machine guns. Scene after scene of hate-filled faces, upraised fists and the bloodied torsos of the marching zealots, all forming one angry montage.

Once again she relived it all like an atonement.

The raucous street rallies with hundreds of thousands of screaming revolutionaries. A sea of waving posters displaying the visage of the sinister Ayatollah. Busses and cars torched in the streets, random slaughter in the universities. All the tension and fragmented uncertainty of an entire society passionately embarked upon the course of its own inevitable destruction.

Abruptly the nightmare dissolved.

Now Brett was back at the beginning. Back in Palm Beach, dancing in the grand ballroom of the Royal Poinciana Hotel. She was loved and deeply in love, amid a blur of celebrated faces, moving beneath the Waterford chandeliers, swaying to the strains of "For Sentimental Reasons."

The music played and the Cristal flowed as she and Simon danced within a magic circle. "Love me," he whispered, as flight after flight of exploding rockets rose and screamed outside into

11

*the sky beyond the terrace. It was a spectacular fireworks display
that illuminated all Palm Beach with a dazzling brilliance.*

*Brett looked into Simon's eyes, eyes that were smoldering with
desire. Lips met . . . he pressed against her and she felt his
hardness.*

*Outside, another round of fireworks soared into space, explod-
ing over Palm Beach like rubies, diamonds, and emeralds falling from the sky.*

Then she was alone.

Weightless and drifting.

There was nothing.

Nothing but a silent deathless void.

Brett knew it was only a dream. Yet it had all been real.

"Miss Farrell . . . we're descending. You said to awaken you."
It was a very Southern voice.

Brett started abruptly. Her beautiful teal-blue eyes widened
and stared up at the smiling flight attendant hovering over her.
For an instant she felt panicked as she tried to re-orient herself.
"Where are we?" she finally managed, still sleepy.

The flight attendant smiled. "West Palm Beach, of course.
Can I get you anything?"

Brett relaxed and sank back against the seat. "Yes . . . thanks.
Some black coffee and a shot of brandy."

The woman rewarded her with a dazzling white smile before
retreating back toward the first class galley. Brett felt the eyes of
her neighboring passengers on her. It was the kind of recognition she'd been receiving ever since her arrival at Kennedy Airport earlier that morning.

Brett's coffee and brandy were served along with a copy of
the Miami *Herald*. Solicitously, the flight attendant had folded
it in order to better display Brett's own photograph on the front
page.

PALM BEACH HEIRESS AWARDED PULITZER PRIZE,
the headline proclaimed.

Brett began to scan the print. As she did so, the words began to waver and dissolve, and the numbing sense of unreality that had accompanied her halfway around the globe continued to deepen. By now the past was like quicksand, while the future loomed ahead like some awesome void that threatened to swallow her completely.

Reading the all too familiar phrases about her life and journalistic achievements had anything but a calming effect on her. Instead, Brett felt even more like an imposter. A feeling that was only compounded by the accompanying photograph that had been taken several years earlier in Beirut.

It showed a tall, slender, dark-haired woman dressed in khaki fatigues and holding a motorized Nikon camera against a backdrop of bombed-out buildings. Dark sunglasses were perched high upon her head.

Anyone viewing the photograph would have agreed that hers was an arresting face, with classical, well-bred features. The chin and nose were strong while the widely spaced blue eyes spoke of distance, taut discipline and calm. It was the face of a beautiful but vulnerable woman.

It was an enduring image, and yet Brett felt as if she were looking at a stranger, someone whose identity she had assumed somewhere along the way. The newspaper fell back into her lap. She turned to stare out of the window, fighting back tears.

By now, the Eastern DC-10 had dropped down out of the cloud cover shrouding the Atlantic seaboard, and the sun was quickly dying. Far below, the Florida Gold Coast spread out over the low-lying coastal terrain, while the sound of the plane's jet engines had muted to a whispered scream.

"Oh, God . . . what am I going to find down there?" she said softly. Ten years on the run had only dulled the pain. So much had been left unresolved and the house on Country Club Drive was now full of ghosts. Full also of unresolved passions, bitter enemies and the tormenting mystery of *why*.

Brett felt herself sinking as the plane continued to descend.

Then, as the sun slipped swiftly below the rim of the world and twilight drew fast, she saw the lights of Palm Beach flickering in the distance—a magical kingdom by the sea.

"Home," Brett whispered.

At long last she had come home.

CHAPTER TWO

THE house at the end of Country Club Drive was reminiscent of the country pavilions built at Versailles by the French nobility in the eighteenth century. Marisol was not really large by Palm Beach standards but it was elegantly proportioned, with long green shutters and a circular drive leading up to a pillared portico.

Set amid lush tropical foliage, the porch was as brightly lit as a stage set. After Brett had paid the taxi driver and slowly mounted the widely curving brick steps, the front door swung open. A familiar figure stepped from out of her past. "Carrida," the woman cried, enfolding Brett in her ample embrace. "I have waited so long for this moment. You have come back to us at last."

Brett wasn't exactly sure what it was she had expected to feel but at the sight of Consuelo, the Farrell family housekeeper, she was immediately cheered. Consuelo was a plump, maternal Cuban woman of middle years with darkly braided hair and a warmly welcoming smile. There were tears of joy glistening on her seamless brown face as Consuelo ushered Brett inside the lower hall with its gleaming parquet floors and graceful staircase rising toward the second story of the house.

Brett was overcome. To her immediate right was the formal living room. Her gaze lingered on the fine French furnishings, the Monet, the Manet, the Van Gogh and the Chinese porcelain vases full of freshly cut flowers from her mother's garden. The air was filled with their sweet scent along with the lemony smell of furniture polish. How familiar it all was.

"Oh, Consuelo," Brett said, hugging her once again. "You don't know how many times I've thought of this house . . . about you and the family. It's as if nothing has changed."

Consuelo's smile faded and with great resignation she sighed, "Much is the same, but much has changed as well." She brightened. "Your mother will be down soon. She's still upstairs dressing. But your aunt is here. She's been waiting for you in the library."

"Laura? Here? Well, what do you know. She always hated Palm Beach. I thought she was still living in Acapulco and married to that Mexican banker."

Consuelo shook her head, pursing her lips as if wanting to say more. Then abruptly, she changed the subject. "Perhaps you will want to freshen up before seeing your mother," she advised, reaching out to gently caress Brett's cheek. "You look tired after your long trip."

Brett turned and noticed her reflection in a tall, gilt rococo mirror. "You're right, I look like hell. Mother'll have a fit."

Brett went over to the mirror. Then delving into her voluminous carryall bag, she produced a comb and proceeded to run it through her dark shoulder-length hair. It was badly in need of washing. Her features were ashen and haggard, with dark smudges of exhaustion around the eyes. Brett looked shadowed and distant in the light of the chandelier. It was the first time in ages she had seen herself as she really was.

"I'm afraid you have come home to many problems," Consuelo whispered almost conspiratorially as Brett touched up her makeup with sure but hasty strokes. "Your aunt is here now for many weeks and she and your mother are like two cats, always clawing and scratching at each other."

Brett turned with a questioning stare, but Consuelo had

already picked up her single battered bag and headed up the stairs. "I will start running a hot bath for you," she called back. "You should try and get some rest before dinner, carrida."

At that moment the library doors to her left swung open and a slender bleached blonde came out into the foyer. She was fashionably bronzed and casually dressed in an outfit that had easily cost a grand. Gold bracelets ran halfway up her arms, diamonds the size of rocks twinkled from her fingers. "Brett, darling," Laura cried in her husky, drawling voice, swaying tipsily forward to throw her arms about Brett in a warm, bubbly embrace. "Christ Almighty, kiddo, you gave us a hell of a scare when we didn't hear from you for so long. Your miserable revolution was on the news every night, but we didn't know if you were lost, strayed or stolen until we read about the Pulitzer in the papers."

"Sometimes, I wasn't sure if I was lost, strayed or stolen myself!" Brett laughed. "After a while these revolutionary shoot-outs begin to get confusing. It's getting hard to tell the good guys from the bad."

Laura arched one artfully penciled brow. "Hell, sweetie, you don't want to go to war to find *that* out. I've had the same problem all my life. Marrying six utter bastards in a row ought to be living proof of that."

They both laughed easily together and hugged once again. Then Laura stepped back to measure Brett with shrewdly appraising eyes. "Quite frankly, love, half the women in Palm Beach would absolutely *kill* to be that thin. But you're never going to make the 'Ten Best Dressed List' in that get-up. Believe me, the dyke look is definitely out."

"In that case I might as well have a drink to celebrate my exclusion and my new-found orientation," Brett said, linking her arm through Laura's as they strolled on into the library. "How about fixing me up with a martini while I collapse and try to get my bearings?"

Laura was already well into a shaker of martinis when Brett

slumped onto the couch and studied her aunt more closely. It had been at least a half-dozen years since they had last seen each other and Brett had to admit that something in Laura, something she couldn't put her finger on, had changed.

At somewhere close to fifty, Laura's lithe and willowy figure was still good, with spectacular breasts and lovely features tanned and siliconed to glowing, waxen perfection. Fashionably attired as always, she wore tawny, gold lame lounging pajamas with a bright silk blouse that made Brett's own safari-slack outfit look bargain basement by comparison.

Mostly, though, the change seemed to be in the eyes. But it was more than the poached, alcoholic glitter and the slight tremor of the bejeweled hands pouring the martinis from a sterling silver shaker. Laura seemed jittery and unfocused. For as long as Brett could remember, Laura Gentry had always been sharp as a whip. There had been a time in her life when she had reigned as one of the most highly publicized glamour girls inhabiting the rarified climes of international society.

There had, of course, been a rather predictable series of mix and match marriages to men of varying degrees of wealth and power. And considering Laura's penchant for fast cars, wild escapades and her consuming passion for living life very close to the edge, perhaps it was a wonder, Brett thought, that she had managed to survive at all.

"I'm simply *dying* to hear all about your latest adventures." Laura prattled on as she turned to clatter across the library in high platform heels. "You live such an exciting life. I can't imagine why you decided to come back to this dull burg."

Then, as if summoning a hovering ghost, Laura handed Brett her drink and lofted her own in a toast. "I know your father would have been terribly proud about your winning a Pulitzer," she said, suddenly subdued. "Let's drink to Dwight. He was such a beautiful man. I don't think there's a woman in Palm Beach who wasn't at least a little bit in love with him."

Tears welled up in Brett's eyes, tears she had been dreading. "How . . . did it happen? Mother didn't say in her letter. Only that he was dead."

Laura turned her face away and something unspoken seemed to settle upon the silence. "Dwight was a very sick man," she said, tracing the rim of her glass with one long, brightly enameled nail. "He missed you a lot, Brett. Dwight kept asking for you, right up until the end."

"I knew that he was desperately ill, but that wasn't it, was it? That wasn't how he died?"

Laura took a drink of her martini and said flatly, "He killed himself, kiddo. Your father blew his brains out and didn't even bother to leave a note."

Brett rose slowly from the couch and began pacing. "I should have known," she said. "That was the way he would have done it. How like him to call the game when he was no longer winning." Brett paced the length of the room before pausing before a silver-framed photograph of her father resting on a Chippendale escritoire. "I remember when this was taken," she said. "It was in Nassau. The summer he won the Bermuda Cup Race."

The photograph was of Dwight Farrell aboard the *Lady Brett*, holding an enormous silver trophy. Tanned, smiling and as handsome as any movie star, he stood poised against a sea and sky of brilliant postcard blue. Something had happened between them that summer and nothing had ever been the same. Instead of the father she had worshipped, he had become a terrifying stranger.

After staring at the photograph for several moments, Brett turned quickly away and jmoved to the bar to pour herself another martini. "I guess you knew that my father was violently opposed to my marrying Simon."

Laura nodded, just as sharp staccato footsteps became audible from the outer hall. They both turned to stare towards the closed library door. Brett stiffened as the doors swung open to admit a fashionable fiftyish woman, smartly attired in a floor-length hostess gown of ice blue satin that exactly matched her eyes.

"Well, here are the two of you," Charlotte Farrell said. "No doubt already conspiring behind my back." She was the only one who laughed. "Welcome home, Brett darling. Sorry I wasn't down to greet you but Phillipe was doing my hair. He's simply booked to the hilt during the season, so one must catch as catch can."

Brett moved forward to brush her mother's cheek with a small, cold kiss. They barely touched, while Charlotte was careful not to disarrange the pale champagne-colored hair, artfully swirled and feathered about her delicately boned features.

"Well, now," Charlotte sighed, stepping back to regard Brett with some distaste. "I can see that Phillipe will be working overtime trying to do something with that hair of yours before the awards ceremony. Quite frankly, you're going to need a complete makeover and certainly some new clothes. You're not in Beirut, Teheran or wherever, any more. We have to maintain an image, a . . . ."

"Oh, really, Charlotte," Laura said. "The girl's hardly even in the door and already you're trying to run her life. Don't you ever learn?"

Charlotte glanced at her sister. "Isn't there some cocktail lounge you could be hanging out in, Laura dear? This is *my* home after all. You're only a guest, and a very *temporary* one at that."

Laura shrugged and headed for the door. "On that typically gracious note, I shall take my leave of you ladies," she announced. "I'm sure the two of you have scads of mother and daughter stuff to catch up on. You needn't bother to keep dinner for me tonight, Charlotte. I'm going to be dining out."

"Naturally," Charlotte smiled. "I hope they don't card him or you'll both end up in jail."

"Now, now," Laura said, exiting.

Charlotte settled herself in a high-backed chair, primly cross-ing her legs with a whisper of satin. "Now, Brett, tell me all about your Pulitzer Prize. Everyone here is simply thrilled. What would you think of having some sort of reception before the awards ceremony?"

Brett crossed to the tall French windows and looked out over the illuminated pool and gardens. "I'm seriously considering having Brad Harroway stand in for me at the awards ceremony, mother. To be perfectly honest, I just don't feel up to it."

"What do you mean you don't feel up to it?" Charlotte said, genuinely shocked. "Darling, you must be suffering from shell shock. The press have been phoning here for hours wanting you. Major press. All the networks. *Time, Newsweek, U.S. News*. . . Need I go on? I thought that proving you were the best at what you do was what all this galavanting around the world was all about. One can't just cancel celebrity, you know."

"I need some time to myself," Brett said. "These past few months haven't been easy. There're still a lot of things I have to sort out. It's going to take some time."

Charlotte Farrell's facial muscles tightened beneath her per-fectly lifted mask. "And I suppose you think it's been a bed of roses around here?"

"I know it must have been very difficult, mother . . ."

"Difficult?" Charlotte repeated. "That was the very least of it. As if your father's death wasn't enough to cope with, Laura has been making a perfect spectacle of herself. She's dead broke, falling down drunk most of the time and throwing herself at any man who'll give her a tumble. Everyone's talking and, quite frankly, Brett, it's beginning to take a toll on me."

Charlotte recited Laura's amorous escapades with a local tennis pro at the Golf and Tennis Club, a pastry chef from the Breakers Hotel, and a parking valet at La Cigale, Palm Beach's swinging new disco. The list went on and on.

"Mother," Brett finally cut in. "I don't give a damn what Palm Beach is saying about Laura. She's an adult and can screw half the county if she wants. It doesn't matter. What does matter is you didn't tell me that father killed himself. I had a right to know."

For several moments Charlotte was silent. Then, "You know he had a very serious drinking problem. The doctors said he had cirrhosis of the liver, but that didn't seem to keep him from guzzling a fifth of Scotch a day. I wrote to you months ago saying that your father was a very sick man, Brett. You didn't make the slightest effort to come home and see him."

"I happened to be on assignment halfway around the world in the midst of a revolution," she shot back. "That's the *real* world out there, mother. Some of us have a job to do."

For a moment, Charlotte examined her freshly manicured nails with elaborate concern. "Well, I'm sure that your father would have understood perfectly," she observed. "Even if I don't. He always did tend to forgive you everything, didn't he, Brett? It's no secret that you were the only one he ever really cared about. Besides himself, of course. Selfish bastard."

Brett suddenly felt completely drained. "Obviously we're getting nowhere with this discussion," she responded wearily. "Now if you don't mind, there's something I want to see on the evening news."

Brett glanced down at her watch and then crossed the room to switch on a large, oversized Sony TV. Her father had loved his library so much. On the plane she had read in the paper that a local television station was planning to rebroadcast her prize-winning documentary on the Iranian revolution. The screen filled with life.

The roaring, chanting crowds. The piercing wail of veiled women and the sharp staccato bursts of machine gun fire. A chilling montage of random violence, hate-filled faces and burning buildings. A blazing firestorm of death and destruction with a background soundtrack of exploding rockets. The grim rattle of small arms fire and the frantic tread of innumerable feet carried along by fear and flight.

Brett had managed to capture something. Something inexplicably poignant that gave her photography an intensely haunting quality. A unique balance between stark beauty and utter horror. An aching sense of alienation from the past and dislocation from the future that denied any emotional commitment beyond the here and now.

For Brett, watching the documentary unfold in scene after scene was like reliving her own worst nightmares. Visions remained etched upon her consciousness with shocking clarity: the curiously detached loneliness of telephone wires hanging slack and silent from splintered poles. A scabrous dog howling beside a burning house. A lifeless hand poking from beneath a pile of rubble with a cheap wristwatch still counting the minutes when time had ceased to matter.

The documentary was only halfway through when Charlotte Farrell rose from the overstuffed chintz-covered couch and crossed the room to switch off the television set. "Brett, darling, forget the past. It's all behind you now. You're home. Relax. Unwind. Besides, no one in Palm Beach wants to listen to bad news, especially me."

CHAPTER THREE

Brett spent the days following her return to Palm Beach trying to moor herself to some kind of reality. The weather was glorious and during the long sun-drenched afternoons she languished by the pool. High above, the Florida sun was baking her skin to a glistening golden hue. It seemed to be enough to simply exist, to allow her senses to absorb the elements while a cool offshore breeze rustled the palm fronds. Sometimes, when she dozed beneath the sun, the barriers dropped and the past crept in . . .

Photographing nature was how it had all begun. Dwight Farrell had given her a camera, a Brownie, for her eighth birthday, after Brett had begged for one for months. By the time she was twelve years of age, she had filled fifteen albums with Brownie snapshots, most of which had been taken in the wildlife sanctuaries of southern Florida, where her father often took her as rewards for good behavior.

Yet, for the following decade, Brett's photography remained little more than an avocation as she went about the business of growing up as the only daughter of one of Palm Beach's wealthiest and most prominent families. Brett had the right schools, a coming out party which Dwight Farrell proudly spent $100,000 on, and finally a reporter's job for the Washington *Post.*

For Brett, along with wealth and lineage, there had always been a keen intelligence, exceptional talent and the endless, restless ambition to succeed. With her slender model's figure and cool good looks, she could have pursued any number of far more glamorous careers, but early on she had decided not to rely on either her appearance or family name to get what she wanted, and subsequently had always been in a hurry to catch up.

Fashion never interested her, and she seldom wore makeup. Dressed as casually and comfortably as possible, Brett worked very hard to learn her craft as a cub reporter during those early years. Her peers at the *Post* recognized her talent both as a reporter and a photographer, and before long Brett was swept up into the highly competitive world of photojournalism.

Thriving in her expanding career, she had, at least in the beginning, little time for romance. But during the anti-war protests of the sixties, she became deeply involved with a firebrand activist spearheading the "Stop the War" movement. It was a passionate love affair from the very beginning.

Simon Lanier. Brilliant. Good-looking. Incredible in bed. Simon Lanier. The exact antithesis of everything Brett had been brought up to represent.

Brett loved him for it.

Her parents, naturally, hated him. In spite of their opposition, Brett and Simon's engagement was finally announced in all the papers. The war was winding down in Southeast Asia, Simon had graduated with honors from medical school, and despite strong reservations, Brett's family finally accepted the fact that she was fully determined to marry the son of a Jewish hardware store owner in West Palm Beach who had some very revolutionary social ideas.

Then, days before the wedding, word was received that her brother, Laddie, had died in Vietnam. It was a devastating blow. Brett decided to call the wedding off. She quit her job in Washington, packed a single bag along with her camera equipment and astounded everybody by taking off for the swamps of Da Nang.

It took Palm Beach years to stop talking about it.

Brett had arrived in Vietnam as a freelance journalist, but very quickly managed to make a name for herself as one of the few women covering the war who refused to stay put in Saigon. She traveled the country by any means at hand and, with her camera, always found herself in the very thick of each battle.

It was while accompanying a search-and-destroy mission into Cam Song that Brett managed to record one of the most unforgettable scenes of the entire war.

What all Americans saw on their T.V. screens, over Sunday dinner, was a pot-smoking, boyishly brutal and decidedly combat-hardened company of marines casually setting fire to a thatched-hut Vietnamese village with Zippo lighters. Livestock was slaughtered and the innocent villagers brutalized in this all-too-graphic image of the war's mindless cruelty and ferocity.

Accompanying the video footage was Brett's on-the-spot commentary with the village in flames around her. *The Rape of Cam Song* flashed across American homes like a whiplash of moral outrage against the soldiers and American policies. Official condemnation of Brett's portrait of America's sons at war was swift and unsparing.

Then, in 1971 she won the Journalist of the Year Award for the Cam Song coverage and found instant international fame. She remained in Vietnam long enough to photograph the victorious Viet Cong tanks breaking through the gates of the presidential palace, then she moved on to Cambodia where the Khmer Rouge were steadily advancing upon the capital of Phnom Penh in the wake of the American retreat from Southeast Asia.

Finally, she returned to the States and published a photo-essay book, *A Camera Goes to War,* to wide critical acclaim and strong sales. Then, when the Yom Kippur War broke out in 1973 she was once again in the midst of the fighting, accompanying the Israeli troops as they crossed the Suez Canal into Egypt. Her photographs were published around the world. She went on to cover the dismemberment of Lebanon, the revolutionary activities in Central America and finally the last bloody months preceding the fall of the shah of Iran.

She had been everywhere and seen it all. During the long, sun-drenched days beside the pool at Marisol, she tried without success to add it all up into some kind of coherent sum, but the totals were never right. Something was missing.

Invariably, however, there was a snapshot quality about the events of her life, as if she were only recalling them in order to award a caption and was afraid to linger over deeper meanings. She was wary of what she might discover in examining her father's long descent into alcoholism and suicide. And she was unwilling to accept her own guilt in the enduring and lacerating conflict with her mother. Finally, she was unable to dwell on the panic and flight that signaled the end to her love affair with Simon Lanier.

In retrospect, she had to admit that her life had always been a very precarious balancing act. She had been driven by the need to experience firsthand what most observed from a safe distance. The taboos had always been there to be broken, the limits extended beyond the point of no return and the unknown made real.

And in that, as in so many other ways, she was very much her father's daughter.

Dwight Farrell still seemed to be everywhere at Marisol. So often Brett had the feeling upon entering a room that he had just left it. At night, she imagined she heard his steps in the hall, or heard his voice somewhere, perhaps in another room.

He was everywhere, and whenever Brett looked into a mirror she saw his eyes staring back at her. Ironic. His legacy had been her eyes, intensely questioning and with an extraordinary depth and clarity. But the legacy of Dwight Farrell continued to be an entirely pervasive influence. In that, nothing had changed over the past ten years. He had always managed to play the role of Prince Charming at all the right times, while Brett was the enchanted princess cherished above all others, including her mother. Together they stood apart from the world around them, sharing intimacy and joy to the exclusion of everyone else.

It was all innocent enough during her childhood years, but as Brett began to blossom into a young woman, their relationship began to undergo a subtle change. Her father had always been her closest friend and confidant, the one with whom she shared dreams. Together they swam, played tennis, rode horseback and explored a magical world that was surfeited with pleasure and gratification. Nobody in the world, Brett thought so many times, was lucky enough to have a father like hers. He was the best anyone could have, and she was delighted that there was only one Dwight Farrell in the world because he was hers.

There were, of course, a variety of young men buzzing around her throughout her teenage years. They were often strikingly handsome and well-muscled young men who were all very much enamoured with Brett. But sexually, Brett had always managed to maintain a certain crucial distance. Where Dwight Farrell was concerned, there was never any competition, and their relationship was one of absolute oneness, of confidences shared and total trust.

Each summer they set sail with Charlotte Farrell aboard the *Lady Brett* to cruise the islands of the Caribbean Sea. Father and daughter sunbathed upon deserted white sand beaches, abandoning themselves to sun and sea, while Charlotte shopped the local ports.

Charlotte had, of course, bitterly resented the closeness of Brett and her father, and the time came when Charlotte simply withdrew beyond a screen of icy politeness. A discarded wife and bitter enemy unbeknownst to Brett, her glacial poise seldom betrayed the razor's edge of her enmity.

Then Brett met Simon Lanier. Theirs had been a passionate and all consuming love affair from the very beginning, and the one who lost out, she would realize much later, at least in his own eyes, was her father. The relationship with him was never again quite the same. Brett had grown from Daddy's girl to Simon's woman. Dwight never forgave her.

Brett didn't want to think about the past anymore, at least not now. She had spent the morning lying in a poolside lounger while the sun poured down on her. She felt completely relaxed in the simmering hush of noon. There was no need to do anything. No plans to be made or appointments to be kept.

In a little while she would dive into the pool and the cool water would revive her before lunch was served. Consuelo would bring it out, as instructed, on their terra-cotta tiled terrace. For the moment, it was enough to allow her mind, her senses and her body to absorb the elements: the sun burning hot upon her flesh, the gentle tropic breezes dusting her limbs, the pure sea air slowly rejuvenating her lungs from her foreign travels.

Still, she could not seem to banish thoughts of Simon or the first time they had made love together. Brett had relived it all so many times . . . speaking to his lips inflaming her without words, but with warmth and urgency, his body over hers, protecting her from everything except his showering love. As they melted together, there came a moment of both betrayal and surrender, when all the barriers she had thrown up to protect the relationship with her father disappeared like the morning mists upon the sea.

Brett stretched and a shiver ran through her. She felt a warmth between her legs that did not come from the sun.

"I hope I'm not interruptiung some delicious sexual fantasy, darling," Laura purred out of nowhere, jolting Brett back to the present. Brett lifted her head to find Laura standing on the pool terrace with a martini glass poised in her hand. Her face was largely obscured behind huge, dark, Jackie O sunglasses. She lazily fanned herself with a big, floppy brimmed straw hat embossed with cabbage roses. Her blond hair was bound up peasant-style in a bright scarf, while she gave every appearance of having been poured into the tight, white slacks she wore along with a flowered silk halter. The halter threatened to spill her breasts at the slightest provocation.

Brett sat up and automatically reached for a cigarette. "You might try daylight more often," Brett said. "I think you'd be amazed how many people get up before noon."

Laura graced her with a tolerant smile. "Not really anyone I'd be interested in, darling. I definitely come alive well after the sun goes down."

"I think I heard something to that effect," Brett murmured. "I've listened to little else ever since I got home."

Laura's laughter was only faintly amused. "Surely you know by now that bitchy gossip is the *raison d'être* here on the magic sandpile. It's all such a bloody bore. Why don't you get dressed and come shopping with me? Then I'll take you out to lunch and we'll dish. You've been away a long time, Brett darling. I think you've got a few surprises in store."

While the northern part of the continent remained frozen in the icy grip of winter, Palm Beach luxuriated in eternal spring. Laura had arranged for a limo to be at their disposal for the afternoon shopping expedition. As they drove through the sun-splashed streets, it was abundantly clear that the Palm Beach season was well under way.

For the past two months the rich and the beautiful had been flocking to the exclusive resort colony from all over the globe. It was a world apart from any other, one with its own rules and rituals as well as the unwritten understanding that it didn't really matter what you did, just as long as you did it with style and flair.

As always, the American aristocracy of wealth was in the vanguard, surrounded by the ubiquitous Eurotrash with their obscure titles and impeccable manners. The French, Italians and flamboyant South Americans had phenomenal fortunes and exotic tastes. There was tennis, golf and polo by day, while by night they gathered to dine in all the chic restaurants and dance until dawn, often ending up in a bedroom somewhere on the island with someone they only vaguely remembered toying with hours before.

The weather was spectacular, with burnished golden days and balmly tropic nights. Waterskiers sliced wakes behind sleek high-powered Riva speedboats, while multi-colored sails careened across the shining expanse of Lake Worth, past flotillas of gleaming yachts and mile after mile of palm-fringed estates where sunbathers basked beside aquamarine pools.

A silver stretch-limousine awaited Laura and Brett in the drive of Marisol. While Laura coyly declined to identify their benefactor, Brett quickly noticed the wet bar was stocked and a chilled martini shaker was filled and ready to be poured, which Laura promptly did. "Cheers!" she gushed.

"Cheers," Brett said quietly.

"Oh, come on, Brett, Auntie Laura's not a lush, just a lot of fun!"

Brett laughed and settled back in the seat.

They drove along South Ocean Boulevard past mansions bathed in soft pastels behind manicured lawns and topiary hedges, with the Atlantic Ocean on their right and the historic Breakers Hotel just beyond a curve.

Beyond the famed hostelry's verdant grounds was Poinciana Way with its sidewalk cafes and upscale collection of trendy shops. They turned west to cruise past Moorish castles and

Tudor estates nearly hidden behind stone gatehouses and sculpted cypress before swinging right onto Worth Avenue, the most elegant and expensive shopping street in the world.

The sidewalks were jammed with well-heeled shoppers in resort wear with lots of gold chains and all the right labels. Dusenbergs, Bentleys and Rolls-Royces lined the avenue along the art galleries, boutiques and pricey emporiums that wouldn't dare to display a price in their windows. If you needed to know, you probably couldn't afford it anyway.

While the chauffeur awaited them at the curb, Laura set forth on a nonstop buying spree that left Brett astounded by its sheer momentum. She made purchases that she obviously didn't need or even particularly want, with frequent visits to various ladies' rooms from which she returned glittery-eyed and flying high on God knows what, only to plunge once more into the fray.

It started at Bonwit's with two of Azzedine Alaia's original designs. A slender, silky sari-like gown that lightly skimmed her figure and a hip-hugging pasha-pajama outfit tapered to the ankles. Then, almost as an afterthought, five silk blouses by Norma Kamali and twelve expensive Valentino scarves, all in different colors.

Twenty minutes later, Laura exercised her passion for shoes by purchasing ten pairs of Italian imports at I. Miller, and then it was only a brisk walk up the street to Gucci where she bought an expensive leather outfit and several handbags before sailing into Magnin's to casually select a $40,000 sable coat.

As the uniformed chauffeur plied back and forth with his arms full of packages, Laura swept like a whirlwind through one boutique after another: Givenchy, Bill Blass, Saks and Cartier, leaving open boxes, reams of tissue paper and order blanks strewn at random along with clusters of whispering browsers staring in disbelief.

"My God, but I do love spending money," Laura said when

they finally returned to the limo and started off for a late lunch at La Scala.

"Well, you certainly must have established a new speed record for buying up Worth Avenue," Brett said. "Which is rather a surprise since mother says your ends are scarcely meeting."

Laura's brittle laughter was somewhat unsettling. "In spite of all those credit cards I was flashing today, the hard truth is that your Auntie Laura hasn't got a blessed kopek to her name. I'm flat busted, kiddo. The wolf is definitely at the door."

"I thought your ex-husband left you with a divorce settlement the size of Nebraska," Brett said. "It's a little confusing trying to keep track . . . but wasn't he the Mexican banker?"

"What he was, dear heart, was a crashing bore and impotent to boot! If truth be told, Ramone was limp as a soggy taco . . . at least what there was of it."

Laura nonchalantly tapped the ash off her cigarette. "In any case, that's all *agua* under the bridge. I only came to Palm Beach this season on a hunting expedition and I'd better find a replacement for the Frito Bandito before all those bills come due. I mean, after all, darling, it's probably going to be my last time out on a very fast and slippery track, so I've got to look my best."

Brett's laughter was low and amused. "From what I've been hearing about your pastry chef, parking valet and young Adonis at the Bath and Tennis Club, I should think that your chances of striking gold aren't all that terrific. I can't really see you getting along on minimum wage."

Laura shrugged and withdrew her compact from her bag to touch up her makeup in the tiny gold-encased mirror. "Even the most dedicated huntress requires a certain amount of recreation," she chided. "You know what they say about all work and no play."

"Anyway," she said, snapping her compact shut with a definitive click, "I have my eye on someone who just might do the trick. His name is Maurice. Rich as God, absolutely *gaga* about yours truly and possibly, hopefully, not too far from terminal. We're going to the Bahamas in a couple of weeks and I may just come back to bounce this town on its ear."

"According to the version circulating, you already seem to be giving *Debbie Does Dallas* and *Deep Throat* some pretty heavy competition. At least, according to mother."

Laura sighed theatrically and lifted her eyes heavenward. "Your mother is an extremely tedious woman with no real sense at all of true hedonism. But not to worry. Nymphomania doesn't necessarily run in the family. I'm perfectly willing to take all the credit for improving relations with the local working class. After all, my pet, social intercourse of one sort or another is what the Palm Beach Season is all about, *n'est pas?*"

With a sly wink, Laura leaned close to whisper *sotto voce.* "What would you say if I told you that the newly widowed ice queen is herself engaged in a merry game of catch me-fuck me with a local man-about-town?"

Brett was clearly astonished. "Mother having an affair?"

"Rather difficult to believe, I'll grant you," Laura conceded. "Charlotte was practically *virgo intacta* when Dwight died and I imagine she thinks that the way to use a birth control pill is to clasp it firmly between the knees."

"This has got to be some kind of joke," Brett laughed.

"It's no joke and not even much of a secret. Everybody's talking about it."

"You have to tell me who he is."

Laura assumed an air of deliberate mystery, prolonging the suspense. "You'll be finding that out for yourself soon enough," she whispered. "I won't say any more except that if poor, naive Charlotte had any idea what this guy's game really is, it would stand her hair on end."

At that moment the limo pulled up in front of La Scala and

the parking valet hurried across the sidewalk to swing open the rear door with a welcoming smile. He was over six feet tall, broad shouldered and beautifully muscled beneath his Lacoste shirt and tennis whites. "Hi, Laura—I mean, Mrs. Gentry. Good to see you."

"Eddie, darling," Laura gushed, as he helped her alight onto the sidewalk. Then leaning close to press her silk-haltered breast against the young man's well muscled arm, continued, "I want you to meet my niece, Brett Farrell. She just hit town and is bored to stone. Why don't you give her a call at Marisol and see if the two of you can't get something going. You already know the number . . ." she teased, cupping his face in both hands and planting a kiss on his lips.

Brett flushed and quickly followed Laura through the glass doors into the restaurant where the maitre d' was hurrying toward them. "So nice to have you beautiful ladies with us today," he said with a dazzling white smile. "La Scala is *à votre service.*"

"Thank you so much, Michel. My niece just arrived in Palm Beach and I wanted to show her where the action is."

Brett nudged her sharply in the ribs in order to forestall any further matchmaking.

"I'll have my usual table and you can put the bill on my sister's tab, *s'il vous plaît.*"

After giving Brett the onceover from head to foot and missing nothing in between, Michel offered a courtly bow and led them past the bar and across the crowded restaurant, with Laura nodding, smiling and occasionally waving along their route of passage.

The decor of La Scala was righly evocative of the Art Deco era: all etched glass, chrome and softly muted lighting with Lalique shades. There were long-stemmed roses on all the tables and drawings by Erté and Beardsley on the walls. There seemed to be attractive young men in abundance. Handsome, sleekly proportioned, suavely mannered and very much in attendance on the languid and bejeweled ladies busy being seen at the best tables.

The bell-like tinkle of silver, crystal and fine china and the low murmur of luncheon conversation grew somewhat hushed in their wake. Brett had the distinct impression that there was something up as diners leaned close to nod and whisper.

Laura, however, appeared to thoroughly enjoy the stir their entrance was causing. She was like an actress intent on convincing every male in the room that she was performing for him alone, exuding a certain throwaway glamour like an exotic feral scent.

The tuxedo-clad head waiter was immediately beside the corner banquette table where Michel had seated them with two attendants hovering nearby. "Good afternoon, ladies. Would you care for a cocktail before ordering lunch?"

"Just bring me a double martini," Laura instructed, batting her long false lashes. "And forget the menu. We'll both have the filet mignon rare with a Caesar salad. She glanced toward Brett for confirmation. Then, after receiving an assenting nod, she went on to add, "And, oh yes . . . bring us the crêpes for dessert and a bottle of your best wine."

"Madame?" the waiter questioned, turning his attention to Brett. "Something for you to drink?"

"I'll have a gin Bloody Mary and a sharp knife to do a little bloodletting, s'il vous plaît."

"Pardonnez moi?" he questioned, clearly puzzled.

"Just a little private joke," Laura cut in. "My niece has a peculiar sense of humor."

As soon as the waiter had departed, Brett turned on Laura and fixed her with a look. "Just for starters, why in hell did you tell that muscle-bound car jockey to give me a call? Teenie-bopping beach boys are not my favorite bill of fare."

Laura occupied herself with taking a cigarette from her case and lighting it with a practiced flick of her gold lighter. "Just trying to spread the wealth," she responded, exhaling twin plumes of smoke. "If truth be told, Brett, a good healthy lay would no doubt do you a world of good. You really have to stop brooding around the house and get out on the town. Besides, I can vouch for our boy Eddie. He's hung like a horse, utterly indefatigable and hasn't got the brain of a retarded gerbil. Trust me, oh naive one, it's a winning combination."

"Now, as for Michel," she went on, "he's a different bag of tricks altogether. Of course, he's only *comme si, comme ça* in the sack but gang busters when it comes to romancing a lady with flowers, dancing, sweet talk and. . . ."

"Thanks, but no thanks," Brett cut her off abruptly. "The last thing I'm looking for is romantic complications. I'm home for a rest and I have no intention of cruising the local night spots looking for cheap thrills."

"You wouldn't still be hung up on Simon Lanier, would you?" Laura said. "He's still around and very much the confirmed bachelor, although not exactly celibate from what I gather."

Their drinks were served and Brett took a long pull on her Bloody Mary before responding. "I haven't seen or heard from Simon in ages. And even if I were interested, I don't suppose he's ever forgiven me for what happened."

"Quite frankly, Brett, I think you missed the boat on that score. Simon is a very successful surgeon now, still gorgeous and from what I hear one of the most eligible bachelors in Palm Beach. A girl could do worse . . . and you aren't exactly getting any firmer! Eventually, you're going to have to give up attending all those silly wars. If you don't, who's going to want you if you're a burntout wreck?"

"As always," Brett laughed, "you have a vivid, if overwrought, imagination. But if you want to know the truth, I've been seriously involved with someone for many years now. The only problem is that we just never seem to be in the same place at the same time."

"Are you sure that's the only problem?" Laura asked, exercising her finely tuned sense of perception.

"There are other complications," Brett admitted. "Brad happens to be very married and he adores his wife and children. The truth is, we only see each other when it happens to coincide with his schedule."

"Sounds like a no-win situation to me," Laura observed. "Listen, what really happened between you and Simon? I was all set to be matron of honor at your wedding when you suddenly cut and ran."

Thoughtfully Brett traced the rim of her glass. "I'm not really sure what happened. It was such a confused time in my life. I was pregnant with Simon's child when I miscarried in Nassau. Laddie had just been killed in Vietnam and somehow none of it made any sense any more." Brett shrugged and took a long drink. She automatically reached for a cigarette and a shadow passed across her face. "There was a terrible row with my father. You know how he hated the idea of my marrying Simon. He got drunk . . . knocked me down a flight of stairs and so I lost the child. When I got out of the hospital, all I wanted to do was to get away. So I shipped out to Vietnam. At the time it seemed to make about as much sense as anything else."

There were tears in her eyes as Brett glanced over the rim of her glass to see an extremely attractive couple being shown to a table on the other side of the room. Brett blinked hard, staring in disbelief at the tall, darkly handsome and expensively dressed figure slipping into a corner banquette next to a beautiful willowy blond. The woman had the look of one of those coolly confident debutante types so often featured in the *Shiny Sheet* social columns. The perfect Dresden features. The fashionable lean body and silky flaxen hair that hung in shining waves about her evenly tanned shoulders. And the man . . .

"Oh, God . . . Simon."

"Well, speak of the devil," Laura said beside her. "And just when the story was getting interesting. "It would seem, Brett darling, that the gods have spoken."

"I have to get out of here," Brett said, suddenly irritated by her drunken dish of an aunt, and desperate to leave.

Simon Lanier looked up to casually scan the room. Their eyes met and held across the crowded luncheon tables. A freeze-frame in time, bridging all the intervening years with a single glance.

Simon smiled that old familiar slightly lopsided smile and something seemed to melt the ice age that had held her in thrall for so long. Was it really finished? Brett wondered. Had it ever really been over between them?

CHAPTER FOUR

CHARLOTTE Farrell was famous in Palm Beach for her style of entertaining. Charlotte had insisted on giving what she termed "an intimate little soirée" to celebrate Brett's homecoming. But descending the staircase on Friday evening, Brett felt like an actress arriving on stage well after the performance had already begun.

Still, she had dressed carefully that evening and the overall effect was simple and to the point. A minimum of makeup, a modest assortment of her favorite keepsake jewelry and a floor-length black sheath that, while many seasons out of fashion, still managed to fit her slender figure like a glove.

As she reached the lower hall, Brett was met by a warmly convivial mix of music, laughter and conversation drifting out of the living room, while the smartly uniformed members of the catering staff swept past bearing trays of Louis Roederer Cristal and a tempting array of hors d'oeuvres. The party was well under way but Brett wished she were anywhere else but there. She had always felt exceedingly uncomfortable among the Palm Beach old guard. All these expensively well-preserved faces. All that well-bred chic with its subterranean tempos and vague subtleties. It was a secret society with a silent language all its own. Full of signals, gestures, signs and unspoken intimations of what *was* and *was not* done. It was not something you could learn. You simply had to live it. The rules were learned by osmosis.

It was so totally different from real life, at least the life she had known for the past ten years, that the very thought of perpetuating the charade for even a night disgusted her. She needed time to pull herself together. Snatching a glass of champagne from a passing tray, Brett quickly dodged into the library and slipped outside onto the terrace to be alone.

It had rained earlier in the evening and the balmy night air was heady with the scent of flowering jasmine. The swimming pool was luminous with light, and as Brett walked slowly along the loggia she had a clear view of her mother's guests through the open windows.

Lithe and burnished women with ageless bodies, streaked or frosted hair and stylishly contoured breasts. The men were equally *au courant*. They were lean and confident, with the slightly bemused smiles of those who were used to receiving a great deal more from life than they were willing to give.

From somewhere Brett heard Laura's laughter rising above the three-piece string ensemble and caught a glimpse of her aunt's radiant face, restless blond mane and braceleted arms entwined about the neck of a middle-aged admirer. Her eyes were glassy and spaced-out. She was clearly flying high on something more interesting than diet pills. But, Laura was a grownup and perfectly free to make her own choices, Brett sighed.

She gazed across the room to where Charlotte Farrell was held rapt by a swarthy, muscular man holding court amid a group of fawning admirers. Dr. Florian Montes. Everyone in Palm Beach invariably treated Dr. Montes like some kind of supreme power. Guessing each other's real ages was one of the most popular subjects at any gathering in Palm Beach and while people talked of little else, Dr. Montes actually did something about it as doctor-in-residence to some of Palm Beach's most celebrated names and faces.

Vanity was no vice as far as Dr. Montes was concerned. He was continually on the prowl, searching out jelly stomachs, drooping breasts, feathered lips, incipient crow's feet and fallen buttocks. Never mind that many of those present that evening bore the glazed formaldehyde-look that was a dead giveaway to Montes' ministrations. Even his detractors had to admit that he was an absolute magician when it came to dramatically reversing the ravages of time.

Nor was it any accident that Palm Beach had become the plastic surgery capital of the world. Many a mansion was a virtual palace of mirrors. There was not the slightest question that Florian Montes was the reigning prince of a culture for whom the aging process held a very special terror.

During the Palm Beach Season, Dr. Montes was an avid participant in the inevitable social whirl and was one of the most dominant personalities. His every move was duly recorded in the local gossip columns. The twice-weekly departures of his private jet were fully booked with Palm Beach socialities flying off to take what was euphemistically termed "the cure" at Montes' posh Golden Portals clinic near Santa Marta, Colombia. Three full weeks of placental injections, rigorous massages, specially formulated diets and perhaps a quick nip and tuck around the eyes. All of which was guaranteed to put anyone this side of the grave back into social circulation.

Yet for all his charisma and social clout, Montes was known, more privately, for jacking up his celebrated clientele with booster rockets loaded with B-12 and a liberal quantity of speed. He dispensed prescription drugs with the casual abandon of a farmer sowing seed, and it was well-known that he made amorous house calls to rich, bored women who considered his services to be as necessary as the air they breathed.

Perhaps more than anything else, Brett thought, Florian Montes was a superb showman, an eternally youthful figure who radiated self-confidence, wore elevator shoes and was always on stage. Just the sight of a society columnist or photographer was enough to turn his flashing Latin smile into a high voltage one.

Brett didn't know him very well, but had always felt an instinctive distrust. She descended the steps into the garden and set off along a graveled path that circled the pool and finally led to a lovely trellised arbor overlooking the moonlit expanse of Lake Worth. It was a solitary place of deep shadow and filtered light, a place of sanctuary where she had often come to be alone in earlier years. The family called it "the summer house" and it was here that her father had come to take his own life.

Her father. . . . Incest was such an ugly word in all that it implied. But Brett knew now that her relationship with her father had bordered on it. How naive she'd been to assume that everything that had transpired between them had been a father's natural response to the feelings he shared with his daughter, and vice versa. She had never had time to grow, to dream and to ripen through a young woman's normal course of puberty.

At least not until she had fallen in love with Simon Lanier and awakened from her long enchantment. After that her father had become a stranger to her, a bitterly vindictive man given to sudden violent outbursts and a growing dependence on alcohol, not to mention ugly accusations of betrayal. Perhaps, Brett thought, that was the way he really was, as he had always been behind the polished, handsome smiling facade of wealth and privilege. She would never know now . . .

"Consuelo said I could probably find you out here," a deep male voice said from behind her.

Brett turned abruptly, her eyes widening in surprise. "Simon . . ." she said, "I didn't know you were coming this evening."

Simon Lanier ambled across the flagstones to fill her empty

champagne glass from a bottle of Chivas Regal. "I thought you might need a booster shot," he said. "I remember you never were too big on your mother's parties."

"I just needed a breath of fresh air before facing the rat pack."

"Rat is right," Simon said, taking her in with his eyes. "How are you, Brett?"

"Fine," she said cheerily. "Just fine."

"Then why did you run out on me at La Scala yesterday?"

"I guess I didn't want to cramp your style. You seemed to be doing rather nicely with your pretty friend. She's very striking, Simon. Laura's been telling me you're the *numero uno* ladies' man in town. I guess she's right."

Simon laughed. "Your aunt's a blast, but she's prone to exaggerate. The girl was just a friend, Brett. Just a friend."

Brett accepted a cigarette from the pack he held out to her and bent her head for a light. She brushed back her hair with one hand. Then, trying to change the subject, "Laura tells me you're on the staff over at Harbor View Hospital. Congratulations, doctor."

"Ah, but you're the one to be congratulated," he said, lifting his glass in a toast. "But where do you go from here? How many fucking Pulitzers do you have to win before getting your lovely ass shot off?"

Brett turned deliberately away from his gaze and drew deeply on her cigarette. "At the moment I'm just running on automatic pilot. I wish I knew."

They were standing very close. She could feel his breath on her and suddenly felt vulnerable and exposed. She stepped back. "Let's talk about you," she said. "For instance, what brought you here tonight?"

Simon smiled as if he'd just been asked a naughty question. "Actually, I'm usually on the 'B' party list. Which I guess isn't really all that bad considering those of the Jewish persuasion seldom get invited at all."

"That large chip on your shoulder is one of your least attractive attributes, Simon. I see you still haven't gotten rid of it."

"I guess it just comes naturally from growing up as the poor Hebe from the other side of the lake."

"Spare me the sad story, Simon. You know how I've always felt about the insufferable arrogance of all these WASPs. Let's talk about something else."

"Let's talk about us," Simon offered.

"What's there to say?" Brett shrugged. "It's been ten years. Things change, people change. It doesn't mean that I ever stopped caring."

"Well I'm glad to hear you still give a damn about the home folks." Simon's rueful expression suddenly turned pained. "Why'd you bail out on me, Brett? How could you just take off like that without even giving me an explanation? Don't you think I deserved that?"

"You're right, Simon. You deserved more than I had to give. I just wasn't ready for marriage. I wanted to achieve something with my life. I didn't feel I could do that married. We were just headed in different directions, I guess."

"That's a nice pat answer, Brett," he said bitterly. "Somehow you constantly manage to reduce everything to a convenient cliché. Maybe it's your journalistic frame of reference. It certainly saves a lot of time and complications. Okay, so you went to Vietnam and became a war junkie instead of marrying me. Am I supposed to just accept that?"

"Simon, please try to understand. My brother died there. I *had* to go. I had to find out why. I couldn't rely simply on the reports being filed out of there. I had to go and see for myself."

Brett turned away and crossed to the railing. Leaning over the side, she stared out at the lights along the far shore and remembered the lights of the rain-slick tarmac at Ben Wah and watching a chopper crew off-loading American soldiers in green body bags. They were laid out side by side in rows and she had captured them from behind the lenses of her cameras.

She turned to Simon and said softly, "The war sucked me in, but getting the story straight was important. Trying to discover what was really going on out there mattered in a way that nothing else did . . . and never has since.

"Listen, Brett, that was a long time ago. It's over with, history. What I want to know about is what happened after that? I lost you, and when I did I lost a part of myself as well." Simon's arms were around her, hugging her. "Something happened the weekend you went to see your father in Nassau, didn't it? He had just won the Bermuda Cup and you'd said there was something you had to tell him. What was it, Brett?"

Brett hugged him tightly, and kissed him very softly on the lips. "Please," she whispered, "forget about all that. Let's not complicate things. I've missed you, Simon. Missed you terribly." She pulled him to her and buried her head against his chest. "Make love to me, Simon . . . now."

They walked hand in hand through the gardens toward the poolhouse. Brett was finally going to have him. After all this time, after all the nights she had longed to have him again, making love as they'd done so long ago.

Inside the poolhouse, with the door safely locked behind them, they spoke no words and none were necessary. Simon undressed her and stepped back, still in awe of the body that had, so many times before, pleased him in a thousand ways.

Brett cupped her breasts and held them up to him. He kissed them hungrily, caressed and sucked them and finally buried himself between them. She pulled his shirt off, then unzipped his pants. She sighed as he laid her down on a large bed in the guest room, and as the moonlight poured in, their bodies rose and fell in the dim light, twisting and merging under the sighs and murmurs of lovers long kept apart but now reunited.

As the strains of distant music drifted out across the garden, Brett felt transformed. Simon's strong hands moved masterfully over her body, touching her every contour with the utmost reverence. She moaned when one hand reached down between her legs and felt herself go completely wet. She wanted him with an intensity that she hadn't felt for any man in years. She wrapped one hand around his penis and tried to guide him in. He got just beyond her lips and then withdrew. She cried out in frustration, but he silenced her with kisses. He entered her again, just barely, and withdrew. Brett felt herself close to coming and wanted him in her, but he was teasing her, driving her crazy. Finally, she moved from beneath him and he lay on his back. She took him in her mouth. From the bottom of his shaft to the very head of his cock, she worked him, sucking his balls, licking him, all the while jerking him off. Then just as he was about to come, she squeezed his shaft and straddled him. Together they rode the waves of ecstasy in a flood of orgasms.

Afterwards, Simon started to speak but Brett silenced him with her lips. She knew he was looking in her eyes for the future, but there were no promises she could give.

"We'd better pull ourselves together and go back to the party," she said, slipping from his arms and starting to get dressed.

It was nearly midnight at the time they returned to the party, which had moved out into the glass enclosed solarium for dancing. After accepting two glasses of champagne from a passing tray, Brett slipped her arm through Simon's and tried to compose herself for what she knew was bound to be an unpleasant confrontation with her mother.

"Brett, darling," Charlotte called out as they made their way across the crowded dance floor. "I was beginning to think that you'd been carried off by gypsies." Then, offering her slimly bejeweled hand to Simon, Charlotte added, "So good of you to put in an appearance, Dr. Lanier. Consuelo told me that you'd arrived and gone out into the garden to find Brett."

Simon did his best to maintain an easy demeanor. "And luckily I found her. We had a lot of catching up to do."

"So I gathered," Charlotte said with a fixed cold smile.

Before Brett could rise to Simon's defense, they were joined by Florian Montes returning from the service bar with fresh drinks in hand. "Well, if it isn't the lovely Pulitzer Prize-winner Brett and my esteemed colleague, Dr. Lanier," he said pleasantly. "Everyone was beginning to wonder what had happened to the two of you. I had just mentioned to Charlotte that perhaps we should send out a search party." Then, turning his full attention to Brett, he added warmly, "Welcome home, Brett. We're all so proud of what you've done."

For all his Latin charm and charisma, Brett was slightly uncomfortable with Florian Montes but didn't know why. Anyway, if her mother *was* involved with him, Brett would have to be especially deferential. "Mother's party seems to be a big success," Brett said, hoping to put an end to any further speculation regarding her absence. "I can't imagine anyone missing me."

"Your Aunt Laura has managed to keep everyone entertained," Charlotte observed tightly. "Of course she was fortified by half a dozen martinis, which probably helped her. Now, however, she too seems to have disappeared. Probably with one of the catering staff."

"Aren't you being rather unfair?" Brett said, suddenly feeling sorry for Laura. "There's no reason to air dirty laundry in front of our guests."

"Now, now, ladies," Florian laughed. "Let's not spoil the evening with such unpleasantness. Especially since we have such a distinguished guest in our midst."

"He's right," Charlotte agreed primly. "Julia DuShane is here tonight and she's very anxious to meet you."

Julia DuShane.

A legend in Palm Beach.

Filthy rich.

For over half a century Julia had ruled over Palm Beach society like an eccentric dowager queen. She was shrewd, high-spirited, unstoppable. When she shopped, stores closed to allow her privacy in choosing her purchases; when she dined, the best table was at her command, even if others were dining at it; and when she came to a party, the occasion was equal to a Papal blessing upon the hostess.

No woman—not a Rockefeller, Post, Mellon, or Whitney—had lived a more spectacularly self-aggrandizing existence. Her arrival at Marisol that evening sparked Charlotte's party into a blaze of unbridled festivity. Julia DuShane was an original in a world of carbon copies. She had built a home to rival the John Deere place in south Florida, the Biltmore House in Asheville, the Basia and Seward Johnson home in New Jersey. At her disposal were a fleet of cars, apartments around the world, a 150-foot yacht complete with eight-passenger helicopter, and endless money to travel. But Julia DuShane stayed in Palm Beach. *Ruled* it with an iron hand in a velvet glove. While she had never married, everyone addressed her as Madame instead of Miss DuShane, just as the Queen of England was addressed as Ma'am.

Julia Tyler DuShane was holding court in the library before a crackling long fire. She was still a magnificent looking woman with her imposing aquiline features, bone-white hair, parchment-pale skin and vivid blue eyes. She was seldom seen in public anymore, yet retained her customary rigid dignity even though confined to a wheelchair, with a nurse—fashionably attired in Adolfo—in constant attendance.

Her legend belonged, unfortunately, to what had been and what would never be again. In spite of advancing age and ill health, Julia's charismatic power remained intact. Although her body had withered, her mind had not. Julia DuShane was still shrewd, brazen and completely aware of the supremacy of her reign. Even though her days were numbered, no one would dare challenge her authority. Not, of course, unless they wished to commit social suicide.

Charlotte reintroduced Brett to Julia, since it *had* been more years than Julia would care to remember since she'd last seen Brett. Brett shook the woman's hand, noticing a slight tremor.

She didn't know whether it was from nerves or the fact that Julia DuShane's hand was overburdened with diamonds.

"My dear Miss Farrell," Julia said in a light, surprisingly mellifluous voice. "You are the sole reason I am here tonight."

Charlotte gritted her teeth silently, hoping no one else had heard the old bag's remarks.

". . . it's been far too many years since I've seen you. And then you were just a little girl," Julia said. "So many things have changed since then, with both of us. There's something I've been wanting to discuss with you for some time. Won't you come for tea tomorrow afternoon at La Caraval?"

Brett was bewildered. "I . . . I would love to talk with you. But tea? I'm not sure if I can—"

"Miss Farrell," Julia DuShane said firmly. "It was not a question."

CHAPTER FIVE

Brett awakened just before dawn in a cold sweat. She sat up in bed and reached to switch on the lamp. She felt completely alone. She'd been in the middle of a nightmare . . . a strange, haunting one whose visions had left her when she'd awakened, leaving only a horrible feeling of impending doom. She quickly lit a cigarette and leaned back against a sea of pillows. She felt hot against the Pratesi cotton sheets, even though the windows were open and a cool breeze swept into the bedroom.

Drawing deeply on her cigarette, she lay listening to the sounds of the night . . . frogs from the lake, catydids beyond, and crickets nearby. In the moonlight she gazed about the room that had been hers for so many years. It was a beautiful room, filled with antiques and a huge four-poster Empire bed. The walls were covered in silk damask. It was a bedroom of luxury, of pleasures to be enjoyed by an indolent and feminine woman. It was a room in which Brett had never felt completely comfortable.

The clock beside her bed indicated it was almost five in the morning. She wasn't going to go back to sleep, she wouldn't be able to. She knew her body well. The years of sleeping under a hail of gunfire had taken their toll on her body's timeclock. Once she was awake there was no going back. She got up and suddenly felt dizzy. She had drunk far too much at the party, but if she'd had her druthers, she would have drunk a lot more.

She went over to the open window and breathed the night air. It helped to clear her head. As she looked out, she saw a black Ferrari still parked in the front drive. No surprise there. Considering that the assembled guests had consumed enough champagne to float the *Bismark,* there had been more than a few unable to make the drive home. Someone had apparently opted to leave his car.

There was a sound below. Glancing down toward the front portico, Brett recognized Florian Montes emerging from the house and hurrying across the drive to the Ferrari. She caught no more than a glimpse of Charlotte standing in the open doorway before the door closed and Montes drove away.

Well, that explains that, Brett told herself. But Montes and her mother? Granted, Laura had told her about the *tête à tête,* but she'd dismissed it as the ramblings of a sometimes not completely coherent woman. Charlotte had always been, in Brett's eyes, somewhat frigid. Her father had vaguely hinted at it from time to time, although she never asked. And Montes had, as everyone knew, a reputation for being a ladies' man and quite capable in bed. Of course, Charlotte was now a widow and a very wealthy one at that. Brett had been left nothing in the will, but did have a trust her father had set up years ago precisely so she wouldn't have to rely on Charlotte should anything happen. And it had. Charlotte was now controlling what was, even by Palm Beach standards, a sizable fortune.

Brett left the window and went into the bathroom, switching on the light. Deliberately, she averted her eyes from the mirrored walls, wrapped a towel around her head and quickly stepped into the shower. The water was hot, but it was just what Brett needed. As the water poured over her and she began soaping herself with a big natural sponge, she felt as if she were cleansing away the dreams, the alcohol, the evening . . . all of it.

Her mother's party had been a huge success and even

though she'd been the guest of honor, she'd felt like an outsider from the moment she and Simon had entered the fray. She had walked through the crowd as during those days in Nam when she had walked through minefields. On every side there were familiar faces, smiling superficially, making banal small talk, all the while nodding, whispering . . .

". . . aged so much."

". . . that's what war does."

". . . no, that's what *love* does."

". . . great figure."

". . . but that dress."

Very little had changed in Palm Beach during her absence. With all the suffocating predictability, there had been several surprises as well. Until now Brett hadn't thought of her unexpected encounter with Simon. And even as she did, she didn't know what to think of it. To say there was still a lot of chemistry there was an understatement. But Simon had changed since his days as a bearded anti-war activist. Being a highly successful doctor was a big change from the old days, but Simon had managed to carry it off with style and élan. Brett thought about going down on him in the poolhouse and smiled. She had been as hungry for him as he had been for her . . . and God, had it been good.

But where would it lead?

She didn't know.

Or did she?

She briskly toweled herself off and dressed in jeans, a sweater and tennis shoes, she silently left the house and went down to the private beach which was part of the family's compound. It was nearly dawn. The sky was beginning to awaken with the early morning light and the water was opalescent and foam flecked with the incoming tide.

She walked along the water's edge, relishing the breeze blowing in off the ocean and the sound of the waves. She loved this beach, had all her life. She had had a tan line stamped and re-stamped on her body throughout all the summers she'd spent on this beach as a child. During her adult years, the tan line faded, but it had never completely disappeared, always reminding her that wherever she was in the world, wherever she was going, there was always a home, and there would always be a Palm Beach.

She had come home, but after last night, the homecoming was behind her now. She'd done her duty to the society which raised her. But what lay ahead?

Simon?

Another war?

Another man?

Overhead a flight of wild swans passed along the shore. They were flying low and traveling very fast. Brett watched them from the water's edge and smiled to herself. There was still a lot of life in the world, even with all the death she had seen. Those swans were just a small part of life, but a beautiful part of it.

She continued walking along the beach, beyond the property lines of Marisol, and at last came upon the high fence bordering the secluded estate of Julia DuShane.

La Caraval. One of the great homes in North America. An Italian palazzo that held enough unique architectural features to be entirely original to Palm Beach, just as Julia DuShane was herself.

Julia DuShane.

She would see her later that afternoon and, even though Madame DuShane had unveiled the invitation as a command, it was a meeting Brett was going to enjoy. Julia DuShane was a compelling enigma to so many, but to Brett she was the ultimate expression of everything that was false and superficial about Palm Beach. Seeing her in all her glory, behind the facade of her fifty-year-old mansion, would be an interesting sight indeed. And besides, Madame DuShane had never said *why* she wanted to see her, which was the most interesting part of it all.

She turned to head back towards home when another flock of wild swans flew past. She looked up just as one of the flock veered off, away from the others. It soared up high into the now brilliant blue sky, moving further and further away. Higher and higher it flew. And for as long as Brett could see it, it never rejoined the flock.

That was an omen, she told herself. But she did not know whether it was good or bad.

CHAPTER SIX

La Caraval was nothing like Marisol. As the imposing wrought-iron gates closed behind her, Brett saw the difference immediately. Julia DuShane's home was a private world of vanished splendors and faded glories. Here, it seemed, time stood still. Marisol was a family home, a place built for and by the *nouveau riche,* something Julia DuShane—and La Caraval—was most definitely not.

The day was hot and clear, and as Brett walked up the drive lined by majestic royal palms and closely barbered lawns, she could see that La Caraval stretched from the ocean to the lake. There was a golf course, clay tennis courts and a magnificent tiled swimming pool encircled by Grecian columns. There were fountains, loggias and a variety of other structures half hidden among verdant gardens of tropical vegetation.

There were glazed tile roofs, white stuccoed exterior walls and long, shaded gallerias beneath gracefully arched colonnades. It was a vast and rambling structure with sprawling wings, jutting mosque-like towers and a huge domed cupola dominating overall.

There had been a time many years before when a good many people in Palm Beach considered La Caraval to be nothing short of a monstrosity. A grandiose fantasia constructed during the depths of the depression merely to satisfy the fancy of an utterly tasteless woman with too much money and a capricious attitude.

Brett was admitted by an aging manservant, a tall and funereal figure dressed in a black cutaway and smiling with ghostly benevolence. He reminded Brett of an undertaker. The echoing marble entrance hall into which she was ushered resembled a royal mausoleum, brooding and somnolent, with a soaring stained glass dome bathing the encircling columns and classical statuary with muted light.

Brett's high heels sounded upon the mosaic Pompeian tiles as the butler led her across the entry hall. She had spent the morning trying to make up her mind what to wear and had finally decided on a summery white linen Saint Laurent pantssuit with a coral silk blouse. She was clean and cool with a minimum of makeup. Her hair was freshly washed and drawn back from her face, highlighting her prominent cheekbones and beautiful blue eyes.

Directly ahead were massive cathedral doors elaborately carved and opening finally upon a vast room with a beamed and frescoed ceiling. The furnishings were primarily Louis Quinze and not a reproduction in sight. The carpets were ancient Persian and the paintings, interspersed among medieval tapestries, ranged from the titans of the Renaissance to El Greco and Goya.

For all the opulence surrounding her, Brett's impression was that everything blended perfectly into a seamless mosaic dominated by a woman who had brought it all into being.

Julia DuShane sat enthroned like an ancient priestess ruling over a dying kingdom. There was an elaborate Georgian silver tea service on the table before her and her satin-slippered feet were up on a tapestried footrest. Behind her was Botticelli's *Birth of Venus*.

"How delightful to see you," Julia said regally. "Do come and meet Helga Nordstrom and Iris Quaid, my nurse and personal secretary."

Brett hadn't even noticed the women. Brett shook hands with a painfully plain and anxious-looking young woman whom Julia introduced as Iris. She clutched a legal-looking portfolio in one hand, extending the other. Her pale eyes were hugely magnified behind horn-rimmed glasses.

Helga Nordstrom was a sort different altogether. Her handshake was perfunctory while her features were bluntly unattractive. Beneath her starchy white nurse's uniform she wore a high-necked black leotard that completely enshrouded her sturdy six-foot frame. A stethoscope hung around her neck and she was carrying a dark leather medical bag. Brett thought she looked like a truck driver in drag.

"Helga has been checking my vital signs to make sure I'm still alive and poor, dear Iris has just witnessed the signing of my last will and testament. Everyone, including the lawyers, seems to think I'm daffy to be giving everything away to charity before I'm even in the grave." Julia gave a regal wave of a pale hand flashing with rings. "Do sit down and make yourself comfortable, my dear. You can smoke if you like. The tea service is only there for show. I always take a brandy at this time of day. You're welcome to join me."

"Brandy would be fine," Brett said, settling herself on the couch and extracting a pack of cigarettes from her bag.

In her own surroundings, Julia was even more of a presence than she had been the previous evening at Marisol. She was gowned in mauve with her bone-white hair upswept in a coronet beneath a matching lace mantilla. There was a single perfect pink rose pinned at her shoulder with a diamond sunburst clip. The scent of attar of roses surrounded her.

"Will there be something else, Madame?" Helga asked.

"No, nothing," Julia said. "Miss Farrell and I have important matters to discuss, so do *not* disturb me."

The butler, who had preceded Brett into the room, was now offering them brandy from a silver tray. Lifting her snifter, Julia made a toast. "Here's to courage, Miss Farrell. From what I understand, you appear to come well endowed with that particular virtue. I'm sure you must find your work extremely challenging."

"It has its moments," Brett admitted, after lighting up a cigarette. "But after you've been doing it as long as I have, all wars tend to melt together. Killing is killing. Only the armies and towns change."

"It sounds rather grim," Julia said, clearly preferring not to dwell on such a depressing topic. "But what really interests me is how you find Palm Beach after being away for so many years."

"To be perfectly frank, it's like going to Disneyworld. Everything's always the same. Everyone doing and saying the same things. It's like nothing has changed in the world during the last ten years. Everything's a fantasy."

"So, we appear to be frozen in aspic!" Julia laughed. She selected a long dark Turkish cigarette with a gold-tipped filter from the silver humidor the butler held out to her. He presented her with a light and silently left the room. "Tell me, my dear, do I intimidate you?"

Brett couldn't help smiling. "As a matter of fact I spent the entire morning trying to decide what to wear today. You are known to be rather formidable, you know."

"Well," Julia sighed, "at least people don't perceive me as a tiresome old recluse living in the past. The one fatal sin in Palm Beach has always been to be boring. I dare say I've never been that."

Julia went on to relate how she first came to Palm Beach in the depths of the depression to find herself totally ignored by a deeply entrenched society with old money and shared prejudices. Her monologue wandered to touch on the scandalous, the amusing and the totally irrelevant. She was like a classical actress playing the part of a *grande dame*. Even her laughter had a light, theatrical quality, while her accompanying gestures had the mannered grace of well rehearsed stage direction.

They talked about random matters and Brett gradually became aware that Julia was carefully scrutinizing her features and measuring her slightest response. Finally, Brett said, "Excuse me for being rather blunt, Madame DuShane, but ever since I arrived here today you've been looking at me as if I were an extraterrestrial. Is something wrong?"

"Oh, forgive me!" Julia said. "But you bear such a striking resemblance to your father. It's really quite extraordinary."

"A lot of people have said that," Brett replied.

"Dwight Farrell was an immensely attractive and charming man," Julia continued. "Of course he was a great hit with all the ladies in Palm Beach, there were few enough who managed to resist his particular brand of charm."

"You knew father well?" Brett asked, not really wanting to know the answer.

Julia smoked quietly for several moments, looking pensive. "I knew him as well, I suppose, as anyone ever gets to know anyone here in Palm Beach. If people get too close, they might discover what monstrous frauds everyone really is."

"I gather you didn't think much of my father?" Brett asked flatly.

"Please, don't be offended. I can't think of five people living or dead I ever sincerely liked. Your father was a delightful man in many ways. But I always knew he'd end up badly."

"And my mother?" Brett probed.

"I've known both your parents for as long as you have been alive," she continued quietly. "They were often guests here at La Caraval and one didn't have to be clairvoyant to know the marriage was a disastrous match from the very beginning. They were fire and ice. Charlotte never forgave Dwight for sleeping around, and he was bored to stone with her social pretensions."

"I don't really see any point in continuing this discussion," Brett said. "My father is dead. I had scarcely even seen him during the past ten years. He was a very sick man who chose to put an end to his own life. I know that you and your friends consider it to be extremely bad manners to blow one's brains out at the opening of the season and all that, but it was his choice and I really don't need to sit here and have his past sins recounted as if we were discussing bridge scores."

Julia was staring at her with the strangest expression. "*Bravo*, Miss Farrell! I do apologize, but you reacted just as I had hoped you would. Please bear with me, there is a point to all this. I know there was a time when you and your father were very close," Julia said. "I must admit I envied that relationship, because, you see, I too adored my father and he also had the bad manners—as you put it—to blow his brains out. It happened just before my twenty-first birthday. I don't think I've ever been able to forgive him. I felt as if there was something dreadfully lacking in me, something I couldn't give him and that he needed. Indeed, I gave my father everything I had to give, Miss Farrell . . . and it wasn't enough."

"What does any of this have to do with me?"

Julia paused to stub out her cigarette in a crystal ashtray. "As the saying goes, the time has come to tell the truth, the whole truth and nothing but the truth. God knows there've been volumes of stories written about me. Everything I ever did was documented by the press. But a lot of it was, quite frankly, bullshit. I want to set the record straight, Miss Farrell, and I need your help."

Brett almost laughed. "Are you asking me to be your official biographer? There are people who do ghostwrite but it's nothing I've ever even wanted to tackle."

"I know exactly who and what you are, Miss Farrell. You don't mince words and neither shall I. The last thing I have in mind is some self-serving whitewash of a book, which is what most of those bird-brained heiresses have written. I've led a very conspicuous kind of life but the truth has seldom been part of my public profile. I'm prepared to tell you things that may very well destroy everything I've spent my life trying to create. I'm not altogether what I appear to be. People have only seen what

I wanted them to see. There are secrets, Miss Farrell. Secrets that I want to reveal to someone in whom I have total trust.

"My only condition," Julia went on to say, "is that you hold everything I tell you in trust until at least six months after my death. What you choose to do with the information after that is entirely up to you. Perhaps you may choose to do nothing. It's irrelevant to me. For you see, my purpose will already have been served."

"Why me?" Brett asked.

"I've chosen you for both practical and perhaps somewhat selfish reasons. You have a journalist's curiosity which will demand answers to questions that I myself cannot supply, and, most importantly, you see the world as it really is. You know death, wasted lives and human tragedy. All of this is going to help you, believe me. You see, Miss Farrell," Julia DuShane said slowly, measuring each word, "I am not just proposing that you become the custodian of my personal history. If you agree to accept this proposal, you may very well find answers that you yourself are looking for."

CHAPTER SEVEN

JULIA DuShane had put out the bait, and Brett bit. Perhaps, Brett thought, that was looking at it rather coldly. Nevertheless, the aimlessness she'd been feeling about her own life, as well as the questions she'd been plagued with about her future, now took a back seat to Julia DuShane's life. Armed with her camera and tape recorder, she met Madame DuShane for several hours each afternoon. Slowly the story of Julia's life began to unfold.

It had all begun in Silver Creek, Colorado, a small mining town where Lucky Strike DuShane had struck it rich. Julia's father had been an itinerant prospector of Irish and Scottish descent who had come to Silver Creek at the turn of the century to work an obscure mining claim he had won in a poker game.

As it turned out, his claim became the greatest silver bonanza in the history of the American West. After earning his first million, Lucky DuShane celebrated his good fortune by marrying a traveling road show dancer, Alma May Tyler, a woman of uncertain past and Rubenesque proportions who, just six months after the wedding, presented her husband with a baby daughter.

Julia's early years were complete bliss. Lucky taught her to ride and shoot and pan gold in rushing mountain streams. But aware that his daughter needed a refinement that his wife didn't have, Lucky had Julia taught by European dance instructors, tutored in arts and languages and classics, and dressed in the very latest fashions shipped out from Boston and New York.

Father and daughter were inseparable. By the time Julia was sixteen, Lucky DuShane ruled over a vast mining complex that made him one of the most powerful figures in American industry, and one of a very few responsible for the country's burgeoning economy.

As his name began to appear in newspapers across the nation, Lucky continued to groom and nurture his lovely highspirited daughter. Alma May Tyler's usefulness to both husband and daughter grew increasingly limited.

Alma May's erratic behavior, long periods of depression and increasing social indiscretions, were the cause of intense embarrassment to Julia and her father, which simply fueled Julia's dislike of her mother. As time went on, Julia cruelly directed her mother's pathetic decline until Alma was finally banished to a private sanitorium.

Julia could not have been happier. She was finally alone with the lusty, brawling, fiery-tempered father she adored.

Lucky DuShane was a man with a raging thirst for spiritous liquors and a passion for women of easy virtue; he could be kind and exceedingly generous, but he also knew the power of intimidation and used it, with his wealth backing him.

Julia learned the meaning of power at a very early age. People were there to be used and anyone could be bought for the right price. She was entirely self-possessed and there was never any competition as far as her father's "other women" were concerned—just being near him was enough for Julia, and Lucky DuShane would move heaven and earth to satisfy her slightest whim.

Lucky had always given lavishly to various political candidates and when he finally managed to buy himself a seat in the United States Senate, it was a triumphant Julia who accompanied her father to Washington to serve as his official hostess. A lavish estate was swiftly acquired in the nation's capital and Julia set about furnishing it with quantities of priceless antique furnishings and important works of art she had purchased on a whirlwind European tour.

Power was always the spur to Lucky's ambitions. He was addicted to it, fought savagely to maintain it and was willing to risk everything in order to get even more. While there were many in Washington who considered him to be a rapacious opportunist, it soon became clear that he was a contender for the White House.

Julia assumed that it was only a matter of time before her father would rule the nation, and she did everything in her power to further his political ambitions. She was the toast of the capital, her smile forever flashing for newspaper photographs. She danced until dawn at the lavish diplomatic balls, dined at the White House and successfully arranged the elaborate entertainments over which both she and her father presided.

It was a splendid time and a wonderful country with everyone celebrating the advent of the great new Industrial Age. The First World War was finally over and vast fortunes were being made in an era of excess and innocence. Everyone was talking about peace and prosperity with wonderous visions of the progress yet to come. In a country lacking any real royalty, Julia DuShane ruled the nation's capital as if it were her divine right. Her mounting celebrity was the result of a great wave of public adulation, and even though men adored her, there was only one man in her life who ever really mattered.

And then, suddenly, her world fell apart.

First came the devastating stock market crash of 1929.

Then her father put a gun in his mouth and blew out his brains.

The suicide caused a sensation in the press and was almost

the death-knell to Julia. But even though her father succumbed to the ultimate weakness of self-hate, he had been a strong man for many years, and Julia drew on that strength to save what was left of the quickly depleting DuShane fortune.

At the age of twenty-one Julia took full charge of her father's estate, determined to rebuild. She was never young and carefree again, and seldom smiled. But in losing her father, she also realized a talent: she had an incredible flair for making money. Within a matter of months she had managed to diversify what was left of the DuShane fortune into oil, railroads and Florida real estate. Slowly, but with steady assuredness, her assets began to rise. Maybe one day, she thought, the DuShane fortune would be returned to its original value, or more. It would be a great tribute to her father.

Her father. There was nothing to fill the emptiness left by her father's tragic demise. While life in the nation's capital had turned grim and cheerless with the depression, Julia needed warmth, sunlight and gaiety. Washington was haunted with memories.

Palm Beach, she eventually discovered, was a world away from the gloomy, depression-ridden capital; a tropical paradise where anyone with money could act out a part against a backdrop of green golf courses, Mediterranean mansions and endless parties.

Palm Beach turned out to be exactly the challenge that Julia so desperately needed. An island of wealth and privilege ruled by a cloistered "Old Guard" elite, an impregnable feudal domain where the unacceptable were tossed aside in a high stakes game of winner-take-all.

Julia started construction on her Palm Beach palazzo in the depths of the depression just twelve months after her father's death. When she wasn't shuttling back and forth to Europe on ocean liners buying boatloads of treasures for the house, she was in Palm Beach tempestuously firing off orders that drove her various architects to the verge of revolt. She hired and fired the biggest names in architecture and finally took on the task herself, exhibiting extraordinary daring and imagination.

No one in Palm Beach was quite sure just what to make of Julia DuShane. She was brash, impulsive and very blunt. She always had her own peculiar notions of social propriety, and as time went on these managed to offend just about everyone. She commissioned a Swedish shipyard to begin construction on the most lavish, ostentatious yacht ever to cruise the seven seas.

It was christened *The Wanderer* and Julia herself designed all the interior appointments with the opulence of a floating Versailles. Upon the completion of her maiden voyage across the Atlantic, Julia took the helm to sail her dream ship across Lake Worth in full sail, dwarfing the collective yachts of Vanderbilts, Whitneys, Mellons and Rockefellers. The press had a field day.

Soon La Caraval was being portrayed as the ultimate monument to conspicuous consumption. Julia was accused of greedily plundering European chateaus, monasteries and Grecian temples of all their treasures.

Julia couldn't have cared less. What did bother her, however, was the fact that she was a queen without a court. The princely paradise still belonged to the blue-blooded aristocrats with vintage money and impressive pedigrees. To them she was nothing but an ill-bred adventuress whose life had become a vulgar spectacle.

Always a law unto herself, Julia refused to accept defeat. If the nobility of Palm Beach thought her to be less than acceptable, she found them to be appallingly stiff, cold and, worst of all, boring. The atmosphere of the island itself was so inhospitable that she began flying in planeloads of celebrities to attend her lavish, spectacular parties.

Film stars, novelists, poets and painters; anyone who happened to be in the public eye at that moment. One by one they were attracted, seduced and discarded for the new, the exciting, the sensational.

Palm Beach slowly began to change. Money, power and

celebrity became the only things that mattered and in this regard Julia DuShane reigned supreme. Eventually the straightlaced dragon ladies of the Old Guard became an endangered species.

Soon Julia was looking for new worlds to conquer. In this way, as in so many other ways, she was very much her father's daughter.

Through a series of exceedingly generous political contributions, Julia finaly managed to secure a titular appointment as cultural ambassador to China. It was a move calculated to give added American support to the failing and despotic reign of General Chiang Kai-shek, although Julia saw the appointment as confirmation of her preeminent status as the foremost jewel in the capitalist crown.

She was photographed everywhere. With Madame Chiang upon the Great Wall of China; distributing money and supplies to help victims of floods, famine and the devastating civil war that was laying waste the world's most populous country; meeting also with various foreign dignitaries as the crisis deepened.

With the attention of the world focused upon China, Julia played her trump card and managed almost overnight to elevate her stature to global proportions. Julia's offer to meet with Mao to mediate an end to the civil war caused a sensation in the media and captured headlines worldwide. Although her diplomatic triumph was monumental in scope, it turned out to be ultimately futile and brief in duration.

Mao had already embarked upon his Great March south to Peking, and before the year was out the victorious Communists had come to power.

Julia, however, had a way of turning defeat into victory. She managed to depart mainland China in possession of perhaps the finest private collection of Chinese art treasures in the world. In the end she returned to Palm Beach a sovereign figure in her own right and her reign after this was never challenged.

It was late afternoon. Brett and Julia had been working together for over a week and were sitting in the garden. Julia wore a filmy, floral, organza gown and a wide-brimmed straw hat with a trailing veil, while Brett was casually attired in khakis and a polo shirt.

Off across the lawns, La Caraval gleamed in the westering sunlight like a massive white stucco wedding cake. All it needed was the traditional bridal figurines on top and a giant knife slashing down to cut it into pieces. It was, of course, inevitable that once Julia was gone the charities, museums and various foundations to which she had left everything would swiftly step in to divide the spoils.

"I want you to have my diaries," Julia said. "I've instructed Iris to give them to you when you get ready to leave today."

Brett wanted to say something, but she had no idea what.

"What are you thinking?" Julia asked. "You look so . . . pensive."

"I hate to see the story come to an end. You've lived this incredible life . . . I guess I don't really feel like going back to the real world yet."

Julia smiled. "All stories come to an end. Mine is no exception. People's lives pass into either myth or oblivion. I don't suppose it really matters one way or the other. The diaries will document everything I've already told you and a great deal more besides." The old woman looked off, as if suddenly wearied and in need of solitude.

For the past eight days, Brett had listened to the story of Julia's life unfold chapter by chapter. There was a cool, factual quality to Julia's recitation, expressing her acceptance of what she was and how she had lived her life. Yet there was something missing—some primary ingredient that Brett was not able to define. What about passion? she wondered. What about love?

"We'll meet again the day after tomorrow," Julia said.

Brett rose reluctantly, taking Julia's outstretched hand. "I'm afraid I've tired you," Brett said. "I'll come the day after tomorrow at the same time, right after lunch."

"I shall look forward to that." Her smile was warm, but her eyes were already somewhere else, as if Brett had suddenly ceased to exist.

As she walked back across the lawn, Brett realized the secret of Julia's long survival was that she never allowed anyone to come too close—the gracious smile and imperious manner always held the world at bay.

Brett envied Julia's insularity. She herself had never felt more vulnerable and uncertain and the feeling wouldn't go away. She felt as if she were being pulled into something that she ultimately would have no control over, and that bothered her. She was actually beginning to care about Julia, a woman who represented everything she found contemptible.

People's lives pass into either myth or oblivion, Julia had said. From the very first, Brett had sensed that Julia was only too aware that the curtain was falling and, that the theater lights were dimming, the stage fading into darkness.

Upon reaching the terrace, Brett paused with her hands resting upon the balustrade and looked back across the lawn toward Julia's solitary figure. She was shading her eyes against the light of the waning afternoon, gazing off toward a flotilla of sailboats skimming across the lake.

It was in that moment that Brett came to understand the tragedy of Julia DuShane. Here was a woman who had pursued life on a grand and monumental scale, and she was going to die . . .

Alone.

CHAPTER EIGHT

BRETT sighed and eased herself into a sitting position on her padded lounger. She had spent the morning by the swimming pool of the Breakers Hotel, and a brief glance at her watch indicated that it was almost eleven. Laura was over an hour late, as usual, and Brett was starving. They had planned to have lunch poolside.

Brett looked around. There was a sultriness she hadn't noticed before on the faces of the other loungers, an easy drift of sensuality as bronze bodies rubbed up against each other's libidos. The astrological sign of Palm Beach was Virgo, Brett mused, but virginity was clearly the last thing on anyone's mind.

There were attractive people everywhere. Lithe and golden women with searching eyes and practiced smiles, all sharing a look of vaguely concealed boredom.

There were also plenty of men, but they were a different breed altogether. Young mostly, with golden limbs and bulging bikini briefs. French, Italian and American beefcake. All suave, sleek and very much on display. They were the type of male common to Palm Beach during the season. They were "walkers" and were invariably on the make. Most were gay and all were too predictable as far as Brett was concerned. Like

exotic hothouse blooms, they were considered prized adornments by the social ladies whose quest was for the best, regardless of cost. They were the perfect escorts to charity balls, and
made the most exquisitely entertaining house guests when hus-
bands were off on their own pursuits, for there wasn't an available man to be found between Sun City and the Everglades
swamp.

The sexual tension in the air bordered on the orgasmic.

Brett took a cigarette from her bag and lit it. As she gazed
about the pool, she caught sight of a man standing poised upon
the high board at the far end. He was quite unlike the others
around the pool. He was older, probably somewhere around
forty and darkly attractive. But that wasn't why he seemed different. There was something familiar about him. Even at a distance Brett was attracted to him, and there was the strangest
feeling that she knew him from somewhere. But it was only a
feeling. She wasn't sure.

He took three long striding steps and arced sharply upward
before doing a perfect double somersault.

Who was he?

"Brett, darling," a voice called out. She turned to see Laura
sweeping toward her with a blond waiter in tow bearing a tray
of drinks. "Sorry to be late, but I come with tidings of great joy
and a morning pick-me-up that will knock your socks off."

Svelt, evenly tanned and displaying an amazingly good figure, Laura was sporting a bright red bikini that was getting
stares from all the males. Her features were partially obscured
behind the Jackie O sunglasses and her blond hair was drawn
up turban-style beneath a white towel.

The waiter placed their drinks on the glass-topped table
between the pool loungers, and Laura rewarded him with an
incandescent smile along with a crisp twenty-dollar bill. "Keep
the change, darling boy, and do come back in about twenty
minutes with refills. I am feeling positively posthumous this
morning."

"What on earth are those slimy green things?" Brett said, staring with disgust at the foaming green concoctions topped with sprigs of mint.

"Where on earth have you been, dear child? Spider ladies are all the rage this season. Vodka, goat's milk and crème de menthe. Absolute nirvana if one just happens to wake up with a hangover the size of North Dakota. A couple of these and a few diet-ups are guaranteed to keep you from falling into the nethermost pits before the cocktail hour."

"Speaking of what you woke up with this morning, where have you been for the past week? Mother was beside herself until I told her you'd called and we were lunching."

Laura smiled and deftly spread a big, brightly striped beach towel on her lounger and arranged herself upon it. "I've been with a friend, sweetheart." Laura produced a jeweled pill box from her voluminous straw bag and swallowed two small yellow capsules with a gulp of her drink. "Now then," she said, "I trust you've been able to keep yourself amused. Palm Beach may not exactly be the center of the universe, intellectually speaking, but there are certain distractions."

"There was a man here that I wanted to ask you about but I don't see him now. He was tall, dark and rather Latin looking."

"Well," Laura giggled, "you've managed to narrow things down to half the hustlers in Palm Beach, since the other half are blond. Was there anything distinguishing about him? Like maybe he was packing an Italian sausage in his bikini briefs? *That* might give me a clue."

"Bigger is not always better," Brett admonished. "Besides, I wasn't looking at his crotch. I was just wondering who he was. Anyway, you're over an hour late and we'll have to skip lunch. I have a very busy afternoon ahead of me. What was so important that you simply had to see me?"

"Well," Laura said, inserting a Benson and Hedges in her holder and igniting it, "what would you say if I told you I was thinking of converting to Judaism?"

Brett almost choked on her Spider Lady. "You . . . the great *shiksa* playing mahjong with the Haddassah ladies?"

"Well, I'm not sure it's as funny as that," Laura pouted. "Elizabeth Taylor did it and you don't see her running around in a *shamatta* with a dowager's hump."

"Frankly, Laura, I'd believe just about anything where you're concerned short of joining the Little Sisters of Charity and taking vows of poverty, chastity and obedience. But what *are* you talking about?"

"I'll show you," Laura said, delving into her straw bag and producing a black velvet jeweler's case from Van Cleef & Arpels. She snapped it open to triumphantly display a spectacular diamond-and-platinum bracelet. "You can take my word for it, kiddo, you don't get ice like that from vows of poverty or chastity. Obedience? Well, there may have to be some room for negotiation in that regard."

"Its gorgeous," Brett said, taking the bracelet from Laura's fingers and looping it around her wrist. "You must have given a world-class performance."

"Try Academy Award. It's no picnic screwing a thousand-year-old antique with a prostate the size of a cantaloupe and a pecker that looks like a kosher pickle. The only way I can get through it is to imagine how he'd look buried under all his money."

Brett tried to stifle her giggles by finishing off her drink. "I assume this is not someone I've run into socially. He certainly doesn't sound like the type you'd find at one of mother's soirées."

Laura snatched the bracelet back and fastened it about her wrist, pausing to admire the flash and sparkle of the stones in the sunlight. "Laugh if you will," she sniffed. "Maurice Begelman isn't just your average millionaire. He's a financial wizard who's down here buying up property for some sort of resort development, and richer than the Federal government. He's kept me occupied for the past week. Actually, it was the other way around. Anyway, we stayed at his place on Palm Beach Shores. Monstrous house, but you wouldn't believe the security. Walls ten feet high, bodyguards that look like sumo wrestlers and a helicopter parked on the lawn for fast getaways to God knows where. I thought I'd died and gone to heaven until he unzipped his fly."

"Are you sure you know what you're doing? You, who're so concerned with appearances, screwing a . . ."

"Oh, give me a break. What good are WASPs? Thanks to your mother and her friends, the Bath and Tennis Club cancelled my guest privileges and every God damned *boîte* in town has cut off my tab. Why shouldn't I go for the gold?"

The waiter appeared with another round of drinks. "Is there something else I can do for you, Mrs. Gentry?" he asked intently, nudging Laura's thigh with his knee.

"I'm sure there is, darling boy. But for the moment I'll settle for a pack of Benson and Hedges." She reached to pat his cheek. "Now do be a dear and hurry right back for a nice surprise.

"Here's the bottom line," Laura said, as he hurried away. "I've simply got to get out of that house. Your mother is driving me up the wall."

"That makes two of us. But where would you go?"

"Maurice wants to put me up in a *cabaña* suite at the Royal Poinciana. Of course, *he* goes along with it. But I'd settle for Godzilla at this point if he had a decent Dun and Bradstreet rating. After that kinky Spic I was married to, with his spike heels and hot wax fetish, I guess I can fake an orgasm right along with the best of them. Now tell me, what's been happening with you and Simon? I've been dying to know."

"He called and asked me out to dinner tonight."

"And? . . ."

"Well, I'm going."

"Of course you're going, fool. I mean, has he got you all hot and bothered again?"

Brett looked thoughtful. "Well, . . . yes, but it's probably just hormones. And no, I'm not going to tell you what he's like in bed. That's privileged information."

"I'll say it is. I only wish the privilege were mine. If I were ten years younger. . . ."

"Down, girl," Brett cut in. "Twenty would be more like it. You were already heading for lost horizons with your fourth husband when Simon was burning his draft card."

Laura sniffed. "The only thing I dislike more than discussing age is talking about poverty. I intend to be raising eyebrows and penises until I'm ninety, and the only problem I intend to have with money is how to spend it. Now this may be a slightly thorny question but what about your media mogul with the sweet little wife and cute kiddies? I assume there's a torrid reunion planned when you go to New York for the awards?"

Brett grew pensive. "That may be a bit of a problem. I don't know whether or not to tell Brad about Simon."

Laura sat up looking incredulous. "Are you entirely out of your mind? The cardinal rule of having affairs is never tell the truth when a lie will do just as well. A little side action never hurt any relationship."

"Brad and I have always been entirely honest with each other. That's what made our relationship so special. I know he still sleeps with his wife. I've accepted that. There hasn't been anyone else . . . not for either of us."

"Do you mean to tell me you've never played around? What on earth were you doing all those nights in lonely hotel rooms with bombs gong off? You had all those hot-blooded revolutionaries shooting off their weapons, why not get them to shoot off something else?"

Brett laughed. "What I was doing all those nights was falling into bed wishing I had the energy to wash my hair. By six I was up and hitching a ride on a helicopter gunship, hoping I wouldn't get my period."

The waiter returned with Laura's cigarettes and she

promptly turned over on her stomach, handing him a bottle of Bain de Soleil. "Please be a darling and cover me in oil. A good tan can hide a multitude of sins but one has to be careful not to end up looking like the curse of King Tut."

Brett finished her drink as Laura's waiter massaged a thin coat of fragrant oil across her back and shoulders. "I have to be going," Brett said, gathering her things together and putting them into her bag. "I have an appointment this afternoon with Monsieur Phillipe and I want to get in some shopping first."

"What a shame to leave when the fun's just starting," Laura said in a drowsy, husky voice. "Auntie Laura will be with you in spirit, dear heart. Sally forth and spend yourself into an orgasm."

Worth Avenue was the ultimate street of dreams, where egos collided, pills were popped, fortunes were squandered and highly strung nerves tended to shatter at the slightest provocation. It was part Monte Carlo, part St-Tropez and part Moorish maze in Marrakech. There were winding stairways, bougainvillaea-hung lattices, and all sorts of interesting alleyways leading off into tiled courtyards embellished with classical sculpture and splashing fountains.

Yet for all its expensive cachet, there was a sense of grace and harmony to the architectural ambience. The shop windows beneath the long cloistered colonnades were resplendent. Diamonds sparkled on indigo velvet at Cartier's. Baccarat crystal, fine linens from Belgium and the very latest in designer fashions dazzled the eye from the windows of exclusive shops and fashionable boutiques.

After years of living out of a single, battered suitcase, Brett scarcely knew where to start. She wasn't sure if it was Laura's spider ladies that made her feel so light-headed and reckless. Brett decided to go with the feeling and shoot for the moon.

Her first foray into the world of pricey chic was into Martha's hallowed, marble-halled salon. After brief consideration,

Brett purchased a beautifully tailored Saint Laurent suit. It was the blue of summer skies and did wonderful things for her eyes. Next, she went a little wild in Ralph Lauren's trendy sports boutique and then found herself at Hattie Carnegie's totally unable to resist a cocktail dress the color of opium poppies.

The Krizia shop in the esplanade had proved to be an oasis of style and originality. The high-tech, ultra-chic look wasn't really *Brett* but "what the hell!" After all, she was riding the crest of a buying binge and everything she tried on just seemed to look fabulous.

When she stopped to stare covetously at a full-length, platinum-flame fox fur in Magnin's window, Brett knew she had passed the point of no return. She saw it, she liked it and she decided to buy it without even asking the price.

Brett arrived late for her four o'clock appointment at Phillipe's salon. Phillipe was one of the few people in Palm Beach that no one kept waiting. Not only was he a veritable cosmetic wizard and hair-styling whiz, Phillipe was also a fount of information that kept the local grapevine buzzing.

Phillipe prided himself on keeping in the know with all the latest gossip fit to spread. His favorite ladies could always count on scandalous disclosures of everyone's worst-kept secrets. He had all but replaced the psychiatrist that many a Palm Beach socialite considered to be as necessary as capped teeth and silicone injections.

Beneath Phillipe's creative and extremely capable hands the ladies of Palm Beach felt glamorous and recharged. By the time they strolled out the mirrored doors of his salon, they had been pampered, manicured, coiffed and ultimately assured that they were stars transcendent—*forever young*.

Phillipe's salon was pleasantly perfumed and climate controlled, with classical music playing softly in the background. At the peak of the season, he employed a dozen other hairdressers as well as a team of beaming young male assistants wearing tight white pants and lavender smocks who helped smooth the various transitions—wash to cut to set to manicure to pedicure—with tiny watercress sandwiches, caviar, and Taittinger champagne.

Phillipe himself was slim as a snake, with a beguiling smile and a mass of chestnut curls framing his sharply delicate features. In spite of Brett's being ten minutes late, he greeted her effusively, then led her into a mirrored cubicle with a tented ceiling and comfortably padded chair.

"How about something really dramatic for the awards?" Phillipe suggested, running his fingers through her hair to gently tickle her scalp. "Something exciting, totally new."

"Whatever you say, as long as I don't end up with blue hair and a tiara!"

Phillipe giggled, then tipped her head back into the sink and began lathering up a fragrant Estée Lauder shampoo. "Just close those beautiful eyes and leave absolutely everything up to me."

Brett did. Inevitably her thoughts drifted to Julia DuShane. When Brett had come back to Palm Beach, Julia was the last person imaginable to have provided an unexpected safety net. Brett was curious about their next meeting. In a way, Julia's life was like some distant mirror of her own.

After a lot of cutting and fluffing, Phillipe switched on a blow dryer and began drying her hair. "I suppose you've already heard about your aunt's latest conquest? It must be all over town by now that she's become the mistress of the most notorious man in all Palm Beach."

Brett said nothing but stared straight into the mirror, eyeing Phillipe. When it came down to it, he was small town, just like most of Palm Beach, regardless of their money. "I'm not sure that I know what you're talking about."

"Well, you can read all about it in the *Shiny Sheet*," Phillipe said, placing the daily Palm Beach tabloid in Brett's hands. "It looks like Palm Beach is about to become Las Vegas East, unless of course they pull up the draw bridges and declare a state of emergency. This time Laura Gentry has outdone herself."

Brett scanned the article.

"FISHERS ISLAND SLATED FOR DEVELOPMENT . . . Representatives of multi-millionaire financier Maurice Begelman have unveiled plans for a five-hundred-million-dollar casino-resort complex just north of Palm Beach, pending passage of the new gambling law currently before the state legislature."

"Oh, God," Brett said, suddenly realizing who Laura had been talking about. Maurice Begelman was reputed to be the Godfather of the Jewish Mafia, a man who knew how to move enormous sums of money, money earned from Las Vegas gambling casinos, while bypassing Federal regulations and banking laws. A man who could also kill as easily as sneezing.

Although proof of his wide-ranging connections with organized crime or reputed rub-outs had never been established, Begelman was without question a very powerful figure in the shady world of gambling.

Brett shook her head. "Well, Phillipe, Aunt Laura is nothing if not dramatically self-destructive."

CHAPTER NINE

W HEN Brett came down the stairs at Marisol that evening Simon was waiting for her in the foyer. He greeted her with a wolfish grin and a low, appreciative whistle.

She wore an elegant Emanuel Ungaro dress with her new fur coat draped casually about her shoulders. Her hair was full and lustrous, shimmering with highlights and beautifully framing her classic features as it curled and waved about her face and shoulders.

She looked sensational.

It was their first date since Brett had returned to Palm Beach and Simon had invited her to dinner at Delmonico's, an old colonial mansion on the outskirts of Delray Beach that had been restored and renovated into a very expensive French restaurant.

They dined in a room that resembled the grand salon of an eighteenth-century brothel, with candle-lit crystal chandeliers, paintings of voluptuous nudes and highly polished dark wood paneling.

"I must say I'm rather surprised," Brett said after the maitre d' had seated them at an intimate corner table surrounded by potted palms. "The last time we had dinner together you were heavily into macrobiotic rice, tofu and bean spouts. You said you'd never eat anything that could look you in the eye."

"Such is the folly of youth," Simon laughed. "As you can see, I've made a few compromises in the face of reality."

"Oh, but what I'm talking about is compromising one's principles . . . something you swore you'd never do."

"And you've got room to talk?" Simon laughed softly. "What about that fur you're sporting? You really should be ashamed of yourself, wearing dead animals killed in ugly iron traps."

Brett leaned close, bracing one elbow on the table and cupping her chin in one hand. "Let me tell you about this coat. In case you hadn't noticed, there's a bitch beneath this calmly smiling exterior. When I first returned to Marisol, Mother accused me of impersonating a bag lady. She told me in no uncertain terms to take myself off to Worth Avenue and do something about my image . . . at her expense, and that's just what I did. The woman you see before you is my mother's child, complete with fur, an Ungaro, Joy perfume and Argenti lingerie. It was revenge, pure and simple. And it cost mother something in the neighborhood of a new Maserati."

"So you and Charlotte still haven't managed to mend the breach?"

"There never was any breach. Mother and I have always been a couple of embattled clichés. But that's very boring subject. Let's please talk about something else."

Simon lit them each a cigarette, then asked, "Do you remember our first date?"

Brett smiled. "How could I forget? It was a warm summer night and we went dancing under the stars. I wore a blue silk dress with a gardenia in my hair. At some point in the evening you said something wonderful and looked very sexy saying it. I guess you simply swept me off my feet."

"I had a hard-on all night," Simon said huskily. "Your dress clung to your body. It molded your breasts . . . and those long marvelous legs of yours. I couldn't wait to get you somewhere alone."

They were holding hands now and smiling into each other's eyes. Brett remembered only too well having lost herself that evening long ago to the wine, the music and the dangerously exciting young man pressing her close in his arms until she could feel his body melting into her own.

As it turned out, they hadn't made love that first night. But when it did happen, Brett had given herself completely and without reservation.

At that moment a tuxedoed waiter appeared at Simon's elbow with his pen poised to take their order. They had completely ignored the menu and hurriedly scanned the elaborately printed selection of French cuisine.

The waiter suggested various *spécialités de la maison* and Brett questioned him briefly in faultless French before choosing the *terrine au deux poissons*. Simon went with the *veau d'anjou*. Then he turned his attention to the extensive wine list presented by the hovering sommelier.

Simon considered himself to be something of a wine connoisseur. He pondered the list and then glanced up. "How about something unusual?" he asked the sommelier. "Something rather complex but well balanced and a bit mysterious. It's called Leoville-Poyferré, a superlative Bordeaux."

Brett had a hard time keeping a straight face. "If you don't mind my saying so, I've always found the Poyferré to be somewhat off-putting. There's something rather eccentric about the bouquet, verging perhaps on the over-ripe. I don't know all that much about French wines, of course, but in my humble opinion, it's just a little too much of a tease. I'd prefer something more along the lines of a Chateau Margaux '57, if your heart is really set on a Bordeaux."

The sommelier was gaping at her, clearly amazed. "*Oui,* Madamoiselle. An excellent suggestion and a most superb vintage. May I say that Madamoiselle certainly knows the Bordeaux wines."

"Thank you," Brett said. She batted her mascaraed lashes at Simon.

Simon was still in shock, but refused to let her get the best of him. Instead, when the wine was served and their glasses filled, he lifted his in toast. "Allow me to propose something befitting the occasion; let's drink to the future."

"To the future," Brett echoed, touching her glass to his. "I'm afraid it's already here but I doubt that Palm Beach is ready for it."

"Smart ass," he teased. "Anyway, at least you were right about the wine and I'm crazy about that perfume you're wearing. It makes my blood race."

Brett sipped her wine. "I know what else makes your blood race, Mr. Lanier. On that particular subject I have instant and perfect recall."

"I'm getting an erection," he whispered urgently. "What do you suggest?"

"What I would suggest," Brett said, "is that you drape your napkin over your lap and get your hand out from under my dress. Here comes the waiter."

The waiter served their entré with elaborate panache and left. Throughout dinner they talked.

"I'm going to hate myself for asking, but when are you packing up and taking off again? I thought you'd be on your way to Tierra del Fuego by now."

Brett looked away. "Do you remember an H. G. Wells story called *The Time Machine*? It was about a man who invented a way of transporting himself into the future."

"Sure, I remember," Simon answered. "One day he discovered the time machine had disappeared. He couldn't find it anymore. He was trapped in a time and place that weren't his own."

"That's me," she said. "For the past ten years, I've been a traveler in a time machine. Invulnerable. Detached. Viewing all the horror, the tragedy and heartbreak through a wide-angle lens. But something happened to me in Iran. The time machine wasn't there anymore. I don't know where I'm going from here or how I'm going to get there."

For a while, neither spoke and then Simon said, "I'll bet you still look gorgeous when you wake up in the morning."

Brett laughed. "You know perfectly well that I look like hell. You couldn't even speak to me until I'd had at least two cups of black coffee." She leaned close to brush his cheek with her lips. "You were my first lover, Simon. In a way, you spoiled me."

"In that case, I think we ought to get out of this place and find the nearest bedroom."

"Yours then, mine's a further drive."

"You're on."

"And you've got a hard-on," Brett said, glancing at his pants. "See what you do to me!"

At Simon's, they had barely shut the door before they were in each other's arms, kissing, caressing, pulling their clothes off. "I want you so much," Simon whispered, exploring her with hands, mouth and tongue.

Brett rubbed herself against his hard-on and moaned, all the while unzipping his pants, finding his cock and stroking it. In a tangle of passion, they moved from the foyer into Simon's study, and lay down upon an expensive Oriental rug.

"You know," he said urgently, "we could always go upstairs, into the bedroom."

"No," she cried, kissing his nipples, sucking them, weaving her fingers through his mounds of chest hair, "I can't wait. I want you, Simon. Here. Now."

He buried himself in her, pulling her beneath him and parting her legs. Her sweet aroma enveloped him as he moved down into the wet, warm inner smoothness between her thighs.

Lingering there, he feasted upon her scented sweetness, eating like a ravished man as her body shuddered and squirmed and writhed and thrust at him.

She begged him to enter her, cried for his cock within her, but his tongue probed deeper, deeper, and then, finding the magic spot, he gave himself to her totally and she to him.

"Fuck me," she moaned hoarsely. "Please fuck me, Simon. I need you to fuck me."

Simon raised himself up and moved inside her. Brett surrendered everything. Over and over he thrust, whispering her name and telling her how beautiful she was. Quickly, Brett came, then Simon's white hot explosion burst within her. But instead of disengaging, he continued to move once again. Slower now, more gently. He told her how much he loved her, desired her, needed her. His thrusts quickened and he caressed her breasts, massaging them with love as Brett moaned approval, until she was coming again, and he was coming again, and they were clinging together in glorious orgasm.

Later, much later, they fell asleep in each other's arms.

CHAPTER TEN

W HEN Brett arrived the next day at La Caraval, she was met at the door by Helga Nordstrom, who showed her in. "Madame is not feeling well today, Miss Farrell. There was a burglary here last night."

"What? Is Julia all right? What happened?"

"She is fine, just shaken. She was having dinner with Dr. Montes last night and planned to wear a diamond and ruby necklace she had laid out. She changed her mind, and forgot to put it back in the safe. Anyway, someone got on the grounds, broke in through the balcony doors in Madame's bedroom and took the necklace."

"Was anything else taken?"

Helga shrugged. "We don't think so. But Madame has asked the police to keep the matter as quiet as possible. Publicity only invites other burglars."

"Perhaps she'd rather I come another day," Brett offered. "I'm leaving for New York tomorrow, but we could meet again the first of next week."

"I suggested that but Madame would not hear of it. She insisted on seeing you today, but please don't mention the robbery. It will only upset her."

Helga took her upstairs, and indicated a pair of intricately carved double doors. "Madame is waiting for you in her bedroom," she said, then left.

Julia's bedroom was more of a boudoir than a bedroom, upholstered and draped in eggshell ivories, muted rose silks and pale yellow brocades. Julia appeared to be sleeping. She was propped up on a Regency chaise against a froth of satin pillows. She looked dangerously frail beneath the goosedown coverlet. Her breathing was shallow and slightly labored. There was a vase of perfect pink roses on the Chippendale table beside her. Julia's hands were folded against her breast, and she was wearing a golden wedding band that Brett had never seen before.

Brett called her name softly and waited. Then again, slightly louder this time.

Julia stirred and her eyes opened. "Oh, Brett, I must have dozed. Do come and sit here beside me so that we may talk."

Brett crossed the room, dropped her voluminous shoulder bag to the floor and seated herself. "I hated to awaken you. You looked so peaceful."

Julia responded with a fleeting wisp of a smile. "I was dreaming of a house party that I gave many years ago for the Duke and Duchess of Windsor. It's strange to think that most of the guests are dead now. It was so vivid. They seemed so very much alive."

"Well then, you should tell me about them. People still talk about the parties you used to give."

"And they should. Garbo was here for that party, and Von Sternberg, her director. Scott and Zelda Fitzgerald arrived hours late and fought the entire time. I can remember it all so clearly. Scott was drinking far too much and cutting up around the pool with Willy Hearst's little starlet friend, Marion Davies."

Julia sighed, arranging herself more comfortably upon the chaise. "The Windsors were the guests of honor and arrived with sixty pieces of Vuitton luggage, four personal servants and six schnauzers that were messing all over the carpets. The Duke was never sober and always talked that dreadful rubbish about Hitler and all those ghastly *Faschisti* he so admired."

Julia sat up and plucked a single long-stemmed rose from the vase beside her. She closed her eyes, inhaling the fragrance. "Of course, in those days the Windsors were considered to be terribly glamorous, making headlines wherever they went and taking marvelous newspaper photographs. They always reminded me of tiny jeweled figurines in a Fabergé egg.

"One couldn't help wondering what the Duke saw in Wallace. She wasn't a particularly attractive woman, although she did manage to put their social life on a paying basis. The Windsors were strictly 'cash and carry.' One could hire them the way you would a plumber. Parties, charity balls, and I dare say that if they were still around today, probably even shopping malls and supermarket openings."

"I've always suspected that La Caraval was full of ghosts," Brett said. "Although I hadn't thought of them as being quite so . . . picturesque."

Julia nodded. "I am surrounded by ghosts, my dear, and not all of them rest quietly in their graves. I asked you to come here today because I wanted to tell you about the ghosts that still haunt me."

Julia paused to light one of her long dark Turkish cigarettes and then sat smoking silently. Finally, she motioned for Brett to switch on her tape recorder. "I knew nothing of men as a young girl. As you know, my father raised me with an iron hand. I was chaperoned everywhere, always sheltered from the realities of life. I knew almost nothing about the sexual relationship between a man and a woman. My father helped me pick out my clothes. Everything I wore was embroidered and edged with lace. You see, my dear, young girls of my class were rather like flirtatious nuns. Delicacy and chastity were necessary requirements for a young gentlewoman in those days. Nothing rough or coarse was ever allowed to touch me. And nothing ever did until the summer I met Don Ramon de Vargas in Havana, Cuba."

For several moments the room was very still, and then Julia continued. "Ours was a reckless and passionate love affair from the beginning. Havana was a paradise. For the first time in my life I allowed myself to fall in love.

"Palm Beach had begun to seem like a prison of my own making. Even when it was filled with people, this house was terribly empty. I was bored with all the parties. Bored by all of it."

Julia lifted her hand to gaze at the golden wedding band. "I imagine I was determined to fall in love with someone, although I didn't know it at the time. It seems odd now to realize that I never even considered the possibility of losing myself to a man. Of marrying him, bearing his children and finally enduring the bitterest disappointment of my life."

Don Ramon de Vargas was like a Latin film star lover. He was a born gambler and womanizer. A Cuban aristocrat whose family bloodlines could be traced all the way back to the Spanish conquest.

By the time Julia had met him just before the Second World War, he had squandered everything but the de Vargas family sugar plantation near Havana. He was a man without visible prospects. But he was also handsome, charismatic and perfectly capable of giving Julia something she desperately needed at that point in her life, a vital masculine excitement that had been missing since the death of Lucky DuShane ten years before.

"We were married by a Catholic priest in Havana," Julia told Brett. "Then we set sail on *The Wanderer* on a honeymoon cruise—Rio, Tahiti, Hong Kong, Bali. It was a wonderful, intoxicating time. I was deliriously happy with Ramon and believed it would go on forever.

"We were in New Zealand when the Japanese bombed Pearl Harbor. I was six months pregnant and eventually gave birth to twins at a private hospital in Sydney. They were christened Luisa and Raphael. By then *The Wanderer* had been commandeered by the American navy, and we had begun to feel more like castaways than romantic vagabonds. It was as if the entire world—everything that I had always taken for granted—was suddenly at war.

"Then I discovered that Don Ramon was being unfaithful. It seemed that once he had me in his power, my affections meant little to him. Of course, there was little enough I could do to stop him from sleeping with other women and gambling my fortune away. I loved him deeply. Somehow, it didn't seem to matter. Just being with him was enough. I was an emotional wreck, but mentally held hostage by him."

Suddenly, Julia coughed hard, almost gagging. She took a sip of water. Brett realized that Julia was a far sicker woman than she had first guessed. She wondered if, somehow knowing her life was drawing to a close, this was what had prompted Julia to reveal so much she had previously kept hidden.

Julia continued. She was just over thirty when she met Don Ramon de Vargas in Havana. It was perhaps inevitable that a man like de Vargas should fall in love with her and, having done so, should determine to possess her completely.

Julia had known he would be unfaithful but being a practical woman, believed that promiscuity was as proper for men as it was improper for women. She would have thought it shocking to even consider taking a lover. For a decent woman there was no possibility of giving herself to anyone but her husband. Marriage was a lasting commitment, and Julia's only real concern was to keep de Vargas from straying beyond her reach.

Don Ramon had first taken up with a nightclub dancer and continued with various chambermaids before becoming bold enough to seduce several of Julia's well-placed women friends.

There was a minor scandal over a fifteen-year-old girl, yet Julia never said a word. Certainly Don Ramon was perceptive enough to realize she was aware of his indiscretions. By then, however, he had her completely in his power and the matter remained unmentioned.

By the time they arrived back in Havana, the war was over and their life on the baronial de Vargas plantation was close to idyllic. Julia settled into motherhood with a serene sense of total fulfillment. Grace, joy and beauty had been bestowed upon her children at birth, along with a thanksgiving of riches. Ever the extravagant and doting mother, Julia watched them grow and flourish and had never been happier in her life.

"It was like living under some kind of enchantment," Julia said. "I knew all about Ramon's other women. I knew who they were and when he went to them, and it only made me desire him all the more. I couldn't wait to have his hands upon me. Night after night, I would lie awake in my bedroom, praying that he would come to me.

"And," she continued slowly, "Even when a trusted servant informed me that she had seen 'something shocking' taking place between my husband and my daughter, Luisa, I still refused to believe the worst."

Julia slowly shook her head. "I knew what kind of man I had married, yet I wasn't able to imagine life without him. At least not until the Marchessa Concha de Vargas appeared upon the scene and threatened to cause a dreadful scandal. And then ... it all ended so badly. Ramon had been married before, although he had told me there had been an annulment. At the time it seemed terribly important to him that we were able to marry in the Catholic church. It never even occurred to me that this, too, was a lie. Then, his legal wife returned to Cuba from Spain, and I discovered myself to be the mother of two illegitimate children, which, back then, was truly shocking. It was exactly the kind of scandal I had always tried to avoid. So, I went aboard my yacht and sailed off, leaving both Don Ramon *and* his wife behind, hoping I could keep the damage control to a minimum."

"And the children?" Brett questioned. "What happened to them?"

"I left them in Cuba to be raised by their father, and up until his death, Ramon de Vargas blackmailed me shamelessly with threats of exposure. I spent a fortune paying him off, yet it was never enough to put an end to the terrible sense of shame, guilt and stupidity I felt. He had made me out to be an utter fool.

"Can you imagine how I felt? It was like looking in a mirror and seeing myself for the first time. I had returned to Palm Beach to inhabit a palace of mirrors reflecting the emptiness of my life into infinity. A shallow, superficial woman who had abandoned her children to a vile and dissolute man in order to save her own pathetic reputation. They were lost to me forever. For all those years I kept sending the money because I had nothing else to give."

"Where are Raphael and Luisa now?" Brett said.

"I've had no word of my children since Castro came to power," Julia admitted in an anguished voice. "Don Ramon is long since dead, and I have no idea where they are. Not even what they look like. But I want to know. . . ."

Julia slipped the wedding ring from her finger and placed it in Brett's hand. It was a band of heavy Florentine gold inscribed with the names, "Julia" and "Ramon."

"I want you to find them for me," Julia said. "You are the only one I can trust. Show them this ring and tell them they have a great inheritance coming to them. But you'll have to work quickly, Miss Farrell. There isn't much time."

"But, I'm not a private detective. I wouldn't even know where to start. . . ."

"Don't be modest. You may not be a detective, but you are a reporter, which is really the same, is it not?"

"Well . . ."

"Find them, Miss Farrell. *Please*. They're all I have in the world, and I desperately want what is rightfully theirs to go to them."

CHAPTER ELEVEN

*T*HE *Huey chopper cut across the sky high above the treetops. In the distance, thunder rolled like kettledrums upon the horizon, while masses of dark clouds rolled past the windshield.*

Brett sat with her back supported by cases of arms and supplies destined for the Somosa forces battling the Sandinista rebels around the village of La Paz. She wore a khaki jumpsuit with her Hasselblad camera strung around her neck on a leather strap.

Directly across from her, a boyish-looking soldier was staring at her. They were all sweating in the torpid heat, and the zipper of Brett's jumpsuit was drawn slightly down, exposing a glimpse of her breasts.

She reached into her camera bag for a pack of cigarettes, and then, after lighting hers with a battered Zippo lighter, she passed them around to the half-dozen soldiers squatting around the open bay of the chopper.

The lighter was her lucky charm. It had belonged to her brother, Laddie, and had accompanied her into battle in both Viet Nam and Cambodia.

One of the soldiers laughed and rattled off something in rapid-fire Spanish, while the others smiled and nodded in her direction. Brett wasn't fluent in the dialect, but it wasn't diffi-

cult to understand what was being said. She was the crazy gringo journalist, who had jumped with the 452nd paratroopers in Nam, been in the thick of the savage street fighting during the Tet offense and had her picture on the cover of Newsweek.

The Nicaraguan revolution was much like any other guerrilla war, and Brett's objective was to get as much of the action on film as possible while at the same time getting it past the censors.

Getting the real story, however, was another matter altogether. The battle lines changed hourly, and in spite of the official version, no one seemed to know just how far the rebel advance had gone—much less who was winning.

The press briefing that morning in San José had been total bullshit. When it was over, Brett decided the only way to get to the truth was by going to La Paz. The rains had let up earlier in the day, and through the open cargo bay, Brett caught glimpses of long green mountain ridges and deep valleys wreathed in mist.

They were still a dozen kilometers from La Paz when Brett saw a puff of smoke rise above the treetops. There was an explosion and suddenly everyone was shouting as the chopper bucked and veered.

Brett struggled to her feet, stumbled and ended up bracing herself against the soldiers, huddling in the open bay as wind and warm tropical rain pelted against her.

Below, in a swampy clearing on the verges of Lake Nicaragua, was the burning wreck of a government helicopter, half covered by reeds and muddy water. Several bodies were sprawled nearby.

"Mira, Cabrone!" a soldier cried out. He was pointing toward a rebel gun emplacement that was by now clearly visible through the trees and wreathing mists. It was too late. They were already well into range. The chopper's rotor sputtered. The ship rapidly lost altitude, and the pilot struggled desperately at the controls to retain command of the chopper.

A burst of tracer fire came from below, and bullets riddled the fuselage. Brett swiftly adjusted her viewfinder and began taking shots.

There was another burst of gunfire. One of the soldiers lurched against her, only to be sprayed with bullets. He screamed and slumped sideways, dragging Brett down to one knee as blood gushed from his mouth.

Pandemonium broke out as the rotor sputtered crazily and bullets raked the ship. They returned fire, one round after another, all the while losing altitude.

They were going down. Down. Down. Brett made a snap decision. In the middle of crossfire, she leapt out of the cargo bay just as the chopper careened into a copse of trees, exploding in a great ball of fire.

And then everything went blank.

When she came to and managed to sit up, a ragged rebel soldier was moving toward her in a low crouch. He stopped about thirty feet away, raised his AK-47 rifle and took careful aim. Brett couldn't believe what she was seeing. Still dazed and disoriented, death was staring her in the face.

"Journalista!" Brett cried out. "Yo estoy journalista. . . . Journalista. . . ."

Brett didn't hear the shot but saw a sudden flash from the rifle barrel and felt a punch in the thigh. There was a rush of blood but no pain, only shock.

"Journalista!" she screamed as she snatched up her camera and began snapping shots.

There was a blinding burst of automatic weapon fire, and the rebel soldier exploded into bloody fragments before Brett's eyes. A man rushed from the tall reeds with an Uzi machine gun clutched tightly in his hands. He was ramming a flesh clip into the Uzi as he came splashing toward her with a ragged red bandana tied about his head.

She watched him spin about and fire off his entire clip into

*the nearby reeds. Her fatigues were soaked with blood, and she
was swimming in and out of consciousness.*

*He bent over her and picked her up roughly into his arms.
She cried out as he stumbled onto drier land and began running with long loping strides.*

Then the world tipped up sideways and everything slid away.

It was three in the morning when the phone rang beside the
bed. It rang again. Then once again. Brett finally picked it up.

It was Iris Quaid's voice. Brett recognized it immediately in
spite of the muffled sobbing. She was hysterical, and her words
tumbled out in a jumbled rush. It was about Julia DuShane.
Something terrible had happened. She must come to La Caraval immediately.

Brett dressed quickly and hurried down the back stairs. She
went out through the kitchen into the garage. The keys were in
the ignition of her father's silver Porsche Spyder. Minutes later
she was speeding along South Ocean Boulevard. The surf was
exploding against the seawall, and the windshield wipers fought
a solid wash of rain. It was one of the worst tropical downpours
of the season.

When Brett reached La Caraval, police cars with flashing
red and blue lights and an ambulance were parked directly in
front of the entrance. Brett came skidding to a halt just as the
paramedics wheeled a white-sheeted gurney out through the
open front doors.

There were shouts from the drive, and Brett recognized
Helga Nordstrom holding an I.V. bottle above the trundling
gurney as it was whisked down the stairs through the rain and
swiftly lifted into the back of the ambulance. She heard someone rapping on her car window and turned to see Iris's pale
and distraught features blurring beyond the streaming glass.

Brett lowered the window. "What's happened to Julia?"

"Oh, Miss Farrell," Iris cried. "I think she's dying. The med-
ics said it was a massive stroke."

"Was anyone with her when it happened?"

"Madame rang her bell in the middle of the night. We found her on the floor with her face . . . just sort of fallen away. She tried to talk but the words wouldn't come out. After we'd called the ambulance she managed to say your name and I called you."

The ambulance was taking off with siren screaming.

"I'm glad you did. I'll call you from the hospital," Brett promised. "Now go inside and for God sakes get out of those wet clothes."

Brett arrived at Harbor View Hospital just as the ambulance backed up to the emergency entrance. The gurney was swiftly wheeled through the glass doors and down a short hall to a waiting elevator. "I'm a relative," she lied as white uniformed medical personnel crowded in around her.

"Julia," Brett whispered urgently as the elevator carried them soundlessly upward. Julia's face was drawn down on one side with one eye partially closed. Her lips moved, but there was no sound.

"I promise," Brett assured her, reaching out to stroke Julia's hair. Brett squeezed the frail hand beneath the sheet and felt the slightest tremor of response. "If it's possible to find them, I promise you that I will."

CHAPTER TWELVE

Brett loosened her seat belt and dropped her head back against the seat. She felt numb and totally drained as the Tri Star executive jet climbed high above the sea, then turned northward.

Only the thought of seeing Brad again had made it possible for her to pull herself together, but even that had been a struggle.

She had spent twelve hours at the hospital.

Seven hundred and twenty minutes watching the large circular clock on the wall outside the intensive care unit.

She had stood staring into where Julia DuShane lay on a white-sheeted bed. The room was clinically austere; totally depersonalized and glaring with hot bright lights. There were no windows. Nothing to break the monotony of the sterile white walls except for banks of flashing video screens and various monitors. The doctors and nurses kept coming and going, their faces covered in green caps, gowns and surgical face masks.

Brett could barely see Julia beyond the coiled turban of bandages completely swathing her head. Her wrists had been bound to the bed to prevent displacement of the tubes, needles and electronic sensors keeping her alive.

She had stared for what seemed like hours at the electrocardiograph monitor, watching the dancing blue line go up and down. At some point many hours earlier, one of the nurses had informed her that Julia's heart had stopped beating twice while she was undergoing emergency brain surgery to release the pressure of her inner-cranial bleeding. They had been able to resuscitate her with massive electrocardial shocks, but she failed to stabilize.

It was almost ten in the morning when Simon Lanier took Brett aside to tell her the worst. He looked exhausted. "I'm sorry, Brett. Julia is brain dead. There's no hope whatsoever for her recovery."

Now six hours later, Brett was on her way to New York City aboard the corporate jet Brad Harraway had sent for her. The Pulitzer Awards ceremony was that evening at the Hilton, but it was the last place Brett wanted to be. Awards, no matter how great, were so trivial against the backdrop of life and death, as were so many other things. She had known that through years of war and had been forced to realize it again in Palm Beach, first with her father, and now Julia.

The plane had by now reached cruising altitude after taking off from West Palm Beach Airport, and beyond the windows was nothing but a sea of white clouds as far as the eye could see. Brett was the only passenger on board. She was drinking a double Scotch and smoking a cigarette.

She really hadn't wanted to come at all after that had taken place, but that was the effect Brad had on her. He had guided and nurtured her journalistic career like an unerring Svengali. She had been green but determined to prove herself to anyone. He had been the Saigon bureau chief of Media International. From the beginning, he had attracted her: tall, well built, vital with clear-cut features, curly graying hair and a clef on his chin. But most important of all, he was a gutsy, first-rate journalist who had immediately recognized her abilities and total dedication to the job. Being a foreign correspondent was considered the glamour job of newspaper reporting. But in reality nothing could have been further from the truth—it was a long and exhausing process of developing news sources and getting the facts.

Brett had made it to the top, but she had made few real friends along the way. From the beginning she had been resented because of her sex, background and the irrefutable fact that she was damned good. If nothing else, Brett thought, winning the Pulitzer Prize should prove that once and for all.

Of course, she owed a lot to Brad. They had been lovers for over a decade, and Brett had come to depend upon him. But over the years, they had failed to make anything other than infrequent and transitory connections in their relationship. Nam, Cambodia, the Sinai, Central America, Beirut, and Afghanistan.

There were passionate reunions and poignant farewells, and ultimately both knew their careers were their first loves.

Now, at fifty-five, Brad had become the man responsible for guiding Media International to its preeminent position as one of the most innovative and aggressive news-gathering services in America. He was also happily married and completely devoted to his wife and family.

It was what he wanted, and Brett accepted it. She had no other choice. But his love was still there for her, as was hers for him.

Brett arrived at Westchester Airport just outside New York City, and was greeted by David Markham, the public relations director for Media International. Brad, he informed her, had been unavoidably detained in Washington, D.C. Russia was intervening in Afghanistan.

"He'll try and get back for the awards ceremony this evening," David said. "But he wants you to cover this. How soon can you be ready to leave for Kabul?"

Brett said nothing but watched as the chauffeur placed her luggage in their limo. Through all their years together, Brad had managed to be there to welcome her. It had become a kind of ritual. Oh hell, she thought, nothing's set in stone.

She pulled her fur coat close about her and settled back in the limousine for the half hour's ride into midtown Manhattan. It had snowed earlier in the day, and the temperature was in the low thirties.

"I know you're disappointed that Brad wasn't able to meet you, but then yours truly isn't exactly the Boston Strangler. Cheer up, Brett. This is going to be the happiest night of your life."

"I'm sorry, David. I'm just extremely tired. I'll be okay after I get to the hotel and get some rest. Now, why don't you fill me in on my schedule for the next twenty-four hours? I have to be back in Palm Beach by late tomorrow afternoon."

"What about Afghanistan?" he questioned. "You didn't exactly look overjoyed when I told you that Brad wanted you over there *poste haste.*"

"I'm afraid the tank is empty, David. I don't think I could handle it right now."

David pulled a comically dubious expression. "I don't believe I'm hearing this. What happened to Brenda Starr, girl reporter? What happened to the woman for whom 'no assignment was too hard or too dangerous'? Not to mention the crack war correspondent who crash-landed in the jungles of Nicaragua and got shot in the ass by some fucking greenhorn guerrilla? Now that's true grit! The kind of reporting that wins Pulitzer Prizes."

They both laughed, but Brett felt close to tears. She was extremely fond of David, a six-foot-tall Texan in his mid-forties with longish wheat-colored hair, roguish good looks and a blond mustache.

He was one of the few people who knew the truth about her and Brad, and his devotion to Brett had long served to deflect more than a hint of gossip about them. Yet, she felt David's feelings for her went deeper, and it was something she had never wanted to deal with.

"Look, Brett," he continued after filling her in on the evening's activities, "you know how I dislike being the harbinger of ill tidings but . . ."

"But what?"

"I don't want you walking into this thing completely cold tonight."

"You don't want me walking *cold* into *what*?"

"Well . . . nothing. It's just that there's been a lot of resentment over your winning the award over all those macho men. You know," he said lightly, "all those heavy journalistic types who like to talk about how they used to get drunk with Hemingway during the Spanish Revolution. It's ridiculous, and totally chauvinistic, but I wanted you to be aware of it. You know how they are. . . ."

Brett sighed. "Yes, David. I know. I don't hang out all night drinking with them. I won't fuck 'em, and while they're still sleeping off hangovers, I'm already half way to ChiChiCastenango. I'll never be 'one of the guys' or even an acceptable female substitute, but I don't give a damn. If they can't handle it, it's their fucking problem, not mine."

"That a girl!"

Brett's smile was grim. "Now what do I do for an encore? I'll probably have to get myself killed just to keep from becoming a has-been. But thanks for the warning. I appreciate your concern. Don't worry, the boys will get over it."

"Watch yourself just the same. There've been a lot of changes. You may be in for a few surprises."

A dismal wintry dusk had settled over the city as the limousine pulled up beneath the porte cochere of the New York Hilton. She kissed David lightly on the cheek and entered the hotel. The lobby was crowded. Most of those attending the ceremony had arrived at the very last minute, and there seemed to be confusion about reservations.

People were milling about, and the management was busy trying to placate everyone because everyone was important.

Slipping on her tinted aviator lenses, Brett worked her way through the crowd and took her place in line at the reception desk as unobtrusively as possible. No one seemed to recognize her, although there were some familiar faces from her own field of television and newsprint journalism.

God knows they were easy enough to spot in any gathering, Brett thought. There was a certain hyper-intensity about the men. They were tough, hard-drinking and sometimes brilliant newsmen she respected more than she liked. They had been around the world a thousand times and met everybody twice. Most suffered from alcoholism, periodic bouts of impotency and a generally jaded view of the human condition.

But she preferred them over the women, who had a very different cut to their sails. Most were professional ball breakers. Blunt, aggressive and flaunting their mental acuity as if jousting to be top dog at all costs. A sense of cross-sexuality prevailed in their clothes, gestures and manner, suggesting they walked somewhere between both sexes.

Authors, poets and playwrights of international repute were also in the lobby. Everyone was meeting and greeting and throwing a lot of whispery little kisses around like used-up lottery tickets. There was a puckish playwright who reminded Brett of a Regency tea cozy in purple velvet, and a Broadway legend sporting her fifth husband and third facelift. She was costumed from head to toe in black leather with a Russian sable draped about her shoulders.

Finally, Brett managed to get her room assignment and started toward the elevators. She had, of course, picked up a stack of congratulatory telegrams and a dozen phone messages that would have to wait until the following day. Curiously, one of them was from Theodore Baxter of Baxter, Barron and Byrne. Baxter had been her father's lawyer and was presently acting as executor in liquidating the estate.

While Brett waited for the elevator, her luck at remaining relatively anonymous ended.

"Excuse me, Miss Farrell. My name is Lisle Brauer, *Frankfurter Zeitung*, Washington Bureau. If you could please spare me a few minutes, I'd like to ask you some questions."

Lisle Brauer was tall, svelt and had all the obvious attributes of a high-fashion model or porno film star. A flawless platinum beauty. For a woman journalist, she was anything but a sexual chameleon.

"There's a press conference at seven this evening, Miss Brauer. You may ask any questions you like at that time. Now if you'll excuse me, I'm rather tired. I want to get to my room."

Just then the elevator doors slid open, and Lisle Brauer stepped forward to effectively block Brett's path. "Please . . . I don't think you would want the questions that I have in mind aired at a press conference. Just a few minutes of your time, Miss Farrell. It's important."

"Just what kind of questions did you have in mind?"

"I'm afraid some rather personal ones."

"I really don't see where my personal life is anyone's business. The prize was given for my profession."

"I understand that, Miss Farrell, but you are going to get some questions anyway."

"What are you talking about?"

"Perhaps we could go into the bar and have a drink. Would you?"

Brett sighed, not at all liking the feeling of where this was leading, but she decided she'd better nip whatever this reporter had in the bud fast. The Candelabra Bar of the Hilton was less crowded than the lobby. Dimly luxurious with a sophisticated ripple of music coming from the piano bar. At Brett's insistence they were seated at a secluded corner banquette.

Drinks arrived and Brett said, "Now what exactly did you want to know?"

"About your relationship with Brad Harraway."

Brett stared coldly at the woman. "What about it? He's my mentor, my friend, my support in times of difficulty."

"That's not what I mean. If we are to be completely frank, Miss Farrell, there are those who feel that it is specifically because of Brad Harraway's interest in your career that led to the Pulitzer."

"There's no denying that, but the Pulitzer Committee could care less *how* I got the assignments, only the way I covered them."

"Listen," the woman said gravely, "there are going to be questions tonight. Planted questions by peers of yours who loathe the idea of you winning this prize. Questions about your relationship with Mr. Harraway, and specifically whether he's divorcing his wife in order to marry you."

Brett sat in stunned silence. This was news to her, if a word of it was true, and she was sure it wasn't. David was right. Things had changed. Someone was trying to smear her, but she was damned if she was going to let this bitch see her squirm.

"If I'm not mistaken, Brad is very happily married and quite a devoted husband. I can assure you that I won't be marrying him."

"Did you know that he's filed suit and his wife has filed a countersuit, naming you as a party to adultery? You can read all about it in tomorrow's papers."

Brett sank back in the banquette, feeling as if she had suddenly walked in on a bad dream from which she couldn't wake up. If any of this were true, certainly he would have told her, wouldn't he? *Of course he would.* This was absurd.

"I think," Lisle said sotto voce, "that it would be wise of you to skip the press conference tonight. Consider the warning a favor from a fellow journalist."

"Wait a minute," Brett said coolly. "Say I do, what's your stake in this? Certainly this is more than just a favor. You don't even know me. We've never met."

Lisle looked at her and smiled. "But I know Brad. He *is*

divorcing his wife, but not to marry you. He's going to be marrying me. We've been lovers for over a year now, and I've worked too hard at getting this divorce pushed through to lose him now because of either his wife . . . or you. She's out of the picture, and I want to be sure that you are, too."

Brett finished her drink in one gulp, rose to her feet and narrowed her eyes on the woman. Her smile was a thin, set line. "Unfortunately, nobody can ever be absolutely sure of anything in this world, can they? That's what makes life so interesting. Good evening, Miss Brauer."

CHAPTER THIRTEEN

Brett was finishing her acceptance speech. "War," she said finally, "*teaches you a great deal about people and even more about yourself. And tonight I wish to acknowledge my colleagues with whom I have shared violent combat situations throughout the world. We were like firemen running to try and help put out a different fire every day, and our being there did make a difference.*

"*Being there meant learning the hard way, because nothing was ever what you thought it would be. We were all out there for a variety of reasons, but the only one that matters is that if decent people are not informed of what's going on in the world, the madness will soon overwhelm us.*

"*There are those who call us 'war lovers,' and it's true that we shared the spirit of excitement that comes with performing near miracles under fire. Perhaps there is nothing that makes you more conscious of being fully alive than coming very close to death and surviving.*

"*But we were never war lovers, because war is never about loving. It's a brutal and dehumanizing experience, and we are only out there because the truth must be told. Whatever our personal motives might be for choosing this exhilarating, impossible and sometimes deeply gratifying profession, . . . we are out there for only one reason. Because someone has to be.*"

Brett left the stage to a prolonged standing ovation.

She pressed the remote control button to switch off the VCR. She felt edgy and preoccupied.

Brett had deliberately slept through the press conference earlier that evening, and while she was dressing, she and David Markham had shared a bottle of champagne. They had arrived at the awards dinner over an hour late in order to avoid the endless round of acceptance speeches. They had made a stunning couple.

Now, back in the hotel suite with Brad snoring softly beside her, Brett felt a restless sense of dissatisfaction. Brad hadn't gotten back from Washington in time for the ceremony and had showed up at the hotel suite afterward exhausted and doggedly apologetic.

He had changed in the six months since Brett had seen him last. He looked every day of his age, and it pained her to see him so worn out. Perhaps she was just seeing him as he really was—a paunchy middle-aged man drained of all the charisma and vitality that had been so much a part of him.

Brett smoothed the graying hair back from his forehead and wondered what had happened. He had been her rock, her source of strength and guidance. The perfect replacement for the man she had only thought her father to be.

She threw back the covers and slipped from bed as quietly as possible. She struggled into the filmy flesh-colored peignoir purchased for their reunion. She might as well have saved the six hundred dollars and worn her favorite flannel nightgown. Neither the sexy peignoir nor her lovemaking had managed to spark Brad to life. Was he thinking of Fraulein Brauer? Or had their passion simply burnt itself out?

She quietly closed the bedroom door, knowing that it was over between them. She switched on a lamp in the living room of the suite and picked up the phone. "I want to place a person-to-person call to Harbor View Hospital in West Palm Beach, Florida," she told the hotel operator. "I'd like to speak with Dr. Simon Lanier."

Julia was still alive, Simon told her when he came on the line, but barely. According to Simon, Julia could continue to exist in that condition for weeks, months or even years, unless of course somebody decided to take her off the life support system. But legally, it had to be a next of kin. Unfortunately, he continued, she didn't have any.

Wrong, Brett thought, but said nothing. . . .

When Brad woke up to use the bathroom, he found Brett curled up on the couch. An empty bottle of champagne stood on the glass-topped coffee table, and Brett was staring out at the glittering midtown view of Manhattan.

Brett didn't even know he was there. He came up behind her and kissed the top of her head. "I missed you," he said softly. "I reached out and you were gone."

"I had to make a phone call about a friend who's in the hospital. It's Julia DuShane. She collapsed last night with a massive stroke."

"I read the United Press release on it this morning. In fact, I've already got someone working on the obit. I didn't know you knew her. I thought she represented everything you hated about Palm Beach."

"I'm not sure what I feel about Palm Beach or Julia DuShane. I'm only sorry she didn't die last night. I'm sure that's what she wanted—a swift dramatic departure with the audience still applauding."

"I'm sorry I was such a bust in bed tonight. Too much pressure and no sleep, I guess. I must have passed out."

"Why didn't you tell me about Lisle Brauer?" she asked quietly. Her voice was blurred with the champagne.

Brad drew away and poured himself a generous bourbon on the rocks from the bar. "I intended to tell you. I'm not sure when . . . but I didn't want to spoil tonight."

"I would have preferred it coming from you. As it was, Fraulein Brauer met me in the lobby this afternoon and staked out her claim in no uncertain terms. She's quite beautiful, Brad. And she's got balls. I rather suspect she'll go a long way in this business. In some ways, she reminded me of myself a decade or so ago."

Brad made a futile gesture with his drink, still refusing to meet her eyes. "I was afraid Lisle might pull a stunt like that. She's very impulsive . . . headstrong—"

"And terrific in bed?"

"Brett . . . I know how lousy all this must look to you."

"The way it looks to me is too mundane for words."

"Whether you want to believe it or not, Lisle really admires the hell out of you. She's always wanted to be a journalist and followed your career since high school. She's twenty-three by the way, and hardly the femme fatale."

"I suppose I should be flattered," Brett shot back. "I was less than flattered, however, to discover from young Lisle, tripping along in my footsteps, that you've decided to divorce your wife. That was always the big no, no, wasn't it Brad? And wasn't I the naive one? How awfully convenient that I was posted off somewhere in the boondocks. All of it strictly business except when you needed a convenient screw. Wars, revolutions and hot sex. That's a hard combination to beat. You certainly proved that tonight."

"I guess she told you my wife is naming you as correspondent in the divorce suit?"

"Now that's something that should make terrific reading in the tabloids. I can just see it now, 'PALM BEACH HEIRESS FUCKS HER WAY TO PULITZER PRIZE.'"

Brad's face was shadowed and haggard. "I'm sorry you got mixed up in this, Brett. Jesus . . . I didn't mean for it to happen. I'll never stop caring about you, Brett. You'll always be important to me. It's been a great ten years. Don't try to cheapen it or make it seem less than it was. Everything got all mixed up. Job pressures, sex, Lisle, the divorce, the way my kids look at me now. My good, dear wife of twenty years turning into a cunt who's out for my blood."

"I was under the impression that it was *my* blood she was after. It's not inconceivable, you know, that she could have named Lisle in the divorce suit."

Brad shook his head. "She's only using you to get to me. I think she must have known about us."

Brett shrugged. "You know what they say about a woman scorned, Brad. I can't say that I blame her. But the truth is, things have changed for me, too. I had planned to tell you about it tonight."

Brad turned to stare at her curled up on the couch. His hands were plunged deep into the pockets of his robe.

"It isn't *just* you and Lisle," Brett continued. "You see there's this journalist who got herself shell-shocked during one too many wars. Suddenly, she doesn't know where she's going anymore, or how she's going to get there. Anyway, she came home and ran into some guy she had almost married once upon a time. His name is Simon Lanier, Brad. And the journalist is beginning to think that she's falling in love with him all over again."

CHAPTER FOURTEEN

THE next morning at eleven, Brett was shown into the office of Theodore Baxter. There were veneered walls, corporate-blue carpeting and a wide expanse of floor-to-ceiling tinted windows. Tall, silver-haired and patrician-looking, Theodore Baxter was immaculately dressed in a Savile Row double-breasted pinstripe suit. He wore a white carnation in his lapel, and his welcoming smile was as bland as a computer printout.

"Miss Farrell," Baxter said, rising to present a well-manicured hand. He had been seated behind a Chippendale desk, perfectly framed by a spectacular view of Central Park and the surrounding skyline.

"I'm so glad you were able to meet with me on such short notice. I know how busy you must be with all this business of the Pulitzer. I thought the time had come for us to have a little chat."

Baxter removed his half-frame reading glasses to regard her with a long, cool, appraising look. "May I say that your newspaper photos fail to do you justice." He motioned to a richly upholstered wingback chair, and Brett came forward to seat herself in front of the desk.

She crossed her long legs with a whisper of silken hosiery, wondering what it was that Theodore Baxter had in mind. She was feeling jittery and hungover from the previous night, but her curiosity had been aroused by Baxter's unexpected request for a meeting. Brett had not met him before.

"You said on the phone that you had something important to discuss with me," Brett said. "I assume it has something to do with settling my father's estate?"

Baxter leaned forward in his chair to open a leather-bound portfolio on the desk. "Certainly you are aware, Miss Farrell, that you were disinherited by your father some ten years ago for reasons that I was not made privy. Dwight Farrell was a very private man and never discussed his personal life with me. I simply carried out whatever instructions he gave me."

"Ah, you mean the messenger is not to be blamed for the bad news, right? Yes, I got your letter while I was covering the war in Viet Nam, telling me I'd been cut off. I was dropped like a bad habit, so to speak."

Baxter cleared his throat and rearranged the papers before him. "Certainly, you may have seen it that way at the time. But I wouldn't judge too harshly if I were you."

Brett looked at him coldly, wondering what Theodore Baxter would think of the *real* reason for her disinheritance. Incest wouldn't play all that well as a topic of polite discussion with him, she guessed.

"In any case," Baxter continued, "your father's previous will left both you and your brother quite a substantial inheritance, while the will in effect at the time of his death left almost his entire estate in trust for your mother. There was also a ten million dollar bequest to the Oceanographic Research Institute in Orlando, which your father had originally endowed."

This was news to Brett. Dwight philanthropic? "I had no idea such a place existed. My father never gave the slightest indication that he was in the least bit philanthropic. I knew, of course, that he was a very wealthy man, but he never discussed money. Not even with my mother. I assume from the way you're talking that he left her very well fixed."

Baxter spread his hands upon the highly polished surface of

the desk and smiled benignly. "At the time of his death, your father's estate was valued at something over seventy-five million dollars. I should think your mother would be able to get along quite well on the yearly interest. A sum somewhere in the neighborhood of six million dollars a year. As you know, your father was extremely secretive about the extent of his wealth."

Brett barely listened. The disinheritance had been a wound that refused to heal, a coldly calculated attempt to undermine her sense of self-worth. Her father's love had always been on loan, and he had merely called in the debt after what had happened in Nassau. She wanted to laugh. Six million a year just on the interest? Her income had been less than thirty thousand dollars last year.

She sighed. Dwight Farrell had been a taker. A user and a destroyer. She was glad he was dead. Glad she had torn up the pathetically pleading letters that had come toward the end. The last thing in the world she had wanted was his blood money.

Baxter paused and cleared his throat. "Are you feeling okay, Miss Farrell? Would you like me to send for something? Coffee, a drink, perhaps?"

"No, no thank you. I'm fine, Mr. Baxter."

"Well, then, I understand perfectly how busy you must be here in New York. So let us proceed. I can understand your displeasure at being cut off from your father's estate. But there is still the trust."

"Trust?" Brett repeated, looking perplexed. "Are you referring to the small trust left by my Grandmother Deveraux?"

"No, I am referring to the trust your father established for you and your brother at birth. At that time he made outright gifts of three hundred seventy-five shares of Tidewater Oil stock. He did, however, insist on the stipulation that no one, not even his wife, was to know about the trust until after his death."

Baxter slipped on his glasses to study the portfolio before him for several moments before continuing. "Now then, with an appreciation of fifteen hundred percent over the past thirty-four years, that makes your present stock holdings in Tidewater quite considerable."

Brett's stomach tightened. She was hovering on the edge of her chair as Baxter studied the long columns of figures before him. Even reading upside down, which she had taught herself to do years earlier, the figures were astronomical.

Baxter leaned back in his chair and folded his hands before him like a judge about to commute a sentence. "I'm pleased to say I have some rather good news for you, Miss Farrell. On your thirty-fifth birthday, you will come into an estimated nine million dollars, based, of course, on current market values."

"Nine million dollars?" Brett gasped.

Baxter nodded. "I thought you might be pleased. But that is not all. There is also a stipulation to the trust that your father inserted. It's what we refer to as an 'ironbound' clause, stipulating that if either sibling predeceased the other, their holdings in Tidewater Oil would automatically revert to the living heir.

"In this instance, Miss Farrell, the trust has reverted to the living heiress. As of the moment, your total stock holdings in Tidewater Oil are worth approximately eighteen million dollars. Congratulations. On your thirty-fifth birthday, you are going to become a very wealthy young woman indeed."

Brett lunched at the Four Seasons with an important syndicated columnist, and arrived at Kennedy Airport for her commercial flight to West Palm Beach just after four in the afternoon.

She was exhausted by the events of the last few days, but also exhilarated. By the time she checked into the VIP lounge at Eastern Airlines, there was a message from Brad waiting for her. She had asked him to try to locate Luisa and Raphael de Vargas, Julia DuShane's children, through his network of contacts.

Brett called his private office number. Their conversation was strained at first, but quickly moved to business.

"Hold on to your hat," he said. According to a top-level informant in the U.S. Immigration Service, Luisa had managed to get out of revolutionary Cuba just as the victorious regime of Fidel Castro issued a warrant for her arrest.

Having been the mistress of a high-ranking general in Battista's corruption-ridden army, Luisa de Vargas would have most likely found herself rotting in a revolutionary jail had she not exercised the forethought to marry an obscure American evangelist named James Earl Carswell.

The Reverend Carswell had been holding Christian revival meetings in Havana when Castro came to power. As the wife of a U.S. citizen, Luisa was able to escape the island by virtue of her husband's American passport.

Together, they returned to New Orleans, where Carswell had a sizable following among poor Southern blacks. It was known as the Cristo Redentor Society. Within a matter of months after her narrow escape from Castro's jails, Luisa de Vargas had been reborn in the guise of Sister Jerusha, who went on to become the hottest road show revival act in the South. A visionary prophetess, preaching a utopian ideal of love, prosperity, and the inherent right of the "poorest of the poor" to inherit the earth.

Faith healing was Sister Jerusha's specialty, and her evangelical services combined a dazzling display of serpent handling, speaking in tongues and a good many carnival aspects of bedrock Southern revivalism. Yet even as her reputation for miraculous healings continued to spread, Jerusha herself began to exhibit increasingly paranoid delusions.

Then, one hot summer night in 1976, after haranguing her parishioners into a state of ecstatic hysteria, Jerusha began handing out dozens of deadly serpents as a test of their commitment and loyalty. When it was finally over, a half-dozen worshippers had been bitten and poisoned to death by the venomous snakes, while another dozen were left blind or severely disabled for life.

It all came out in a trial, and the press made much of the

fact that the Reverend Carswell was among the unfortunate deceased. As the case exploded into the headlines as *The White Witch Murder Trial,* Jerusha's wide-ranging talents were very much in evidence.

Hundreds of her followers held twenty-four-hour prayer vigils in front of the court house. The courtroom itself was packed to the galleries. The atmosphere was emotionally charged and highly volatile when Jerusha took the stand in her own defense.

In the end, the publicly unknown illegitimate daughter of Julia DuShane was acquitted on six counts of manslaughter on grounds of insanity. She was, however, summarily committed to the Louisiana State Hospital for the Criminally Insane.

Brad had not been as successful in getting a lot of information on Raphael de Vargas. But what he did know, he told her.

At eighteen years of age, the son of Don Ramon de Vargas and Julia DuShane had deserted a life of ease and luxury to join up with Fidel Castro's rabble of revolutionaries in the Sierra Maestra Mountains.

During the flight back to Palm Beach, Julia and her children dominated Brett's thoughts. The more Brett discovered, the more she became convinced that she had to find them ... or at least the son. She wanted to know Julia's family, just as she wanted to know her own.

Brett's had been a Sunday supplement kind of family. She had been born into a world of leisure along with privilege and power. Whatever blessings that nature may have overlooked could always be acquired. There had, of course, been a good many more expectations, and as it turned out, many of them had been quite impossible to fulfill.

Despite all the advantages, Brett realized, and perhaps even because of them, the Farrell family had somehow transformed itself into an emotional landscape of incest, loss and despair.

Who was the man she had thought her father to be? Shrouded in contradictions, the question still demanded an answer. An answer she couldn't give. Just as she had been ready to release him, he had turned her world around from the grave and had the last, richest laugh. But for eighteen million dollars, she would let him. After all, she wasn't crazy. Still, the pieces to the puzzle never seemed to fit.

Dwight David Farrell was the son of the founder of Tidewater Oil Company, and a man of immense natural gifts. He was an extremely sexual man who lived for his own gratification, for sexual conquest, sailing, drinking, and playing championship polo for very high stakes.

Born under the sign of Cancer the crab, Brett's father had always been impossible for her to read. Whenever he appeared to be going in one direction, he was actually going in another. No one ever knew what he was thinking, and he invariably bought his pleasures at the expense of others.

He was domineering but immature. Hidden but affable. Abstracted, yet surprisingly shrewd and always fiercely competitive. He could be suavely charming or cruelly cutting. Wealth, family, power and position—all of it existed for the sole purpose of satisfying his every whim, desire or twisted sexual perversion.

Brett had lied to Laura about what had happened in Nassau that summer after her father had won the Bermuda Cup Race. But there was no possible way she could have lied to herself.

She had flown down from Washington to help celebrate his victory. But she had also come to tell him something she knew her father would never be able to accept—she was pregnant and determined to marry Simon Lanier in spite of everything.

The wedding date had already been cancelled, and Brett was getting panicky. She hated the rift that had fallen between them. Laddie's death had cast a pall over the entire family, and Brett couldn't bear the idea of further estrangement.

Dwight Farrell had at first accepted the news of her pregnancy during a riotous shipboard celebration aboard the Lady

Brett. But back on shore later that same night, following an evening of heavy drinking, Brett's life had crumbled.

There had been a knock on the door of her hotel room. Her father was standing there in the doorway, and the change in his appearance was frightening. His features distorted, his face flushed. His eyes were glazed, staring out with a look of almost feral hatred.

Without a word he had locked the door behind him and knocked the breath out of her with a violent blow to the stomach. He was striking out at her unborn child, and the blow sent Brett doubled up and reeling, with a scream cut off in her throat. He hit her so hard that Brett crashed back against the bureau and crumpled to the floor, gasping with pain and shock.

She felt the hysteria rising within her as he beat her again and again with his fists. Dragging her to her feet time after time only to send her smashing up against the furniture until she was nearly unconscious.

She fought back, struggled against him, but it only seemed to increase his rage. He finally dragged her to the bed and threw her bruised and bleeding body down upon it.

With his last assault, her struggles ceased, and Brett turned her face away from him, deliberately avoiding his eyes. She willed him into anonymity as his full weight came down hard upon her with a tearing stab of pain.

She was gasping for breath and choking on her own vomit while the room spun around and around. He pounded away at her, rasping obscenities. "Whore . . . slut . . . never marry . . . fucking Jew bastard! Never have . . . his fucking kid!"

Dwight Farrell had succeeded in seeing to that. Brett had never borne Simon's child, and in the days and weeks that followed, she had come very near to losing her sanity. Escape was her only way out, and the place farthest away was Viet Nam.

Never again could she allow herself the luxury of trust, and there was no longer any question of being afraid since she'd already faced the worst. Nor could she permit herself to think of Simon and the solace of his embrace. Too much had happened, and all she wanted to do was forget.

In time Brett had begun to rebuild her life, but nothing was ever the same. Nor would it be. Not ever again. There were wounds that continued to bleed.

As soon as Brett arrived back at the airport in West Palm Beach, she took a taxi to Harbor View Hospital. While she had been emotionally bracing herself for the worst, nothing could have prepared her for the discovery of what had taken place during her short absence.

That morning Julia had been taken from the hospital by the daughter she had condemned to oblivion almost forty years before. Simon filled Brett in on what had taken place.

After Brett had left for New York City, Simon had received a call from Dr. Florian Montes, asking about Julia's condition. As a professional courtesy, Simon had given him the facts and gone on to say that he had no intention of employing any further artificial means of prolonging Julia's life.

At that point, Montes had demanded that Simon use any possible means at his disposal to keep Julia DuShane "alive at any cost." Should he fail to comply, Montes hinted darkly at a possible malpractice suit brought on behalf of Luisa de Vargas. Montes even went so far as to threaten to bring Simon up on charges before the State Medical Examiner.

To everyone's astonishment, Luisa de Vargas had appeared at Harbor View Hospital, flanked by Dr. Montes and a high-powered Miami lawyer named Bull Dunham-Cartwright, who had political connections throughout Florida.

Dunham-Cartwright had gained himself a well-deserved reputation for being a legal barracuda. Much of his notoriety had been earned through his defense of millionaire drug smugglers and corrupt public officials.

Still, there was just no contesting the fact that Cartwright had somehow managed to procure a court order appointing Luisa de Vargas as the sole legal surrogate for all of her mother's affairs. It was a mind-boggling premise, considering Luisa's background. But this was, after all, Florida, where corruption in high places was the name of the game.

Simon had no choice in the matter but to comply to the letter of the law. A private ambulance had taken Julia home to La Caraval, and she was currently under the exclusive care of Dr. Montes.

"The only thing I know for sure," Simon told Brett, "is that Julia DuShane is only technically alive."

CHAPTER FIFTEEN

THE dunes of Singers Island were a welcome escape for Brett. It was a place of marsh and mangrove, of shallow salt-water ponds and meadows ablaze with wildflowers in spring. It had always been a haven for wildlife. Seabirds abounded and giant sea turtles still came ashore to bury their eggs among the dunes, just as they had since the dunes were formed.

Carrying her surfboard beneath her arm, Brett walked for over a mile up the beach after parking the Porsche near the fire station. Far in the distance, thunderheads gathered upon the horizon and sunlight streamed through clouds to throw patches of light upon the sea.

Spring was the time when the sea came into its wild season along the Florida shoreline. There was a storm coming, and Brett estimated that she would just have time to catch the leading edge of the waves before they became too treacherous to maneuver. The sea was already running high with dangerous riptides and erratic waves that gathered farther out and then came rushing upon the beach.

The long sandy isthmus stretching from the northern perimeter of Palm Beach Shores to the exclusive Country Club enclave at Turtle Beach was a very special place for her. As a child her father used to bring her here to gather shells and brightly colored bits of sea glass. It had been a time when the world was a beautiful place and life itself was imbued with a lyrical sweetness.

Brett paused to draw the fresh sea air deep into her lungs, taking one long deep breath after another. She stripped off her jeans and sweatshirt.

Ever since her return from New York, she and Simon had become a couple again. He sensed exactly what she needed, and their relationship was one of warm, comfortable intimacy.

Simon made love to her with great tenderness, thoughtfully yet naturally and with complete understanding. For the first time since her return to Palm Beach, Brett was able to unwind during the hours they spent together. Simon was the kind of man whose quiet strength and reasoned response to life had gradually begun to give her the sense of emotional security and balance she needed. They spent as much time as possible together, with long moonlit walks along the beach and lazy stolen mornings in bed when Brett stayed overnight at Simon's apartment.

Palm Beach was alive with gossip about the relationship. But Brett ignored the looks and whispers. There were more important things in life. Julia's tragedy was never far from her thoughts, nor was the mysterious Sister Jerusha, whose sudden appearance upon the scene made Brett inexplicably nervous and suspicious.

Upon her return from New York, Brett had moved into the pool house at Marisol. She had set up a darkroom and worked tirelessly developing the photographs she had taken at La Caraval and reading through the diaries entrusted to her safekeeping. Sometimes Brett lingered for hours, endlessly rereading the most intimate passages of Julia's life.

But it was the fifteen hours of recorded conversations that had come to haunt her.

"The last thing I want in the world is a hopeless and lingering death connected to a room full of machines."

Brett had needed to get away from the house, to be alone

with herself and her thoughts. On this particular afternoon the dunes were deserted. The beach was empty and strewn with driftwood and seaweed washed up by the morning tide. She shielded her eyes against the harsh glare and watched the waves pile in from far out at sea without break or pause. Then Brett started running down the beach to throw her board into the shallows. She leaped on top of it while the board was still in motion. Although she hadn't surfed in years, the skill had never left her. Brett slid her weight backward as the nose of the board struck each successive wave to send great masses of frothy sea water rushing over her.

The sea was running high and she paddled hard, sending the surfboard shooting through the rushing white water until she was well beyond the booming surfline. Brett swung the board around and slid up into a sitting position. She watched the huge combers as they rose up beneath her to fall away and hurtle toward the shore.

She recalled that there was a dangerous shoal of rocks submerged somewhere off to her left, about halfway in to shore. But exactly where it was, Brett couldn't remember.

She had been out there for only a few minutes when Brett heard someone calling her name in the distance. Scanning the dunes, she finally saw Simon's distant figure running along the shoreline with a surfboard held high overhead. He threw his board into the shallows and was soon paddling toward her.

"What the hell are you doing out here alone?" he shouted as his board drew nearer. "You've got to be crazy to be surfing in this place on a day like this. They don't call it the 'suicide pipeline' for nothing."

"You worry too much," Brett said as Simon drew near. "How did you know where to find me?"

"I went by the house and Consuelo told me," Simon said. "She was worried because of the storm coming. I think you are out of your mind to come out here alone."

"Sanity is relative," she threw back at him with a taunting smile. "Anyway, I wanted to see Singers Island one last time before the bulldozers turn it into a parking lot."

The wind was stronger now, whipping across the tops of the waves humping up beneath them as Simon looked back over his shoulder to scan the horizon. "Holy shit," he said, frantically starting to backwater. "We have to get farther out. This next set looks like the jaws of death."

Simon turned his board and began paddling straight out while Brett remained where she was, watching as a massive wave rose up out of the sea to suddenly block out the horizon. It was a monster of colossal proportions whose color had begun to change from deep ocean blue to translucent green.

By now the roar was deafening as the wave rose even higher to display a big stingray with its massive batlike wings spread wide as if for flight. Simon yelled another warning, but Brett had already begun to paddle hard until she was swept suddenly to the breaking crest.

She was hurtled forward by an awesome thrust. The fear she experienced was overwhelming, but now she was on her feet with the board skimming down the massive concave face of the wave at an incredible speed.

Simon feared Brett wouldn't see the rocks in time and launched his own board sideways to angle off across the churning face of the wave. He sliced down upon her from above.

Then, directly ahead, the jagged rocks thundered up out of the surf, and Brett was nearly upon them. She tried to cut sharply away but it was already too late. The board seemed to explode beneath her, and the next thing that Brett knew, her nose and throat were filled with salty water. Her heart was thundering against her ribs and her mind became possessed with blank white terror.

Simon's arms were around her as they were hurtled against the rocks and then thrown clear. Their close bodies tumbled over and over as they were dragged along the bottom through boiling clouds of sand and twisting ropes of kelp that whipped about them like coiling tentacles.

The wave had come to possess them, and it seemed to go on forever. Brett's lungs were bursting and her muscles were cramping. She was aware only of being engulfed by forces completely beyond her own control. This was where it would end, she thought, as the sea swirled crazily upward. Above, the sunlit surface shimmered, but Brett felt herself being pulled away into a fathomless black infinity.

She found herself lying on the beach with Simon anxiously bending over her. She coughed and vomited up salt water as he pulled her hard against his chest. He held her tightly, drawing the sand-matted hair back from her face.

"That was a goddamned stupid thing to do," he said. "If I hadn't been out there, you would have bought the ranch."

Her entire body was trembling. She clung to him tightly and then lifted her face to kiss his salty lips. "I do love you," she whispered. "Always remember that."

CHAPTER SIXTEEN

THINGS had already changed at La Caraval the following afternoon. The first thing Brett noticed was a newly painted sign emblazoned with the legend *Cristo Redentor Society* when she and Simon drove through the entrance, and when they pulled up to park in front of the mansion, a group of hostile-looking young blacks materialized, regarding them with narrow and suspicious eyes.

There had been others guarding the gate, and the overall impression was that of an armed camp. Nothing was said as Brett and Simon alighted from the car. The blacks simply stood there watching impassively as they mounted the stairs, crossed the terrace and entered the mansion through the open front doors.

Simon was limping slightly and his arm was in a sling due to a disjointed shoulder injury sustained the previous day. Brett herself had escaped with various superficial cuts and scrapes, even though, once again in her life, she had come very close to death.

It was cool inside the marble entry hall and quiet except for the splashing fountain. Their footsteps echoed against the tiles, and quite unconsciously, Brett slipped her arm through Simon's, their fingers meshing.

"I wonder why the place is wide open?" Brett said. "And who were all those goons with the hard stares?"

"It looks to me like somebody's been rearranging the furniture," Simon said.

Brett made a quick survey and noticed that all the statuary had been removed, along with the paintings that had hung along the staircase. They paused beside the fountain, staring around in puzzlement. It was far too quiet.

They heard a soft swishing sound from above and looked up to see a tall slim figure in white descending the staircase.

There was not the slightest doubt in Brett's mind who the woman was. She bore an almost uncanny resemblance to Julia DuShane. The same classic features, long slender throat, high forehead and dark straight brows were clearly in evidence. But Luisa had a stern Latin beauty, hawkish and proud, yet as luminously poised as a Dior mannequin.

She was standing above them now on the landing, looking down over the carved bannister with her long dark hair drawn back into a single braid. Luisa de Vargas was a commanding figure.

"I have been awaiting your arrival," she said in a full voice. Then she continued on down the stairs with her long white robe sweeping the steps in her wake.

When she reached the bottom of the staircase, Luisa came forward to clasp both of Brett's hands. "You are most welcome in this house, Miss Farrell. I hope that we are going to be friends."

Brett was taken off guard by Luisa's poise and gracious manner; her elegance was something sheer, while the firm cool grasp of her hands seemed to transmit some underlying power. Overall, she was very attractive.

"I hope it isn't inconvenient, our arriving unannounced like this," Brett said. "I know I should have called but I was afraid you'd refuse to see us."

"As I said, Miss Farrell, you were expected. I gave instructions for the doors to be left open for your arrival. There is much we have to discuss."

Then, lifting an eyebrow to Simon, she said, "You, Dr. Lanier, are less than welcome here. I've been told by Dr. Montes about your callous attitude toward my mother's recovery."

Simon glanced at Brett, appearing entirely perplexed. "I'm afraid I haven't the slightest idea what you're talking about. Your mother received the very best medical care available at Harbor View. We did everything possible for her."

"I am not referring to your medical expertise, Dr. Lanier. You would have allowed my mother to die if it had been left up to you. You failed your trust. You are a man bereft of faith . . . without compassion."

Simon was suddenly flushed and angry. "Listen, Luisa or Jerusha or whoever the hell you really are, I'm a physician, not some witch doctor. We did everything possible to save your mother's life. But the fact is no earthly purpose can be served by keeping her heart beating by artificial means. Faith is fine in the abstract, but you might as well face the truth—Julia DuShane is brain dead, and nothing can change that."

"Enough!" Luisa said, her eyes flashing. "There are matters I wish to discuss privately with Miss Farrell. You will be kind enough to excuse us."

Simon glanced at Brett. "Sure. Why not? I'll wait outside with the troops. I don't have any choice, since you and Montes appear to be legally in control—at least for now."

"Simon, please," Brett entreated. "Do as she asks. I won't be long."

After Simon left, Luisa preceded Brett down a long corridor from which all the furnishings had been removed. The lower floor of the mansion seemed to slumber beneath a musty brooding silence, while the familiar rooms opening off on either side of the corridor were steeped in darkness. The heavy draperies were drawn against the day, and shadowy forms bulked up beneath ghostly dustcovers.

Luisa paused to throw open the library doors, motioning for Brett to follow her inside. A flood of light poured in through the bank of French windows at the far end of the room, opening onto a cloistered garden blooming with light and color. A soft breeze blew in at the open windows, billowing the white lace curtains and casting fluttering shadows over the wine red carpet. The air carried the illusive scent of roses.

The room was baronial and out of another era, with leather-bound volumes lining the walls and heavy dark Victorian furnishings. The only sound was the ponderous tick-tocking of a mahogany grandfather clock standing in the corner.

"Do you know who the man is in that painting?" Luisa asked, gesturing toward the gilt-framed portrait hanging over the paneled mantelpiece.

"Your grandfather," Brett said. "Your mother and I spent many hours in this room. Julia told me this library was a perfectly restored replica of his study in Silver Creek. It was her favorite room."

Lucky DuShane had been painted in white tie and tails, holding a silver-headed Malacca walking stick and sporting a walrus mustache. Brett thought he had one of the most arrogant faces she had ever seen.

"My grandfather was a very ruthless and evil man," Luisa said. "Greed was his only God, and it destroyed him in the end."

"But your mother worshipped him. This room is a testament to the influence he held over her life. I had the feeling she felt closest to him here. Almost as if she was experiencing some kind of communion."

Luisa laughed. "The heart of evil is ever iniquitous. You, if anyone, should know that the spirits of the dead continue to inhabit the lives of the living."

It was a curious comment, but then everything about Luisa de Vargas was strangely unnerving. "I was wondering about the servants. I haven't seen any of them about, and I wanted to talk with Iris Quaid."

"I've sent them all away," Luisa replied. "It's important that my mother be surrounded only by those who believe. Soon many of my followers will be joining me here at La Caraval. Perhaps you would like to be present for one of our prayer vigils?"

Luisa paused to stand looking out over the garden through the open windows. "How I envy you, Miss Farrell. You know everything about my mother's life and I know almost nothing."

"We spent a lot of time together," Brett explained. "Your mother and I became very close. I valued her trust and friendship."

"She entrusted you with all her innermost secrets, things she had never revealed to anyone before."

"How do you know that?"

"Helga Nordstrom is still charged with my mother's care. She told me that you came here often. She said my mother had even turned over her personal diaries to you. I have the feeling that you have something to tell me, Miss Farrell. Some communication from my mother."

Brett sank down on the edge of a chair and went through the motions of lighting a cigarette in order to gather herself. "It's true that Julia asked me to find you," she said at last. "It was terribly important to her. I promised I'd try."

Luisa remained poised before the windows. "And were you able to find me . . . after my being lost for so many years?"

Brett nodded. "At least I found out what had happened to you after Castro came to power in Cuba. I know why you had to leave."

"I see," Luisa said very quietly. "Then you know about my marriage to Reverend Carswell. About the trial and my . . . hospitalization."

"I also know what you were committed to a state institution

for the criminally insane. Now suddenly, you appear here in Palm Beach as your mother's legal guardian. It doesn't add up. What do you hope to gain by prolonging her agony?"

"I'm going to be honest with you, Miss Farrell. As strange as it may seem, I do have certain powers. Even as a child I was able to predict the future and heal the sick. I've often thought that my mother may have abandoned me because she feared these powers."

Luisa waved her hand as if to rid the air of an unpleasant thought. "I can assure you that I have long since forgiven her. My only wish is to restore her to life. That is my single mission—my only purpose. I want nothing for myself."

A silence fell between them.

"Do you think I'm a lunatic, Miss Farrell? Some woman full of paranoid delusions?"

"Listen, Luisa, you've been declared criminally insane. You tell me you have powers—that you can give your mother life—but the record shows that you're responsible for the deaths of six people, including your husband. I have no idea what to think."

"I had a vision," Luisa said. "I saw you taken by the sea and very close to death. There was a voice. A man's voice—tortured with guilt and bitter regret. A voice coming from the other side—begging forgiveness."

"What else did you see—or know?" Brett asked.

"I know you are troubled. You feel yourself to be a stranger here. You have grave doubts about finding your rightful place. What I have to say to you has been given to me. You will always be a stranger in the world for that is your true calling. Always seeking, always traveling in search of answers to life. Asking questions. Trying to awaken those that sleep. This is your true calling. But when the call comes, you must be prepared to risk everything—even death.

"Soon, very soon, there will be signs and portents. It will be a time of terrible calamity. Of revolutions, plagues and natural disasters. Great numbers of people will be displaced. Even this island will not be immune from the conflagration to come."

At that moment there was a light knock at the door, and Brett turned to see a thin young black girl wearing an ill-fitting maid's uniform standing in the doorway. She was very dark and extremely pretty with the delicate features of an African water bird. Her straight black hair was preened precisely in the middle, and her worshipful gaze was brightly fixed upon Luisa's face.

"You must excuse me," Luisa said. "Sister Sarah has to speak with me about something."

Brett rose and began browsing about the room. She paused before the fireplace and stared up at the portrait of Lucky DuShane. Behind it was a steel-reinforced safe containing the fortune in jewels that Julia had intended her children should have. The fabulous Manchu treasure that had once belonged to the last Dowager Empress of China.

Up until that moment Brett had remained undecided about informing Luisa of the legacy. But now she realized clearly that it might be the only bargaining chip she possessed.

"I'll return you to Dr. Lanier," Luisa said from the doorway. "I must go to my mother now. Thank you for coming, Miss Farrell. I'm so glad that we were able to have this talk."

"I want to see Julia myself," Brett pursued. "It's very important to me."

Luisa's expression was cool. "I only wish that were possible. For now at least, Dr. Montes has forbidden any visitors. Soon perhaps, when her condition improves."

"I came here today to try to convince you that what you are doing is wrong," Brett said firmly. "To be kept alive like that is the last thing Julia would have wanted."

"Are you so sure that you know what my mother would have wanted?" Luisa asked.

Without a word, Brett reached into her bag and produced the small tape recorder she always carried. She switched it on, and Julia's voice drifted out.

"The last thing I want in the world is a hopeless and lingering death connected to a room full of machines."

Brett clicked off the recorder. "There it is, Luisa. Those are her words, not mine. For your mother's condition to improve would take nothing short of a miracle."

Luisa's smile was enigmatic but luminous. "Fortunately, I happen to be in the business of performing miracles."

CHAPTER SEVENTEEN

BRETT was still pondering Luisa de Vargas when she arrived home at Marisol. Luisa was brazen. Shrewd. Uncanny. Julia DuShane's daughter had more than lived up to her advance billing as the seductively dangerous Sister Jerusha.

According to Consuelo, Brad had called in Brett's absence, leaving an urgent message to call him in Washington.

As always, Brad was a man who got things done. And by the time he had related all that he had been able to discover about Raphael de Vargas, Brett knew she was on the trail of something big.

Well, chalk one up for Luisa, who had been right. Less than an hour after leaving La Caraval, her prediction had started to come true. The call had come, and Brett's life was going to take an unexpected and dangerous turn.

The darkly intense young boy who had been born Crown Prince of a great American dynasty and grown up to become the firebrand poet of Castro's revolution, had gone on to become the most elusive and feared revolutionary in the western hemisphere.

As a super-nationalistic zealot, de Vargas had ultimately broken with Fidel Castro over various ideological differences that were reflected in his writings. His politics had veered sharply to the right, and after publishing a particularly scathing portrait of the Cuban dictator, he was arrested, charged with treason and sentenced to life imprisonment in a Cuban military prison.

When he eventually managed to escape in the early seventies, de Vargas assumed the name of Santos and vowed vengeance against Castro as his single consuming purpose in life. Santos was swiftly condemned to death in absentia in the Cuban courts and went on to leave a trail of revolutionary mayhem in his wake that was unmatched in its ferocity and total disregard for human sensibility.

It was Santos who masterminded the kidnapping of a half-dozen Cuban athletes attending the Pan American Games in 1973. And it was Santos as well who fired a surface-to-air missile at an Aero Cubaña airliner taking off from Rio de Janeiro with a group of important Cuban officials aboard.

Even though the Cuban plane was finally able to land safely after very nearly being blasted out of the sky, both incidents had cost Fidel Castro greatly in terms of international prestige. Yet, they were nothing compared to the embarrassment brought about by the Cuban Embassy bombing in New York in September of 1976. Or the subsequent assassination of the Cuban ambassador to the United Nations in 1978. This was the same man who had brutally tortured and degraded Santos throughout his long years of imprisonment.

Clearly Santos was gradually upping the ante. He was a lone wolf on the prowl, and he was out for blood. He was being hunted relentlessly by the FBI, Europe's Interpol and one of Castro's own death squads. Even so, Santos continued to elude them all, intent on pursuing his deadly vendetta against Fidel Castro with a single-mindedness that was unequaled in revolutionary terrorism.

According to the most recent Interpol reports that Brad had been able to obtain, Santos was believed to be somewhere in the Florida Keys. But he was elusive, and intelligence reports were always sketchy and fragmented. Still, the consensus was that Santos was getting ready to make a move . . . and soon.

There was evidence that he had been instrumental in the purchase of a large quantity of Columbian cocaine; a multi-million dollar deal that authorities believed was intended to finance the assassination of Fidel Castro.

There was one other piece of information Brett thought might help her in her quest to find Santos. A woman by the name of Gabriella Marquez, a prostitute, heroin addict and sometimes nightclub entertainer had recently taken up residence in Key West after being run out of town by the Miami vice squad. She was known to have once been the mistress of Castro and had been involved in a disastrously bungled CIA plot to assassinate the Cuban dictator during the early sixties.

Gabriella Marquez was her best hope in tracking down Santos, Brett decided. According to sources in Miami, they had once been lovers, and it was Gabriella who had fronted the cocaine buy in South America, with Santos calling the shots.

A warm rush of air came through the open car windows as Brett drove south along the Inter-Island Causeway spanning the Florida Keys. It was nighttime, and hanging low above the water, the moon covered the passing islands with a silvery radiance.

The Florida Keys were a broken strand of glittering gems that had been cast in the sea. Key West was the free-wheeling playground of the islands. It had always been America's jumping-off place, just short of the shadowy spectre of Cuba only ninety miles to the south.

The island was fully *en fête* when Brett arrived that evening. It was Mardi Gras time, and elaborately costumed partiers cavorted in the streets, jammed the bars and restaurants and kept the local discos throbbing.

Brett liked the old seafaring town with its shadowy banyon

trees, Victorian gingerbread mansions with widow's walks and tiny conch houses clustered in garden compounds of lush subtropical foliage. Its population included a sizable number of gays, Bahamian blacks and U.S. Naval personnel; all of them genially living with an impressive contingent of artists and writers.

Not really knowing what to expect, Brett had dressed in condom-tight jeans, a slinky full-sleeved crepe de chine blouse with a plunging neckline and spike stiletto heels. She had made herself up to look like a Miami Beach hooker slumming for Mardi Gras in Key West.

Brett parked the Porche on the fringes of "Old Town" with its garden restaurants, small shops and numerous art galleries. As soon as she turned the corner into Duval Street, she was instantly swept up by the chanting, dancing crowd. Thousands of extravagantly costumed people filled the street and sidewalks, accompanied by a flotilla of colorful floats and marching bands.

After being grabbed, kissed and having her breasts squeezed in the insane explosion of bodies, she was finally able to break away, escaping into Captain Tony's landmark saloon, where she made discreet inquiries of the bartender over a double Scotch mist.

She located Gabriella Marquez at the Club Paradiso, where she was singing with a merengué band. The waterfront club was dimly lit and just off the Mallory Docks. There were prostitutes perched provocatively along the bar, with dozens of rowdy sailors crowding the tables.

"Anything I can help you with, pretty lady?" a large man with dangerous eyes and a powerful build asked. His white suit made him appear all the more gigantic, with the coat straining across his massive chest and shoulders. His blunt brutal features were ambiguous, while his skin was very dark with kinky greased black hair.

"I want to see Gabriella," Brett said with far more assurance than she actually felt.

"What if she don't wanna see *you?*" he said.

"I'm sure you can convince her," she said, handing him a sealed envelope from her shoulder bag along with two new crisp twenty-dollar bills. "See that she gets this envelope and I'll double that. I'll be waiting in the bar."

At that moment the house lights dimmed. The stage lights came on and a striking woman came out. She was tall and feline, with a brazen, savage beauty. She wore long black gloves and stiletto heels. She was Gabriella Marquez, and she started dancing in a leather G-string with her bare breasts and sinuous body moving to the beat, cracking a whip at all the right movements of the music.

There were whistles, catcalls and suggestive shouts as Brett walked to the end of the bar. She ordered a stiff drink and watched as Gabriella jiggled her breasts, allowing the music to carry her into the number.

Slowly her gloved arms came up to draw the audience to her before moving in to clutch the microphone. Then she started singing in a throaty resonant voice.

Gradually Brett became aware of the change in the atmosphere. A hush settled over the dim smoky room. Everyone was listening. Gabriella had them all within her grasp. The crowd was with her now. Eager. Hot. Booze mixed with sexual tension was a powerful combination. Gabriella stalked the stage, her whip flailing out to slice through the hazy blue air as she sang.

The fever rose. The audience joined her in a foot-stomping frenzy that had them all up and out of their chairs by the time the number ended.

Without waiting for the whistles and deafening applause to abate, Gabriella licked into a low smoky ballad that quickly reduced them to silence. All along the bar the whores brooded over their drinks with their dresses hiked up. Indifferent. Available. Listening to Gabriella's earthly lament and allowing the vagrant sailors to fondle their breasts and fumble beneath their skirts.

Suddenly Brett's view was cut off by a husky six-footer in navy whites. "Ain't you kind of off your turf, princess? You know the animals 'round here get mighty restless 'bout this time of night."

Brett drew deeply on her cigarette and eyed him coolly. The sailor was blond and well built with attractive all-American features, bloodshot blue eyes and a smooth face. "Fuck off, sailor. I'm waiting for someone."

"How do you know it ain't me?" he asked, brushing his hand across her breasts. "I mean, I been three months at sea. How 'bout lettin' me buy you a drink for starters?"

"Sorry," she said. "Like I said, I'm otherwise engaged. Why don't you hit on one of these other ladies? They're open for business."

"Hey, I don't want them. I got three month's pay in my wallet. So what's the problem? You got it, you sell it to me, and you still got it. What's better than that? Right?"

The music had come to an end, and at that moment the bouncer loomed out of the smoky dimness to elbow the sailor aside. "Fuck off, swabbie," he grunted. "The lady's got business backstage."

"Hey, what is this shit?" the sailor complained. "We were just gettin' acquainted. Why don't *you* fuck off?"

Everything happened so quickly. Brett was shoved aside as the bouncer landed a deadly powerhouse right squarely in the sailor's gut. It was a solid, damaging blow, and he doubled over with a groan and staggered backward. The bouncer then moved in to cold cock him with a powerful karate chop to the back of the neck. He turned to Brett and his mashed-in, brutal features were smiling in a way that made her blood run cold. "Come with me, pretty lady. Gabriella wants to see ya in her dressing room."

Gabriella Marquez was sprawled on a shabby couch, legs spread, smoking a cigarette. "What do you want?" she asked as Brett closed the door behind her. Gabriella looked—and sounded—used and hostile.

"I want to talk."

"I'm not so good at speakin' English. The words . . . I forget."

"Maybe this will jog your memory." Brett reached into her bag and withdrew an old photograph. She crossed the room, seated herself on a rickety cane-back wicker chair and placed the photograph in Gabriella's hand.

Gabriella regarded the photo with veiled eyes. She looked older than she did onstage. She was wearing a garish floral-print dressing gown, falling open in front to partially expose her breasts and thighs. She wore no panties.

"You think maybe I know who this is?" Gabriella asked, grinding out her cigarette with a sullen gesture.

"I think you know very well who it is. That photo was made over thirty years ago. It's a picture of Raphael de Vargas taken in Havana. He was just a child. The woman with him is Julia DuShane, his mother."

Gabriella tossed the photo aside, shrugged her shoulders and reached for a small lacquered music box on the table beside her. She opened it to a brief sprinkle of Latin musical notes and reached in to withdraw a thin, deftly rolled, brown paper joint. "Very good shit," she announced, sinking back against the mass of pillows.

Gabriella placed the joint between her brightly painted lips and lit it with a cheap plastic lighter. She inhaled deeply. "You can see I got expensive habits," she purred. "All you paid for was talk—not information. So maybe I do know this de Vargas. Who was it that told you about me?"

"Everybody in Miami knows about you. You, Castro . . . the CIA spiriting you out of Havana after you failed to poison him. The Miami vice squad knows all about your heroin addiction and your 'working' in Miami Beach hotels—even the big coke score you made a few weeks ago in Bogota, Columbia. I'd cool it for a while if I were you, Gabriella. A lot of people know a lot about you."

With the joint dangling from her lips, Gabriella uncoiled from the couch and crossed to her dressing table. She sat down and switched on the illuminated mirror, reflecting her heavily made-up features in a fluid wash of harsh white light. Taking up a hairbrush, she began brushing her wild dark hair with short attacking strokes.

"Who are you?" she asked finally.

"I'm a reporter," Brett responded. "All I want you to do is to give something to Santos for me. Tell him to get in touch with me. The five hundred dollars I enclosed in the envelope was just a down payment. When I've heard from Santos, it's worth a couple of thousand more."

The brushing stopped with the brush poised in midstroke like a defensive weapon. Their eyes met and held in the mirror. "What do you want me to give him?"

Brett removed the Florentine gold wedding band from her finger and held it up to catch the light. "I want you to give Santos this ring for me. He'll know what it means. Tell him I want a meeting."

CHAPTER EIGHTEEN

CHARLOTTE Devereaux Farrell was a deeply ambitious and extremely resourceful woman who had mastered the art of social celebrity.

Forever graciously smiling, she had a steely self-confidence born of habitual wealth and generations of selective breeding.

The illustrious Devereaux clan of North Carolina was one of the most aristocratic families in the South. For twelve generations they had been famous for their beautiful women, brilliant military officers and superb Arabian horse stock of equally aristocratic lineage.

Brett's relationship with her mother had continued to smoulder ever since her return from New York. Charlotte was furious over not being allowed to bask in her daughter's celebrity, and Brett was appalled but not surprised at her mother's predatory instincts. The Queen was not yet dead and already the two foremost contenders for the throne were engaged in a fearsome cat fight for succession.

Social sovereignty in Palm Beach had always been a ruthless contest. Charlotte knew everyone who was anyone, and it had long been assumed that she was next in line of succession. But that was before Monique Von Helsen came to town.

The charity gala at the Galleria that evening was being staged to celebrate the appointment of Charlotte Farrell and

Monique Von Helsen as co-chairwomen of the Diamond Tiara Ball. It was the season's most spectacular event, founded and presided over by Julia DuShane herself for over a quarter of a century. The ball marked the end of the Palm Beach Season, and speculation was running high on who would emerge as the clear front-runner.

The two women could not have been more different in style and temperament. Sleek, daring and blatantly self-promoting, the Baroness Von Helsen had founded a vast cosmetics empire on guile, guts and sheer determination. Though her origins were decidedly obscure, she had managed to amass a huge fortune, marry a European title and was well on her way to making Palm Beach her own private fiefdom.

The Baron and Baroness Von Helsen were the platinum-plated darlings of those who commuted between the Hamptons, St. Moritz, Acapulco, and Palm Beach. By anyone's measure, Hugo and Monique were a high-octane duet with the right combination of title, charm, glitz and good looks.

With a nightly agenda of events crowding one another, no one wanted to miss a moment of the action. On that particular evening, the Galleria was definitely the place to be and to be seen. Over two hundred luminaries of one wattage or another had been invited to attend a charity showing of Pablo Picasso's paintings on loan from various local collectors.

Charlotte and Brett were taken to the opening in the family Rolls. They were already over an hour late as the white Corniche pulled out of the drive at Marisol and headed north along South Ocean Boulevard. Charlotte was in a dark mood.

"You have to admit, I've been extremely patient with Laura. But this time she's gone too far," Charlotte complained. "Begelman's nothing but a mobster. How can she do this to me after all I've done for her? What about the family? We'll *never* live this down."

"For the record, Mother, Begelman's never been arrested, not so much as a parking violation. If Laura chooses to sleep with him, that's her business. Granted, I think she's making a big mistake, but there's absolutely nothing anyone can do about it."

"It's the scandal of Palm Beach," Charlotte shot back. "I'm so humiliated. I'm ashamed to even show my face in public."

"Actually, the scandal of Palm Beach is you and that Von Helsen woman—scheming and plotting to take over the Diamond Tiara Ball. Julia DuShane isn't even dead and you two are already circling her throne like vultures. I think it's disgusting. Julia deserves better than that."

"How dare you talk to me like that with *your* name splashed all over the scandal sheets. Carrying on all these years with a married man! Honestly, you talk about 'pursuit of excellence' and all this time you were excelling at being someone's whore. Really."

"Brad and I were lovers for ten years. It's over now. He isn't divorcing his wife for me. It's for someone else."

"Well," Charlotte scoffed, "I can assure you the sordid details are not of the slightest interest to me, although I'm sure that they must come as a shock to Simon. You're obviously sleeping together and don't care who knows it! You certainly turned out to be your father's daughter, Brett. A Farrell through and through. No scandal ever touched *my* side of the family, that's for damned sure."

"Oh, really? What about all those black slaves the Devereaux clan used to breed like cattle and sell off at auction? I don't suppose your conscience was ever particularly troubled by that little slice of Devereaux family history."

Just then the chauffeur swung around the corner onto Worth Avenue, and Brett turned away from her mother. She stared out the window at the brightly lit shops lining the street of ultimate dreams. She hadn't wanted to come at all that evening, but Charlotte had insisted.

It had been a week since Brett's visit to La Caraval. And she had still heard nothing from Santos. She felt tense, moody and increasingly anxious.

Simon had accepted her explanation about the publicity over Brad's divorce, but Brett's emotions, coupled with her growing frustration with inactivity, had become a web too complicated to negotiate anywhere but in bed.

There was a crowd gathered in front of the Galleria. As the Rolls cruised up to the curb, a smartly uniformed doorman hurried across the sidewalk to open the rear door. Brett and Charlotte were ushered past the onlookers and on through the double glass doors, with cameras flashing in their wake.

The charity gala was in full swing. The Galleria was packed, and they had scarcely stepped inside when Monique Von Helsen came forward to greet them. Heads turned, necks craned, bodies swiveled. They were the focus of all attention.

"Charlotte, darling," Monique crooned as they exchanged chilly cheek brushings. "We've all been wondering what happened to you. When you don't see someone in this town for over a week, it's a pretty good sign they're dead—at least socially."

Monique Von Helson was a surprisingly tiny woman, considering her larger than life image. She was bronzed, of course, and loaded down with jewels, not to mention painted, powdered and costumed in a filmy blue caftan. She was at least thirty years older than her titled Austrian husband, yet she was still a strikingly attractive women with Middle Eastern eyes, flame-colored hair and extraordinary breasts, perfected, Charlotte guessed, by an expensive plastic surgeon.

"Good evening, Charlotte," Hugo Von Helson said before turning his blue-eyed gaze on Brett. "So you are the mysterious Brett Farrell we've all been hearing so much about. I can assure you the pleasure is *all* mine."

Hugo feyly lifted Brett's hand to his lips. He had the kind of blond dissipated good looks that one saw on the ski slopes of St.

Anton or Gstaad during the winter season and was rumored to be as gay as pink ink. She was polite and returned the greeting, but it was clear the evening ahead promised to be something that would have to be *endured,* not enjoyed.

"I'm so glad your daughter was able to join us," Monique observed. "But I was hoping she'd bring Dr. Lanier along. We've read so much about the two of them. Such a divine man," she sighed. "I was just saying to Hugo that there don't seem to be any *real* men left in Palm Beach this season. Just a lot of bimbos and gigolos."

"Well, aren't you fortunate, Monique," Charlotte said. "You got the entire package all wrapped up with a title to boot."

Monique's face froze in a glacial smile. "At least I haven't found my husband's cerebral cortex decorating a rose trellis. How terribly impolite it was of Dwight and how messy for the gardener. But then, you certainly know how hard it is to keep help these days."

"Now, ladies." It was Florian Montes appearing on the scene to cast oil on troubled waters. "This is a charity gala after all. Why don't the two of you make a supreme effort to be charitable." He presented his arm to Charlotte. "Shall we circulate, my dear?"

Brett managed to keep her smile intact throughout a flurry of introductions as they made their way into the crowded gallery. Ever since seven that evening, limousines had been pulling up to the curb to drop off a stream of guests.

For Brett it was all too predictable. The strained and vacant laughter. The jewels. The gowns. The perpetually pasted smiles, and all that endlessly diverting social chatter. The gossip. The whispered innuendo. The polite flirtations with a glance or a touch. She had never felt at ease with these people.

While sipping from a glass of champagne with a gloved hand, Brett gradually drifted away to view the paintings. She had never known quite what to make of Picasso, but her attention was immediately drawn to a painting on the far wall.

It had been painted by Picasso during his early blue period and was titled *The Harlequin*: a sinuously androgynous figure whose pose and gesture proclaimed some tragic and disquieting torment. A subliminal struggle between the life and death of the self.

Someone tapped her on the shoulder. She turned to find herself confronted by a burly, dark-suited man. "Laura Gentry wants to see you in the women's john," he grunted, jerking his head toward the door of the nearby ladies room, where an identical figure stood guard. "We'll see you ain't disturbed."

Laura was touching up her makeup when Brett entered carrying a bottle of champagne with an extra glass. Laura wore a Dior chiffon gown with spirals of matching ostrich feathers that accentuated her perfect tan, dramatic bone structure and bountiful cleavage. She looked sexy and sophisticated with a ruby necklace and matching pendants at her ears.

"Thank God you're here, Brett," she cried with a glittery-eyed smile. "I simply couldn't resist popping in tonight, but from the looks I got, I had the impression that I might end up the victim of a *très* genteel lynching."

"Well, you said you were going to bounce this town on its ear," Brett said, pouring them each a glass of champagne. "You were only scandalous before Begelman . . . now you're positively notorious!"

Laura capped her dark red lipstick and leaned close to the mirror to deftly apply a smudge of smoky eyeliner. "Trust me, dear heart. They ain't seen nothin' yet. Auntie Laura still has a few tricks up her skirt." She turned, wiggling her finger to display a huge ice cubelike diamond engagement ring. "I think a toast is in order to the future Mrs. Begelman. Maurice finally popped the question. We're flying to Nassau next week to officially tie the knot."

Brett lifted her glass. "Well, since Maurice and I are going to be in-laws, the least you can do is introduce me to this character."

"Of course I will, kitten. In due time. . . . What do you think of my Mafia-chic look? It's definitely me."

"Laura, I said I wanted to meet Begelman."

"Do you think I'm insane, Brett?"

"More often than not."

Laura eyed her ring critically, turning it to catch the light in all its shimmering facets. "Listen, don't take this personally, but Maurice is absolutely death on reporters, and I'm not about to scare him off at this point. You understand, don't you?"

"I shouldn't think he'd scare all that easily, from the look of those two bozos out there."

Laura shrugged her shoulders and adjusted her décolletage for maximum exposure. "Primitives, perhaps. But kind of sexy in a grungy, sinister way. Maurice won't let me out of his sight without *beaucoup* security. He's just wild about these tits—silicone and all—and doesn't want to lose them or me. If you're hot, you're hot. What can I tell you?"

"Laura, I hate dropping a turd in your punchbowl, but Begelman's mob—real mob. This isn't a movie, you know. These people kill or are killed. What happens if the don's wife gets killed in the cross fire?"

Laura downed her champagne in a single gulp and quickly poured herself another. "In case you hadn't noticed, kiddo, I'm a fifty-year-old broad with a lot of mileage and no foreseeable future. At this point in my life, I'm just not about to rush down the path of respectability and rightness. To be perfectly candid, cold hard cash is the only evidence of God I've yet seen on the planet."

Brett paused to light a cigarette. She sighed deeply. "On lighter subjects, you'll be glad to know that Mother's convinced that your latest antics totally screwed her chances of being the undisputed Queen of the Ball. Charlotte sharing the chairmanship of the Diamond Tiara with Monique Von Helsen is like sharing a death wish. They're already at each other's throats—fang, claw and mandible."

Laura laughed. After atomizing herself in a cloud of Chanel, Laura removed a small cellophane packet from her sequined purse and poured a mound of crystaline white powder on her thumbnail.

"Aren't you going a little heavy on that stuff?" Brett asked.

Laura took another hit of the coke, sniffed twice and blinked hard into the mirror. Then she rose rather unsteadily, slimmed her dress down over her hips and started toward the door, where she sketched a dramatic pirouette. "Lighten up, Brett. You only won a Pulitzer . . . not the Nobel Humanitarian Award. Don't bother trying to reform me. I've been convinced beyond any reasonable shadow of a doubt that crime really does pay. Oh, what divine decadence to be utterly free of scruples. Now, let's go get 'em!"

The gala was in full swing. No one seemed to mind the heat, the crush and the high-decibel band playing for dancing.

Strolling arm in arm, Brett and Laura browsed from painting to painting, allowing the natural momentum of the party to carry them toward the glass-enclosed atrium at the rear of the gallery. They paused at the top of the stairs and surveyed the scene below, where dancing couples made splashes of color against the white marble tiles: a glittering array of names and faces mixing, mingling and swilling Moët & Chandon, surrounded by the sculptural art works of Pablo Picasso.

White-gloved waiters moved about offering freshly opened oysters and tiny brochettes of grilled pompano. It was laughter and music and brightness and a mix of expensive perfumes. Laura was prattling on until suddenly Brett was no longer paying the slightest attention.

She saw him standing there on the other side of the atrium. Tall. Slim. Saturnine of feature. The stranger from the pool at the Royal Poinciana.

This time he wore formal attire, dinner clothes, perfectly cut. "That's him," Brett whispered, clutching Laura's arm. "He's the one who saved me. It's him . . . I know it is. The beard is what did it. I didn't recognize him last time because he didn't have the beard."

Laura said, "I just adore hearing you speak in tongues, dear heart, but the end may be nearer than you think. Here comes the Graf Zepplen in drag, and it looks like she's on a bombing run."

Brett looked away, and in a fraction of a second he was gone. She was nearly beside herself with frustration as Daphne Shelldrake swept down upon them. She was a monstrously obese woman given to mascarading in circus tent dresses with little girl bows in her curly blond coif. Her face was as smooth as glass and painted like that of a Kewpie doll. She looked like the legendary Elsa Maxwell on a good day. She wagged one brightly taloned finger in Brett's face. "You haven't bothered to return my calls," Daphne drawled. "You naughty, naughty girl, you. I was beginning to think you'd missed the article I wrote about you in *People Parade*."

Brett hadn't missed it. "JET SET JOURNALIST CITED AS MISTRESS IN MEDIA MOGUL DIVORCE" read the head-line. Brett had wanted to forget the rest.

"How perfectly *marvelous* to see you, Daphne," Laura gushed. "But then who but the deaf, dumb or blind could miss someone the size of the Houston Astrodome dressed up like Henry the Eighth in drag? I see you're still scavenging around for all sorts of malicious gossip to titillate the vulgar little minds of your brain-dead readers."

Daphne theatrically batted her false lashes. "Where you're concerned, Laura dear, I haven't even begun to scavenge. Don't fret. I'll get around to you eventually. At the moment, though, I'm more interested in Julia DuShane."

"It's okay," Brett said. "I'll handle this, Laura."

"Well, I hate to dash off when I just know I'm going to miss a perfectly fascinating exchange of confidences. But then, who knows, I might just get lucky on the dance floor."

"All right, Daphne, here it is. Brad Harraway is not divorcing his wife to marry me. Actually, he dumped me for another woman. It's hardly headline material, but use it if you like."

"Oh, come off it, darlin'. All that horseshit is last week's news. What I have is twenty million salivatin', palpitatin' readers simply dyin' to know all about the secret life of Julia DuShane. My sources inform me that you've been initiated into the mysterious inner chamber of Julia's life, so to speak. So she spilled her guts to you? For a book perhaps?"

"If you're asking me if I'm planning on doing some sort of biography, the answer is no. Not now at least. Julia and I did spend a lot of time together and became very close. That's all."

"I know you have her diaries, and what good are they except in a book? Come on, give a fellow journalist a break. Who is this Jerusha person who claims to be Julia's illegitimate daughter? What the hell is going on over there at La Caraval, anyway? I hear it's beginning to look like something out of *Porgy and Bess*."

"That, Miss Shelldrake, is one question too many," a familiar baritone voice intoned. "Now I'm afraid you'll have to excuse us."

Florian Montes took Brett's arm, and as they circled the dance floor, Brett caught sight of Laura, who had somehow fallen into the arms of a handsome young man wearing a white dinner jacket and a red carnation in his lapel. Laura appeared oblivious to everything but the pulsing rhythms of the music. Brett didn't want to think about the two hoods watching from the sidelines or the report they would be taking back to Maurice Begelman.

It was a warm and balmy night, and the garden surrounding the outer patio was a bower of tropical fern trees, rare orchids and hundreds of tiny lights twinkling among the foliage.

"Thanks for playing referee. I was just about to go down for the count," Brett told Montes.

Montes withdrew a slim platinum case from his inside coat

pocket and offered her a cigarette. "No thanks, what I need is some fresh air and some straight talk."

Montes fitted a Soubrani Oval into his cigarette holder and lit it. "I can appreciate both, Brett. But since I've managed to so conveniently place you in my debt, I'd like a straight answer from you first."

"Feel free," Brett agreed, seating herself on a cushioned chair of ornamental wrought iron. Overhead the sky was awash with stars, luminous pale and infinite.

"I've gotten the impression that you go out of your way to avoid me," Montes suggested casually. "Whenever I visit Charlotte at Marisol, you always manage to be out or hermetically sealed up in the pool house. Tell me, am I such an ogre?"

"Dr. Montes . . ." she started.

"Call me Florian . . . please."

"All right, Florian it is. I suppose I have been avoiding you. But it's because there are many things I just don't understand."

"And one of them is my relationship with your mother? Perhaps you resent anyone trying to replace your father in Charlotte's affections?"

"My mother's affections are her own affair. Quite frankly, I'm surprised she has any. You no doubt know by now that our relationship is anything but cordial."

"Your mother, Brett, is not an easy woman to comprehend. Her marriage to your father was, I fear, not a happy one. For far too long Charlotte has closed herself off from her deepest emotions. You are both strong women and both very competitive. Who knows how these situations come about? Perhaps you were competing for the same man all these years."

"There was that, of course," Brett admitted. "My father thrived on that sort of thing, and we both adored him, each in our own way. For the longest time I think I actually hated my mother. But not anymore. In a strange way, I envy her for being so absolutely sure of who she is and what she wants out of life. It is so much easier that way."

"You're a very complex young woman. There are so many things I like about you. One of them is your candor. It is most refreshing, especially here in Palm Beach."

"Julia said the same thing to me. She said you were all monsters of one sort or another, and that illusion was the most powerful weapon of all. Tell me, Florian, what exactly is your stake in keeping Julia DuShane imprisoned in a living death? Julia knew she was dying and she wasn't afraid. It was really quite moving to see the way she faced up to her mortality toward the end. Julia accepted herself for what she was, and when she began to taste the ashes, she knew it was time to bring down the curtain."

Montes smoked thoughtfully for a moment. "The decision of whether Julia lives or dies is not mine to make. No matter what you think, I am merely the attending physician, acting on the instructions of the next of kin. Luisa desires to preserve her mother's life in any way possible. I am merely the servant, not the master."

"I suppose you know that I came to La Caraval to try to see Julia."

"Yes, Luisa told me. She also said you appeared to be advocating some form of euthanasia where her mother was concerned."

"It's only what Julia herself wanted," Brett insisted. "Luisa heard Julia voice those exact sentiments on tape. You're a realist, Florian. What possible purpose can be served keeping her hooked up to a lot of machines? If she could, Julia would pull the plug herself."

"What exactly do you intend to do with the diaries and tapes?" he asked quietly.

"I haven't decided to do anything yet," Brett said. "Julia entrusted them to my safekeeping with the implicit proviso that nothing was to be made public until at least six months after her death. I gave her my word . . . but only in regard to publication. Tell me, Florian, does Luisa know that you were giving her mother a series of highly controversial injections just previous to her collapse? And, if so, have you also informed her that a certain percentage of people receiving those rejuvenation drug treatments have been known to stroke and go comatose?"

Florian Montes looked at her with his piercing dark eyes. "Let me give you a piece of very practical advice," he said. "Stay out of it. Julia DuShane is no longer any of your concern. If you continue interfering in this matter, I wouldn't want to be responsible for the consequences."

CHAPTER NINETEEN

THE call that Brett had been awaiting came several nights later. It was Gabriella Marquéz, speaking in hushed tones.

Santos had agreed to meet with her. But there were certain conditions . . .

Brett was to drive south along the Florida Keys that evening without telling anyone her destination. Upon her arrival in Key West, Santos promised to meet her at a roadside truck stop near the charter fishing marina.

It was, of course, a chancy gamble. However, chancy gambles had often paid large dividends in the past for her, and she had carefully laid the bait on her last visit to Key West. Now Santos had taken the hook.

Brett had counted on this happening because of his psychological profile. That and the valid assumption that the major goal of all revolutionary assassins was drama and publicity. Santos was clearly a showman.

Upon examining the sketchy details Brett had been able to gather thus far, a picture had begun to emerge portraying him as a man of almost indecipherable politics. Radical right and radical left curved around in his twisted psyche to meet each other going the other way. He was a brilliant intellectual and an outcast, traveling endlessly around the world with forged passports, relentlessly laying the groundwork for his big score against Fidel Castro.

After reading some of his writings, Brett was convinced his vendetta was entirely personal. His hatred of Castro and determination to destroy him would prove to be the ultimate springboard that would play him into her own hands.

Following Gabriella's call, Brett dressed quickly in dark slacks and a black cotton turtleneck sweater. She pulled on an old blue nylon windbreaker, grabbed her bag, and took off for Key West without a word to anyone.

The radio was playing softly as the odometer clicked off the miles between Palm Beach and Key West. When the first news bulletin was transmitted across the airwaves, Brett couldn't believe it. Castro had opened the doors of his prisons and mental asylums to unleash tens of thousands of criminals and mental defectives. At that very moment hundreds of boats had begun plying back and forth between the Cuban port of Mariel and Key West, Florida. As many as one hundred twenty-five thousand people were being flushed out of Castro's Cuba to seek asylum in the United States.

Great, she thought glumly. She parked her Porsche in front of the roadhouse on the outskirts of Key West and walked through the front door of the diner. She was engulfed by laughter, blaring country-western music, and booming male voices. The tables were crowded with truckers, and most of them stared as Brett crossed the room to take a seat at the counter. She ordered toast and coffee from the waitress, a washed-out blond with a pitted complexion, sullen manner, and a slovenly twitch to her behind.

The smell of fried eggs scorching on the griddle was enough to make Brett's stomach turn, but she remembered she hadn't had anything to eat since lunch. She suddenly felt nauseous.

Probably just nerves, she thought, making her way to the restroom at the end of a long, narrow, dimly lit corridor. There were two doors with one leading outside into the parking lot.

Across the hall the restroom was small, windowless, and claustrophobic with walls that were painted a sickly green.

The air was close and reeked of strong urine. Brett didn't even have time to latch the door behind her before retching miserably into the filthy toilet bowl.

Finally, when the sickness had passed, she splashed cold water on her face, took a couple of aspirin and then lifted her gaze to the cracked and yellowed mirror.

She looked strained and ghostly in the feeble light of the single naked hanging bulb. She put on some lipstick and ran a brush through the cloud of her dark hair.

Where the hell was Santos? She glanced at her watch. What if he had decided not to come or was somehow involved in the Mariel boatlift? It was just the kind of diversion he would make use of, she was sure of it.

Quite suddenly, the sound of heavy footsteps came from the outer hall. Then the door banged open and she spun around to find Cujo, the bouncer from the Club Paradiso, looming over her. She would have known him anywhere.

"Santos sent me," he said. He suddenly spun her back around and pressed her up against the wall. His huge hands moved swiftly and expertly over her body in a thorough frisk.

"I'm not carrying any weapons if that's what you're after. There's a tape recorder in my purse—that's all. No camera, no explosives, no gun—nothing. Now would you be so kind as to take your fucking hands off me?"

Brett pushed him away and started to say something else but Cujo slapped her hard. The blow was deafening. Her body flew up against the wall only to reel sideways as she was caught with a stinging backhand that sent her crumpling to the floor. Cujo pulled out a hypodermic syringe and held it up against the light. "Well, baby, this is the only way you're gonna get to Raphael—asleep. And when you wake up you're gonna wish you never heard the name Raphael de Vargas."

Several hours later Brett came to and found herself aboard the schooner *Callisto* somewhere in the Florida Straits. She had awakened lying on a cramped bunk in the schooner's main cabin as the boat pitched and rolled through the heavy swells of an early spring squall. A man was seated on the bunk across the cabin from her, staring impassively.

There was something arresting about the bearded and gauntly handsome face. *It could have been the face of a saint or an executioner.* His eyes were pale blue-green, but they were eyes that had, one could tell, seen a lot.

Slowly, Brett raised herself into a sitting position, pulling the blanket about her shoulders and drawing her legs up beneath her. She felt drugged and woozy with a thundering sick headache.

Then comprehension slowly dawned.

"I know you," she said, groggy, still sedated.

The faintest flicker of a smile spread across the man's lips. "Yes, you do know me," he said. The voice was deeply resonant without the slightest trace of an accent. Only the Latin cadences and intonations gave him away.

He prolonged the moment, taking his time to shake a Gauloise Bleu from his cigarette pack and inserting it between his lips. Then he lit it with a battered Zippo lighter. "If I recall, Miss Farrell, your ass was dead meat when I hauled you out of that swamp in Nicaragua."

With that, he tossed the lighter across the cabin, and Brett only barely managed to catch it with both hands. There was no mistake about it. Laddie's initials were etched across the top. For a moment, Brett clutched it to her breast, trying desperately to control her emotions.

"I don't actually know what happened to me that day," she said finally. "I woke up in a Medivac helicopter flying me to a hospital in San José. They said someone had sent up a distress flare. All I know was that my leg had been bandaged and I'd been given a shot of morphine for the pain. It *was* you, wasn't it?"

He smiled. "I also stole your lighter and the cigarettes you had in your bag. Civilized amenities were few and far between with the Sandinistas. I know you had some pretty good shots in that camera of yours. I saw them later in the newspapers."

"You were one of them, weren't you? You were fighting with the Sandinistas that day in the swamp."

Santos flicked his ash with studied negligence. "In those days I was one with *all* revolutionaries. I suppose I was naive enough to believe in the perfectability of man."

"The one you shot—he was just a boy. . . . I don't think I'll ever forget the look on his face."

Santos nodded gravely. His face was a study in planes and hollows, moving in and out of shadow as the hanging lamp swayed gently with the motion of the boat. He and Luisa were not identical twins; there was, in fact, only the faintest resemblance. Their eyes, however, were very much Julia DuShane's. Penetrating. Intense.

"Yes, he was just a boy with a gun about to kill an unarmed woman," Santos intoned, "just to show his *cajones*. A big man with his AK-47. But you already know the tragedy of giving guns to children and sending them off to war. You've photographed them all over the world. The only difference was that that particular youngster was going to kill *you*."

"Yes, but what was one less *journalista* to a man like you? A man who shows his *cajones* by shooting rockets at airliners and assassinating United Nation's diplomats."

Santos shrugged. "Morality is contraband in war. Anyway, where would terrorists be without the press? The relationship is symbiotic. Who knows? Perhaps I thought that someday you'd return the favor."

"May I have a cigarette?" she asked. "I'm still feeling rather fuzzy around the edges."

Santos tossed her the pack of Gauloise, and Brett leaned back against the bulkhead and lit a cigarette, using Laddie's lighter. She inhaled deeply. They sat smoking and staring across at one another, immersed in silence and listening to the storm.

"So here you are," he mused at last. "The famous journalist who wanted to meet with Santos, the notorious terrorist. What exactly do you want from me, Miss Farrell? And what were you doing with my mother's wedding ring?"

"Are you aware of what's happened to Julia?"

"I do read the papers," he said, going over to the galley and pouring some coffee.

Their fingers touched as he handed her a mug.

"If you were expecting some kind of sympathetic reaction to the news that my mother is hovering at death's door, forget it. Julia DuShane means absolutely nothing to me. She's history."

Brett sipped the coffee. "I guess I didn't answer your question," she said. "Your mother gave me the ring and asked me to find you. Julia told me everything."

He softly, slowly paced the cabin. As Brett watched him, she realized she was strongly attracted to him. And at the same time, she knew that she could easily be afraid of him as well.

Santos said, "If my mother told you everything, then you know she discarded her children like toys that had ceased to amuse her. Yes, I remember her very well, Brett. She was the pretty lady who smelled so good and didn't speak our language very well. For all of her obvious talents, linguistics was not my mother's forté. Memory does play tricks, but I do remember that she was like a goddess. She was also a mother who deserted the children who worshipped her, and that was the end of the fairy story. One day she just sailed away on her big white yacht and was never seen again."

"Julia never forgave herself for that," Brett said quietly. "She knew she had lost the only thing that money could never replace. If only you could have seen her toward the end. So utterly alone with her regrets. If you had, you might be able to think more kindly of her now. Julia paid for her sins and she's still paying. I don't believe she hoped for forgiveness—only atonement."

Santos paused in his pacing and turned to face her. "And that brings us to the question of the moment, doesn't it? Why did you want to see me? Was all this just a clever way of gaining an interview, perhaps? Or is it something far more personal?"

"Listen," Brett said. "Julia entrusted me with a legacy she wanted you to have. A fortune in jewels. I'm the only one who knows where they are and how you can get your hands on them. Is that candid enough for you?"

Santos regarded her with narrowed and suspicious eyes. "How do I know that this isn't some kind of trap? Someone could be using you to try to destroy me."

"They could, but they aren't. For several good reasons. First of all, I'm a journalist. I'm not a fool and I'm not in the least political. I'm far too rich to be bought and I'm not asking you to trust me. I know all about the Cuban death squad hunting you down. Just hear me out—that's all."

"Gabriella said you told her things . . ." Santos ventured carefully, ". . . gave her certain information."

Brett leaned forward, clasping her arms about her knees. "Look, there's no mystery or secret about your intention to assassinate Castro. God knows you've made the threat public enough. The CIA and Interpol each have a file on you a mile long. I also know that you broke into La Caraval and stole a very valuable necklace. My guess is that you did it to finance the dope deal that's become the worst kept secret around greater Miami."

Santos propped himself against the far bunk. He seemed to meditate for several moments. Then he said, "You're certainly a woman who does her homework."

Brett couldn't help smiling. "Well, I have my sources, not to mention my powers of observation. You were in Palm Beach the night the necklace was stolen, staying at the Royal Poinciana Hotel, doubtless under one of your assumed identities. You are a very elusive and resourceful man, Señor de Vargas. I saw you there at the pool and again several nights ago at a charity gala at the Galleria. For someone who pretends to loathe everything that Julia DuShane stands for, you seem to be spending an inordinate amount of time in Palm Beach."

He gave her a long, hard, appraising look. "Are you some kind of psychic? If so, perhaps you'd be good enough to foretell my future. It interests me far more than the past."

"No problem," she agreed. "I don't have to read your palm to know that you are going to need a great deal of money to carry out your plan to kill Castro. This is one prediction you can count on. I know where you can get the money and I'm willing to help you."

"You like taking chances don't you, *journalista*? I knew that the first time I saw you. You feel drawn to dangerous circumstances. It's only then that you really come alive. Perhaps you and I are very much alike in certain ways."

"I don't take sides," Brett said coldly. "I'm just an observer playing the odds, that's all. It's what I've always done. My reasons for doing this are entirely my own. They actually have very little to do with you personally. Maybe this is just the favor I owe you for saving my life. Let's not complicate it any more than that, okay?"

"Okay, *journalista*. Have it your way. But first you have to prove yourself. Just so you know that you are taking a very big chance of getting yourself killed."

"Hey, it's been my whole professional life," Brett said. "In that way at least, we are much alike."

They talked for a long time. Santos told her about his disenchantment with Castro. And underneath Raphael de Vargas, in the guise of Santos the terrorist, there was a man obsessed with a single compelling mission in life—the destruction of Castro. He dismissed his mother's lingering agony as her fate, and one she deserved. He damned his sister, Luisa, as a "traitorous whore" who had brought only shame and degradation upon the proud de Vargas family name.

Santos had been chain smoking throughout their conversation, and now he dropped his cigarette and ground it out beneath his heel. "The only legacy my mother left me was that of hatred," he said finally. "I don't need anything else. After tonight I'll have all the money I need to blow Fidel Castro halfway to Venezuela. We're going ashore in the Dry Tortugas to pick up a very large shipment of very high-grade cocaine."

He smiled. "This little adventure should be right up your alley, *journalista*. Dope running can be a very dangerous and exciting business. There's a war going on out there and you're going to find yourself in the middle of it once again. Only this time you won't have a camera to hide behind."

CHAPTER TWENTY

Brett clung to the railing of the schooner and peered out into the gray dawn. In the far distance, the Tortugas rose out of the mists, a small dry enclave of rocky islands the color of bleached bones, stark against the morning sky. They had long been deserted by all but the seabirds that came to nest along the limestone cliffs. The storm had passed northward into the Florida Keys, while a thick white fog had swept in from the south to envelope the islands like a shroud.

As Santos, Brett, and two crewmen set out from the *Callisto* in a power launch, the mists billowed in from the sea to completely obscure the towers and battlements of the ancient stone fortress crowning the largest island's rocky cliffs. From far out at sea came the deep gorged blast of a foghorn from a passing tanker.

The launch went foaming and hissing through the heaving black swells. Santos was at the wheel. He throttled down as they approached an old wharf. Visibility was less than a dozen yards. They were practically upon it when powerful yellow searchlights flashed on to guide them in.

As the launch's bow scraped against the rotting pilings, two crewmen leaped onto the wharf, weapons drawn. Santos felt uneasy in the fog. Brett could tell by the look on his face. She thought he was just being paranoid until there was a burst of rapid gunfire and he shoved her down in the launch. Gunfire riddled the launch below the waterline.

Covering Brett, he whipped an Uzi off his shoulder and shattered the twin spotlights on the wharf. The launch's powerful engine roared to life and they shot away from the wharf amidst repeated blasts of automatic weapons' fire.

"Stay down!" he yelled. Crouching low over the wheel, Santos swerved sharply away as gunfire shattered the windscreen and ammunition went whizzing by. Water was filling the launch as he headed for the harbor exit, but fog made visibility nonexistent.

Brett could hear a tolling buoy coming closer. Just as she spotted the blinking red light from the buoy she was suddenly thrown hard against the windscreen frame. The launch had crashed into the wooden pilings of a partially submerged pier. It was swiftly sinking.

Santos half dragged her up a rickety ladder onto the rotted planks of the pier.

"It's Castro's death squad," Santos spat out at Brett. "Someone has betrayed me."

He was hurting her with the steely grip of his hands, and Brett realized she was shaking uncontrollably.

"Now listen carefully," he said. "Our only chance is to reach the beach on the other side of this pier. We can hold them off from there until the *Callisto* comes in to take us out."

"What about the others?" Brett asked. "The crewmen we left on the wharf?"

"There's nothing we can do for them," he shrugged, thrusting a .45 caliber automatic into her hand. "You know how to use a gun? If you want to get out of this alive, don't hesitate to shoot anything that moves."

The fog became an ally as they ran crouching and stumbling over the broken timbers of the pier. It was so dense that Brett could barely see Santos ahead of her. He stopped abruptly, then pressed her back against the wall of an old warehouse. Breathing heavily, they tried to remain still and listened for the distant shouts and angry voices coming from across the harbor.

There was more gunfire, then, suddenly, an enormous explosion. Flames erupted through the fog. The wharf was burning. They took off, running for their lives.

Brett stumbled and fell, but Santos jerked her to her feet. He dragged her down a flight of steps, and seconds later they were on their bellies slithering downward over a rocky embankment until they came to the edge of a six foot drop.

"Jump!" he hissed.

"I can't . . . my goddamned ankle. I must have turned it when I fell."

Santos cursed and leaped to the slope below. He pulled her into his arms. His body was pressed against hers. He could feel the heat of her body and she could feel his. It scared and excited Brett at the same time. He was more of a man than any man she'd ever known. He picked her up and carried her down a steep embankment to the beach. Brett remembered that terrifying day in the swamp in Nicaragua. He had saved her twice now.

She was limping badly and Santos was pulling her along. The beach before them widened and the cliffs loomed up ahead out of the mists. She was short of breath. The distant voices shouted from behind them on the pier. Santos had the Uzi slung over his arm, while Brett clutched the gun he'd given her. It felt so cold and lethal. She hated it, but knew she needed it. If anything happened to him . . .

The fog had begun to lift and the sky was opening up. Quickly they had become easier targets. They zig-zagged up the beach to take advantage of the deep inky shadow cast by the towering cliffs below the fortress. Farther on they came to a series of dilapidated storage shacks facing outward toward the sea.

The old buildings offered welcome cover. They ducked down between the last two structures in the line. It would take the

Cubans time to check out all the others. They crouched there in the sand, pressed flat against the rusted, corrugated tin siding, remaining perfectly still. Listening and waiting.

Every few minutes Santos poked his head out and scanned the beach for some sign of the Cubans, then scanned the fog-obscured sea, hoping for a signal light from the *Callisto*.

They waited five minutes. Then ten. It seemed forever. Brett's teeth had begun to chatter and her ankle was throbbing with pain.

It was a misplaced pebble that finally gave them warning. A very faint sound, but one that instantly alerted them. Brett turned around, trying to see where the pebble had come from on the cliffs directly behind them. Then, almost miraculously, the fog lifted slightly and she saw a figure poised on the edge of the cliff, pointing a gun directly at them. Santos, however, still hadn't noticed.

In a fraction of a second, Brett dropped to one knee, clasped the .45 tightly in both hands, and fired off three shots. The figure crumpled, buckling backward before lurching to one side and then toppling over the edge of the cliff to the jagged rocks below.

Brett turned and stared directly into Santos's eyes. He made a thumbs-up gesture and they were on the move. They ran down the beach, dodging from side to side as a fusillade of bullets whistled past their heads.

The fog still hung low over the water, but by now they could hear the powerful throb of the *Callisto*'s twin diesel engines as the schooner moved in toward the shore. There were more shots. They kept running until Santos slumped against her. One of the bullets had torn into his shoulder and the wound was gushing blood that quickly soaked his shirt.

The Cubans were converging on them. Brett and Santos made a final staggering run into waist-deep water. Santos's hung onto Brett's neck and he was gasping for breath. The water wasn't deep enough to swim but the breakers were huge.

There was a powerful riptide sweeping them outward and buckling their legs beneath them.

Brett was frantic. She was a strong swimmer but Santos was dragging her down. The signal light from the *Callisto* appeared, blinking like a beacon of hope through the fog.

Santos was dead weight by now. He passed out from loss of blood, and it was easier to make progress. The shooting had stopped, but Brett could still hear voices shouting from the beach.

Don't panic, Brett told herself. Panic invited sharks, and the blood trailing behind them didn't help.

All she had to do was concentrate on reaching the blinking signal light.

All she had to do was keep her arms and legs moving with Santos locked in a dead man's crawl.

All she had to do was pray.

Brett didn't hear the outboard until it was practically upon them. It materialized out of the mist, swerving abruptly at the very last moment so that Brett swam right into the side of it.

The outboard rolled in the swells, looming and dipping as a huge dark hand reached out and roughly grabbed her wrist. Then Cujo was hovering above her. Never in her life had Brett been so glad to see someone she loathed so much.

CHAPTER TWENTY-ONE

BRETT *blinked her eyes, trying to focus in the dim light. The only light came through a partially open door, illuminating the shadowy figure of a man moving slowly toward her bed.*

Santos.

Santos leaned over her and kissed her. Their bodies came together. Brett felt as if this was, somehow, the way it was always meant to be. Each kiss, each touch of his hand, made her feel as if she were being kissed for the first time, touched for the first time. It was a wonderful feeling. A sense of peace and calm came over her. He knew her. She knew him. It was mystifying, and terrifying at the same time. Two souls, in flight, connecting as one. Being one. They made love again. And again. His body was over hers and then she was over him. Melting together. Getting to know each other and yet already knowing more about each other than most know their lovers in a lifetime.

She was free at last.

He had saved her.

And she him.

There was nothing, nothing, that would keep them apart.

Brett was awakened by the touch of a hand. A man's hand. She heard a strong familiar voice talking to her. But it was not Santos.

It had only been a dream. Blinking against the light from the bed lamp, Brett looked up at the face of Simon Lanier. His features were blurred, swimming in and out of her vision as she tried to focus.

"You were dreaming, Brett," Simon said. "It woke me up. Must have been some dream." He paused. "I feel that you're slipping away from me. I don't know how or why ... but I don't know what to do about it."

Brett sat up, drawing the sheet around her. "What do you want from me, Simon?"

"What do you want from me?"

Brett reached for her cigarettes on the night table. I don't know ... something. . . . You're pressing me."

"Something isn't enough," he said. "You've got to be more precise than that. You know, I'd love to know what's really behind that face you put on. Sometimes I stare at you and can't see anyone I know."

Brett sighed. "I'm not so mysterious. I'm human. I think I may even be in love with you, but I'm not sure."

Simon relaxed. His smile was boyishly beguiling. "Give me your hand and I'll put it on something you can definitely be sure of."

She laughed. "Your cock does have a mind of its own."

"No conscience either," he grinned. "It's utterly shameless. Not to mention insatiable where you're concerned. Do you have any idea how much you turn me on?"

Brett helped Simon take off his shorts. Then, without a word, she gently guided him back on the bed and draped herself languorously on top of him, thighs and bellies pressed together. Her face was buried in the crook of his neck and she hugged him tightly.

They lay together for a long time without speaking or disengaging. Then Brett leaned on one elbow. "Dear Simon . . ." she whispered. "What are you thinking of?"

Simon stretched. "How you still look beautiful in the morning," he murmured, burying his face between her breasts. Simon nuzzled and kissed her breasts.

"I hate to rain on your parade, Dr. Lanier, but you have just over an hour to be at the hospital. Why don't I fix breakfast while you take a shower and dress?"

After Simon had left for the hospital, Brett took a leisurely bath in the Jacuzzi, then dressed in the clothes she had worn the night before and browsed restlessly around the condo, deliberately delaying her return to Marisol.

Simon's apartment was a statement of good taste. There were shelves of fine books, rare oriental carpets, and an impressive collection of abstract art.

Brett made herself a double Bloody Mary and stepped out onto the terrace and into the early morning sunshine.

From the towering condominiums lining the southern perimeter of the island, the view of Palm Beach was spectacular. It had never looked more beautiful to Brett, with its green golf courses, its spectacular mansions, and all the gleaming white yachts sparkling on the sea.

She leaned against the railing and sipped her Bloody Mary. She remembered the dream . . . and Santos. He had stirred something up deep inside her, and yet he was remote, untouchable. She had never known anyone like him.

And then she thought of Simon. There had always been a sense of inevitability about her and Simon. They balanced one another. Brett had come to depend upon his steadying influence since her return to Palm Beach, and as far as Simon was concerned, there had never been anyone else, nor would there be anyone else.

Yet, when they were in bed that morning, it was the face of Santos that had crossed her mind—tantalizing and enigmatic.

Simon had been right about her drifting away. For reasons she could not comprehend she had become obsessed with Julia DuShane. The tragic legacy Julia had bequeathed was casting a long shadow over her. But there was more to it than that. Her instincts told her she was onto the most sensational story of her career; there was no turning back.

Brett hadn't seen Santos since their rescue. He was unconscious when they had lifted him aboard the schooner, and Brett was locked in a small forward cabin throughout the voyage back to Key West. The finale of her voyage into the world of drug smuggling had been entirely anticlimactic. Cujo had put her ashore at the charter fishing marina, and Brett had returned to civilization to find her car conveniently parked in the adjacent lot.

Everything that had taken place seemed like a dream. Brett realized she was still suffering from the emotional bends, the predictable aftereffects that usually plagued her after an adventure. But there was something else—she had been in a situation and had been forced to kill. It didn't bother her. If anything, she was surprised how easily she had done it. How easily she could do it again. She was afraid to admit it, but she liked the feeling. She was changing. In fact, already had.

Driving home to Marisol, Brett heard the insistent wail of sirens rising above the tiled rooftops of Palm Beach. It was ten o'clock, a Sunday morning, and she instinctively followed the speeding police cars along South Ocean Boulevard. They eventually turned left on Los Cielos Drive and sped down the palm-lined avenue to the gates of Casa Encantada.

At least a dozen reporters and photographers had already arrived on the scene, as well as several ambulances and a fire truck.

"It looks a lot like those freak killings they get out in California," a police sergeant on duty outside the gates told her.

He pointed off toward the pink stucco wall bordering the long drive leading up to the mansion. Brett could clearly make out imprints of a bloody hand, along with the scrawled message *CUBA LIBRE* encircled by a writhing snake design.

At one-thirty that morning, the officer said a call had come into the police switchboard. The caller was a woman, hysterically screaming, *"Hombres del muerto! Murder . . . bodies . . . blood!"*

"We figure it must have been one of the servants, but nobody really knows," the sergeant explained. "By the time the fire department got here the place was in flames. We didn't find out till this morning that there were eight people inside, all hacked to death. The bodies were all over the house like they'd been chased, hunted down and slaughtered like pigs."

The officer took off his hat and wiped the beaded sweat from his brow. He looked pale and his eyes were disbelieving. "You should've seen the pair we just hauled out of the basement. . . . It was enough to make a dog throw up."

"And the others?" Brett asked.

"Barbecued. Every last one of 'em. Six rich people and two illegals, probably Haitian. Both women."

The reporters were finally allowed into the grounds for an official briefing and were led up the drive toward what was left of the mansion. Brett remained impassive behind her tinted oval glasses. She paused here and there to snap off random shots of the topiary gardens, the pool and the sleek expensive cars parked along the drive. From the kennels somewhere in the back out of sight came the frantic, incessant barking of small dogs.

Brett's steps began to lag as she approached the blackened walls that were all that was left of the impressive Spanish villa. It was a ruin, a vast desolate shell, and the sickly sweet smell of human flesh seemed to hang over everything.

A uniformed man Brett assumed was the police chief was talking to reporters on the lawn while a television minicam was panning the entire scene.

"You wanna see the two we pulled out of the wine cellar?" the sergeant asked Brett. "You can have a look while the others are still interviewing the chief."

He motioned for Brett to follow him. Together they made their way across the neatly trimmed grass toward the two inert forms lying beneath white sheets inside a latticed gazebo. Here it was very still and quiet. It was going to be hot, she thought. The air was already stifling with the high humidity.

The covers were drawn back. The first body was that of a male Caucasian whose face had been horribly battered beyond any recognition. On the other side of the fountain was the body of a woman in a silver gown that had been drenched with her own blood. Her skin was alabaster white and her body had been slashed and stabbed with dozens of knife wounds.

Brett recognized Monique Von Helsen immediately.

Brett thought she was going to get sick. She slowly bent to pick up a scorched silver satin slipper that had fallen from Monique's foot. She held it for a moment in her hands. Then quickly handed it to the sergeant and suddenly, without a word, hurried away across the lawn and on down the drive. Covered with perspiration, she fumbled through her bag trying to locate her car keys. She started out again for Marisol, praying she wouldn't throw up.

As Brett turned onto Palmetto Drive, she pulled over to the side of the curb and pressed her head against the wheel. She moaned softly, fighting back the bile that churned suddenly up from her stomach.

She realized the killing zone had extended to Palm Beach. And it began to seem that she couldn't run far enough or fast enough to escape it. That villa was only a prelude. There would be more to come.

She was sure of it.

CHAPTER TWENTY-TWO

WORD of the murders spread through Palm Beach.

The scene of the crime was the palatial home of a man by the name of Roberto Castillo, who had lived there with his beautiful Brazilian wife, Kiki, and a dozen purebred prize-winning poodles. After immigrating to Palm Beach a decade earlier, the Castillos had managed to master the art of social celebrity. Roberto Castillo was a multi-millionaire expatriate from South America who was known for his polo playing. His wife was famous for giving some of the most entertaining parties and winning blue ribbons at national dog shows.

On the night of the murders, the couple had been hosting an intimate supper party, and the guest list had contained several prominent Palm Beachers. Now they were all dead, butchered by persons unknown.

The only leads the police had been able to come up with was the reported sighting of a boatload of Cuban refugees just south of Palm Beach hours before the murders and a blood-stained machete found at the beach near the villa.

When Brett finally reached Marisol on Sunday morning, she discovered that her mother had been invited to the Castillos' party on that fateful evening. "Florian saved my life," Charlotte cried. "He insisted on driving down to Boca Raton for dinner. I had to call Kiki to cancel at the very last minute. Thank God I did."

Brett was so relieved at her mother's narrow escape from death that she didn't even think about the circumstances. But later, she began to wonder what it was that had made Florian Montes decide against Charlotte going to the doomed dinner party. She knew she was speculating wildly, but still . . . Montes had never made her feel totally comfortable.

The following day Brad Harraway called from New York and asked Brett to do a series of articles on Palm Beach for Media International.

Dave Markham was flying down for a broadcasters convention and he was going to bring Brett some confidential information. Brett was to meet with him that same evening at the Hawaiiana Hotel in Fort Lauderdale.

They drank too many Mai Tais before dinner and were both a little tipsy by the time they sat down at their poolside table. The setting was so theatrically exotic that they both decided it was terribly amusing. Palm trees fringed the floodlit dance floor, candles flickered in storm glasses on each table, and the waitresses were wearing grass skirts with flowers in their hair.

The mahi-mahi dinner was excellent. A Hawaiian steel guitar band was playing romantic island favorites. Then came the Polynesian revue. It occurred to Brett during the Tahitian flaming sword dance that she could never have enjoyed such an evening with Brad. He would have made her feel that it was all too ridiculous and tacky. "Tourist city," he would have said.

Brad.

She hardly thought of him anymore.

According to David, Lisle Brauer had been hired by Media International and sent to Afghanistan with a three-man camera crew to cover the fighting. Brad was still in love with her, but Lisle had caused quite a stir among the foreign press corps. Brett could have cared less.

After dinner they retired to the lanai of David's suite for coffee and Kahlua. The wind had risen, fluttering the luau torches placed along the beach. The waves washed in upon the sand while the moon shone down with a brightly cool brilliance.

After they were comfortably sitting in deeply cushioned bamboo lounge chairs, David showed Brett an investigative report from Brad. She was not surprised to discover that it had been Dr. Florian Montes who had arranged for Luisa's release from the Louisiana State Mental Institution.

Brett already knew that Julia DuShane had been secretly receiving a series of rejuvenating drug treatments from Montes, and Iris, Julia's companion, had told Brett that he had visited Julia at La Caraval only hours before her collapse. The reason for his visit? To give Julia another of the injections.

None of the information was incriminating in itself, Brett knew. Still . . . it did pose further questions, and she was convinced that Montes was orchestrating the current situation at La Caraval.

But what, Brett asked herself, did Florian Montes have to gain from such a scheme? Julia had already given everything of value away. What reason could there be for Montes to keep Julia alive? Clearly, Luisa herself was merely a convenient pawn.

"Okay," Brett finally said to David, "what do you have so far on the Palm Beach murders? Brad said the DEA has come up with something but he didn't want to discuss it over the phone."

David leaned slightly forward, looking terribly pleased with himself. "Roberto Castillo was not the man that everyone thought he was."

"I'm not surprised. Who the hell was he?"

"In Palm Beach Castillo was just another rich South American, but in his native Colombia he was the king of coke. Casa Encantada, that villa of his, was a front and his headquarters! And, Castillo's cocaine operation earned his organization over one hundred million dollars last year alone. That has to have made him the biggest drug czar in South Florida, and one very heavy-duty dude indeed."

"And they were never able to pin anything directly on him, were they?"

"Of course not. The man was head and shoulders above all the sleazy dealings and the Miami crowd. I also think it helped a great deal that he owned enough politicians to have the statehouse quivering at this very moment."

"What did Castillo do with the money he bagged from the sale of the drugs, and who do they think killed him?" Brett questioned.

David smiled. "The money was laundered through a chain of banks that Castillo controlled under another name all over Florida. That's the easy one. As to who it was who did the dirty deed, everybody's got his head up his ass. There is, however, one interesting theory. The DEA is convinced that the Casa Encantada murders were ordered by someone determined to muscle in on the Colombia cocaine connection. They are convinced that, within a matter of months, whoever this is has already managed to transform the South Florida drug industry into a smoothly flowing pipeline that runs from South America through Florida to New York and points west. Five drug biggies have been eliminated recently with the same modus operandi. Castillo is the biggest hit. He was the top dog. Nothing like eliminating competition."

Palm Beach—Media International
by Brett Farrell, on special assignment

Palm Beach—the name evokes images of high society and high jinks; of playboys and polo ponies; of dowagers in diamonds and palaces in pink. For over one hundred years it has been the dignified playground for America's creme de la creme.

People of wealth and privilege have always come here to live out their favorite dreams. But there is a darker side to Palm Beach now. War zones are no longer half a world away. The flashing machete is as deadly on Los Cielos Drive—one of Palm Beach's most exclusive drives—as it is in war-torn jungles. It has finally struck the paradise that nobody ever leaves, as the inhabitants are so fond of saying, unless they die or go broke.

Panic has come to Palm Beach since the night that six prominent Palm Beach socialites fell victim to savagery and mindless brutality. Body guards are being hired, chauffeurs have started carrying side arms, and there has been a rush to install state-of-the-art electronic security systems. The local police force has begun training a crack SWAT team in antiterrorist and hostage release tactics, while all servants working on the island are being fingerprinted, photographed, and required to carry I.D. cards at all times.

A system has been set up so that if violence should erupt, a Code Red signal would be flashed across the island and all three drawbridges linking Palm Beach to the mainland would be raised, cutting off road access from the outside world.

With its golden shores, ageless people, and long green lawns sloping to the sea, Palm Beach is still considered by many to approximate the fabled Garden of Eden. Yet, even with its great mansions, bounteous boutiques, gleaming yachts, tropic sun, and blue Gulf Stream, the fabled resort is no longer immune from the fears of impending chaos.

Ever since the Casa Encantada murders, rumors abound. The glittering necklace of islands stretching across the Caribbean from the Bahamas to South America has become an arc of crisis and political unrest. Central America is exploding with violence, and Mexico, with its vast overpopulation and underemployment, is like a volcano ready to erupt.

Many here fear the dominos have already begun to fall and that Palm Beach—a symbol of America's greatest prosperity—will fall as well. . . .

In spite of the Casa Encantada murders, as far as the Palm Beach social season was concerned, it was still party time as usual. Not a single gathering was cancelled, and the island's exclusive clubs and hotel ballrooms continued to celebrate without missing a beat.

Even so, there was now a sense of apprehension in the air.

Gossip abounded. The fact that Monique Von Helsen was discovered to have been clutching a jeweled Star of David at the moment of her demise had raised eyebrows as well as a ritual drumbeat of speculation. The death of her husband, the Baron Hugo, had stimulated another fire storm of rumors because he had been found with his *genitalia* summarily transferred from his groin to his mouth.

Hugo was well known to have entertained a penchant for black rough trade in the seamy gay leather bars of West Palm Beach. There were a good many who saw the murders as some sort of bizarre psychosexual aberration brought about by his preference for leather men and sado masochism.

There was, after all, a rather large homosexual community within the multilayered makeup of the Palm Beach scene. A woman needed at least one gay intimate to help her keep up with the gossip on the social circuit. Someone bright and clever who would also look good next to her at a formal dinner. These men were a lavender elite of well-preserved middle-aged men who were for the most part discreet and extremely sophisticated about their sexual proclivities.

They existed within a charmed circle, impressively redolent with pleasure and sensual gratification. Their cruising was usually confined to a little flirtation at cocktail parties and the chic "tea dances" aboard their yachts. But rough trade was out, and the West Palm Beach bar scene had turned grimly suspicious and not nearly so freewheeling as before, since the Casa Encantada murders.

Conversation at any and all Palm Beach parties was a complex combination of valentines and vitriol. But no one had anything good to say about La Caraval. Jerusha's messianic crusade was not a bit amusing to them; she was always referred to as "that mad woman and her troop of niggers."

After establishing La Caraval as the headquarters of the Cristo Redentor Society, Sister Jerusha had begun bussing in hundreds of poor Southern blacks for daily prayer vigils. All of the original servants had been replaced by Jerusha's highly militant black followers, and the mayor's office had been working around the clock to find a solution to her newly established residency.

Everyone was outraged. Committees were formed, petitions were signed, and the town council was called into emergency session. But even as the public pressure mounted, there didn't seem to be anything anyone could do about the situation. Everything was legal, and no high official was prepared to make too many waves as long as Julia DuShane still remained alive.

Dr. Florian Montes continued to monitor Julia's condition while trying at the same time to calm the furor. But it was only a matter of time, according to most people, before Julia died. Then Sister Jerusha and her rabble of followers would be gone, they hoped, and everything would be the way that it had been. The Cristo Redentor Society would become nothing more than a bad dream, an amusing anecdote to regale dinner guests in Monaco, Cap d'Antibes and Acapulco.

From the beginning, Brett had seen Julia's life as a puzzle. But now, after all that had transpired, a far truer analogy indicated multiple puzzles, none of which was entirely complete. Every time a visible pattern began to emerge, there were always gaping holes or pieces left over that just didn't fit. The riddle of Jerusha. The enigma of Santos. Dr. Florian Montes, who seemed to hover over all and then to vanish like a shadow melting into mists whenever Brett got too close.

Brett had come to realize that there was at least one single constant—Julia DuShane herself. Julia was still a presence, and Brett felt she had to see her. Only this time, no one was going to stand in her way. . . .

CHAPTER TWENTY-THREE

As soon as Brett stepped in the door and switched on the light she knew something was wrong.

The pool house at Marisol was actually a one-bedroom guest cottage separate from the main house. There was a fieldstone fireplace in the sunken living room with a nineteen foot ceiling, rough-hewn crossbeams, and a large skylight. It was airy, spacious, and secluded by the surrounding gardens encircling the pool.

At first, nothing looked different, but Brett couldn't shake off the feeling that something was wrong. She switched on the lights in the kitchen, checked out the small darkroom, and then slowly climbed the spiral staircase to the bedroom loft above.

Consuelo insisted on keeping Brett's domestic life well ordered and neatly predictable. But Brett remembered that Consuelo had been visiting relatives in Orlando for the past week. No one else was permitted to enter the pool house during Brett's absence. Now she stood looking around the loft with a perplexed expression. Everything appeared to be as she had left it, but there was a subtle feeling of difference.

Crossing to the rosewood desk, Brett opened the top drawer to find that her papers had been shifted ever so slightly. And in the drawers of her bureau, some anonymous hand had riffled through her undergarments.

Nothing appeared to be missing. Her jewelry was intact, as were several hundred dollars in mad money she kept in a Chinese porcelain pot.

She went back downstairs. Although she didn't know what an intruder may have been searching for or who they may have been, she did know it was *not* a matter for the police. Fortunately, she had locked Julia's tapes and diaries in the library safe inside the main house.

The phone began to ring as she returned to the living room, and as soon as she heard Simon's deep comforting voice, she blurted out what had apparently taken place.

Simon was clearly alarmed. "Are you sure nothing of value was stolen?"

"Yes . . . it wasn't that kind of a break-in. It's something else, I'm sure. I'm afraid it has to do with Julia."

They were both silent for a moment. Then Simon said, "It'll take me about twenty minutes to dress and get over there. Promise me you won't do anything before I arrive. I think it's time we had a serious talk about what you've gotten yourself into."

Immediately upon his arrival Simon began searching for the bugging devices he suspected had been planted. Brett watched with narrowed eyes as he ran his hands beneath the edges of the carpet, checked behind the hanging wall pictures, and finally dismantled the phone.

"Just as I thought," Simon said. He produced a small amplifying device no larger than a martini olive, then placed it in Brett's hand. "State of the art. Your phone calls can be picked up as far as a mile away."

"I can hardly believe this . . ." Brett said. She stood staring down at the bug in her hand. "So all my calls may have been monitored?"

"*We're* being monitored. I can tell by the oxidation that this bug has been in place for some time. Let's hope your calls were *all* that was being monitored," Simon added.

He nodded toward the loft and the color in Brett's face drained as the implications of another bug planted in her bedroom took hold. Climbing the stairs, Brett couldn't decide what would be more damaging—the calls from Brad detailing all the information he'd given her or the invasion of her love life.

Upstairs, Simon circled the big brass bed, feeling beneath the frame with his fingers. Brett couldn't watch, and turned away, clasping her arms. She stood staring out through the skylight windows toward the pool. Her mind was racing frantically through a maze of possibilities. There might be nothing in the bedroom. She prayed there wasn't.

"Here's another one," Simon soon confirmed. He got up off his knees to toss an additional device onto the quilted bedspread. "Well, someone wants to get something on you real bad."

Simon was looking gravely across the bed at her with the device lying between them. "I think you should call the police. This looks like you've interested some serious people. . . ."

Brett shook her head. "I'm afraid calling the police wouldn't help, Simon. It's already gone beyond that."

"Are you going to tell me what this is all about? Talk to me, Brett. Something's going on. I've known it ever since you got back from that mysterious trip of yours last week. I know it was Key West because the mileage checks out on the Porsche."

"So now *you're* spying on me," she snapped. She got up and walked through the open bathroom door, slamming and locking it behind her.

Her head was spinning. She braced herself against the wash basin, resisting the dry heaves. She had drunk far too much earlier that evening with David in Fort Lauderdale. The bathroom spun around in a sickening montage of tiles, towels, and hand-painted porcelain fixtures. Even the softly diffused light seemed harsh.

Simon had every right to be concerned by what was going on. But what could she tell him? About Santos?

No. For someone who courted death, Santos seemed to be charged with life. But if she was going to be a part of that world, she'd have to be stronger than this.

She felt as if she had tasted too deeply of some potent brew, of having trespassed into some forbidden zone where life was very close to death, and Raphael de Vargas was the grim master of the rebels.

Twenty minutes later, she made her way down the staircase still feeling shaky. Her hair was freshly brushed and her pale features were slashed by a fresh application of lipstick.

"I need a drink," Brett said, going to the liquor cabinet and pouring herself a brandy. Simon had started a fire in the fireplace.

"You're right, Simon. . . . I haven't been entirely honest with you. But you'll have to promise me that you won't try to interfere. I know now that whoever came here earlier tonight was looking for Julia's diaries and tapes."

Pacing back and forth before the hearth, Brett told Simon everything from the beginning to end. All about Santos and what had happened in Key West and the Tortugas. The only thing she failed to mention was the depth of her own attraction for Santos.

Simon was silent for a while. His lanky frame was sprawled on the rug with his back braced up against the couch. His angular features were somber.

"Brett," he said at last, "I want you out of this thing."

"I can't quit . . . can't you see that?

"I say get out while you still can. You're getting into deep waters that even you can't negotiate."

"I'm just following the story wherever it leads. I'm a journalist and a damned good one—that's what this is all about."

Simon shook his head. "Do you really believe that's all there is to it? Are you sure there aren't some things you haven't told me?"

"Please understand, Simon. All I'm saying is that I have to find out. . . ."

Simon ran his fingers back through his wavy dark hair and looked thoughtful. Then he got up, went over to the fireplace, and pitched two logs onto the fire. They were standing very close together.

"Hasn't the light begun to dawn yet, Brett? You're living out Julia's life for her. You've become obsessed. Can't you see that she's using you, just as she's always used everyone?"

His words struck her. "Isn't it more likely that you've always resented any commitment I've ever made to anything except you? You're just like all the rest of them, Simon. It's that damn male ego of yours."

"Perhaps you're right about that, but I've never been willing to purchase success at the expense of my own values. This entire DuShane business has somehow managed to warp your values. You're out of your mind thinking you can play in Santos's league. He'll use you and then destroy you once you've served his purpose."

Brett leaned forward, pressing her hands against the mantel while staring into the flames. "Santos isn't like that. And this assassination plan isn't just an ordinary political killing. It's a vendetta. It's vengeance, pure and simple. It's striking down the God he stopped believing in. He's not really a terrorist, no matter what anyone says. His aim goes much deeper."

"Are you serious? It's crazy to play Russian roulette with a man like that. Do you honestly think you're immortal?"

Brett turned to face him. "I've got the whole incredible story at my fingertips. Do you really think I'd let this one pass me by?"

"Look, you've been out in the field for over ten years and your odds for survival are getting slimmer all the time. One of these days your luck will run out."

"My luck, darling, is operating very nicely, thank you. This is a story every journalist dreams of. It's just not possible to play it safe on this one, Simon. I'm going to follow it wherever it leads me and to hell with the odds. Raphael de Vargas might very well change the course of history. I have every intention of being there to see it happen when he does."

Simon reached out to draw her to him. He kissed Brett gently and held her tightly in his arms. "Okay . . . but I wouldn't get too close if I were you. And for godsakes, cover your ass at all times."

"I always do," she said.

CHAPTER TWENTY-FOUR

T HE following evening Brett, accompanied by Consuelo, went to La Caraval to attend one of Jerusha's impassioned prayer vigils. There was a string of buses parked along the drive. Several hundred of her followers were already gathered together in the great hall of the mansion.

All the fine antique furnishings and priceless art works had been removed, and the vacant walls and uncovered floors seemed to echo like an empty cathedral.

Jerusha's followers were seated on wooden folding chairs lined up in rows, and dozens more were standing around the fringe or jammed together at the back of the vast room where Julia DuShane once held court.

Brett had made no attempt to disguise her identity, yet no one seemed to pay any attention as she and Consuelo slipped inside the huge cathedral-like doors and took their places at the rear.

Within a matter of minutes, Jerusha made a poised entrance on the low dais at the far end of the room. She looked less like a real person than a theatrical figure from some biblical movie. This was a very different woman than Brett had encountered during their initial meeting.

Sister Jerusha seemed subdued. Upon reaching the microphone at center stage, she turned and said slowly, "Friends and seekers of truth, I welcome you here tonight."

Her voice was compelling, haunting, as it echoed out over the speaker system. The silence in the great room that followed was even more haunting. There wasn't a sound among the hundreds of people.

"We have gathered here together for a high purpose," she continued. "Throughout these past weeks we have been praying and meditating . . . preparing ourselves for a miracle. We have asked the Lord to guide our search for perfect truth. The healing miracle I have promised you is about to reveal itself. Now we must all join together in preparing the way. It cannot come from our own wills and desires. Oh no, my brothers and sisters, it will only come if we open our hearts and minds to the great power that is flowing out to us at this moment."

Jerusha held them in thrall, like a mystical priestess of some dark and ancient rite. Her eyes were luminous, shimmering with light as she lifted her arms and tilted back her head in supplication to the heavens.

Brett thought she looked like she was offering herself up as a martyr. The audience began swaying rhythmically, with voices crying out as if to confirm her vision.

"Restoring my mother to life," Jerusha explained in a sharper, stronger voice, "is only the beginning of our great crusade. Many wonderful and extraordinary things are about to be revealed, and each one of you will go forth to spread the healing light of love. It has been made known to me . . . that only through our prayers and efforts will this troubled place be brought out of its dreadful pain and darkness."

Jerusha slowly allowed her eyes to traverse the room. "There are those who seek to destroy our mission and drive us from this house," she warned. "But there is no need for fear among those who truly believe. At this very moment we are at the center of a powerful spiritual field of tremendous strength. All dark and evil shadows are being cast away . . . peace and light are all around us."

With her words still echoing against the bare sandstone walls, Jerusha seated herself upon a simple wooden folding chair situated in the center of the small stage. She spread her voluminous robe about her as if she were seated upon a throne. She closed her eyes and clasped her slender hands before her. The lights in the hall slowly dimmed as she sat smiling in dreamy contemplation.

Finally, when she spoke it was in a crooning incantation. *"Let the healing light steam forth. . . . Let the spirit of love renew the hearts of men. . . . Let the forgiveness of God descend upon the earth so that we may be bathed in light and receive the healing power."*

By now the room had fallen into semidarkness. The only illumination came from two giant silver candelabra flanking Jerusha's chair.

Brett whispered something to Consuelo and slipped away unnoticed. Brett paused for a moment in the shadowy rotunda outside the great hall to gain her bearings. Then she hurried off along a darkened corridor, stepping quickly inside the first door she saw. She crossed the empty room toward the French doors that opened to the outside, and passed through them to find herself on a wide pillared loggia, floored with terra-cotta tiles. Moorish arches framed the view of the moonlit lake and ran along past a series of shuttered rooms.

At the far end of the loggia there was a small door of carved cypress hidden by bougainvillea climbing to the gabled roof. She cautiously tried the brass handle—it wasn't locked. Circular walls closed in around her as she stepped inside and fumbled for a light switch.

When she finally succeeded in finding it, she switched on a brass Moroccan lantern hanging from the ceiling, illuminating a narrow flight of steps curving upward above her head. She couldn't help smiling as she recalled the delight Julia had taken in showing her all the secret passages she had so lovingly built into her palace of mirrors. Julia had said, "The fantasy that makes you happy is better than the reality that makes you sad." How right she was, Brett thought.

Holding onto the railing, Brett ascended the stairs and was out of breath by the time she reached the top. She stepped into a room. Julia had called it "The Golden Ballroom," with its goldleaf ceiling, gleaming parquet floor, mirrored walls, and spacious minstral's gallery large enough to accommodate a twelve-piece orchestra. The room was enormous. Moonlight washed in through banks of diamond-paned windows. Delicate French chairs of tarnished gilt and frayed satin still stood in place along the walls like patient guests waiting for the music and dancing to begin.

Brett could hear distant voices from very far away. Jerusha's followers were singing "Nearer My God To Thee," and it appeared that her absence had not been noted. Otherwise, Brett was sure Jerusha's militant black storm troopers would have been after her by now. Brett had seen them posted at the gates, along the drive and standing guard in front of the house upon her arrival.

Whenever Julia gave one of her fabulous, legendary balls, it had been her habit to suddenly vanish at the stroke of midnight. The secret of the Golden Ballroom was a *trompe de L'oeil* door painted to replicate the marbled walls. It was partially hidden behind velvet brocade draperies. The small, invisible door led into Julia's private suite of rooms on the second floor of the mansion.

Brett entered the suite through a series of commodious wardrobe rooms, where everything was neatly labeled and notated with instructions for the coordination of accessories. Brett could still detect the faint illusive scent of Julia's Attar of Roses perfume as she passed through a room full of gowns hanging on racks and sealed in clear plastic.

Next she found herself moving through a vault full of furs

that was climate-controlled and walled in fragrant cedar paneling. This gave way to rooms containing less formal wear and shelved passages displaying thousands of shoes, hundreds of hats, and finally a mirrored dressing room whose door was slightly ajar.

Through the crack in the door, Brett could see Julia's nurse, Helga Nordstrom. She was standing beside the bed with her back turned while making notations on a medical chart.

The tension was excruciating as the minutes dragged by. Brett stood frozen in place for what seemed to be like eternity. Then Helga disappeared from view, and Brett heard the soft click of the outer door closing behind her.

Brett entered the familiar bedroom and went over to Julia's gilded-swan bed. There were so many things—the heart and lung machine illuminated with flashing multicolored lights, the smell of hospital disinfectant, and the pulsing bleep of the pulmonary scanner. Overall was the background soundtrack of human lungs, highly magnified and mechanically gasping for breath.

Julia DuShane lay curled like a fetal child inside her plastic oxygen tent. She was frail, wasted, and ominously still, with a variety of needles and plastic tubes extended from her emaciated form. Brett crept up close beside the bed. She felt an angry choking sensation in her throat, and tears formed at the corners of her eyes.

It was then that Brett knew there was no longer a decision to be made. There was only an act of liberation to be carried out. She owed Julia that much at least.

"I shouldn't even think about it if I were you," a familiar voice said suddenly from behind her. "In any case, not unless you're prepared to spend the next fifteen to twenty years in prison for murder."

Brett spun around to find Florian Montes standing in the doorway leading to the adjacent chinoiserie. Sleekly self-assured, impeccably groomed, and as always, courteous to a fault. He was smiling at her as if they had come to share some grotesque private joke.

During lunch the following day at Café L'Europe, Charlotte angrily informed Brett that news of her disastrous confrontation with Florian Montes was all over Palm Beach.

"This entire business with Julia DuShane is becoming too ghoulish for words," Charlotte snapped. "Florian is absolutely furious. If you don't stop interfering, he's threatening to file charges of criminal trespass and get a restraining order on you."

Every Friday afternoon Brett maintained a standing four o'clock hair appointment. After walking out on Charlotte at lunch, she waited an hour, window-shopping, then hurried across the sidewalk to stroll through the swinging glass doors of Phillipe's salon, arriving five minutes early.

For once she didn't want to be late. Too much depended on gaining Phillipe's cooperation.

"So how is my beauty today?" Phillipe cooed after making a dramatic entrance through the tall mirrored doors leading to the inner sanctum. He brushed her cheek lightly with his lips. Then he stood back scowling owlishly over the tops of his half-frame glasses. "Tsk, tsk, tsk . . ." he said. "Do I detect some frown lines around that lovely mouth?"

They laughed comfortably together and moved arm in arm into the salon, where a bevy of Palm Beach matrons were being pampered, coiffed and manicured beneath the dexterous hands of Phillips's lavender-smocked staff. Brett had come to look forward to her weekly visit to Phillipe's, and thoroughly enjoyed his outrageously wicked sense of humor. The extravagant pretenses of the ladies of Palm Beach had become the butt of all their private jokes.

Brett was used to causing a stir wherever she went in Palm Beach; but for once, she was totally, pointedly ignored. The second syndicated installment of her Palm Beach profile had been published that morning in the *Miami Herald* and there was a chill in the richly perfumed air.

Phillipe led her into the narrowed cubicle reserved for his most prestigious clientele. Brett settled herself into the comfortably padded chair. "I got the impression on the way in here that I'm about as welcome as a pair of cellulite thighs," she said cryptically. "Or am I just being paranoid?"

Phillipe was busily bustling about arranging the tools of his trade for easy access. "I wouldn't be too surprised if I were you, considering those poisoned articles you've been penning. You've stirred up a hornet's nest, dear."

"Mother did say the local gentry are upset. I can't imagine why."

"Come out of the woods, Bambi," Phillipe said. "We're talking about the wild kingdom here. Even as we speak, fluffed heads of hair in tints from white to blue are bobbing up and down talking about you. It must have been that 'let them eat cake' attitude you managed to capture so well. I loved the charity ball hostess who said, 'What disease are we going to celebrate this year? Or are we going to have to invent a new one?'

"In fact," he added, "I'm putting my career at risk even letting you in here, much less making you absolutely gorgeous when you walk out the door. The ladies who lunch may be giving you the cold shoulder in public but they're talking of little else beside you-know-who in private."

"What are they saying?" Brett asked as he dropped the chair into a horizontal position, tipped her head back into the basin, and began lathering up a fragrantly foaming shampoo.

"Well," Phillipe continued, obviously relishing the opportunity to recount the latest gossip, "I've heard a variety of retaliatory suggestions that range from clawing your face off to electrocuting you under a faulty hair dryer. The one thing you always have to remember in Palm Beach is that no one wants to hear bad news . . . especially about themselves. That's why they hire press agents."

"A reporter's job is *not* to make people happy," Brett said, her eyes squeezed tightly shut to avoid the soap. "My job is to tell the truth."

"Be that as it may," Phillipe replied primly, "but if you plan to stick around this burg for any length of time, I'd suggest a coif of shorn locks worn with sack cloth and ashes. For penance, you could crawl down Worth Avenue over broken glass and kneel in front of Cartier's handing out printed retractions. Trust me . . . you've managed to ruffle up a hen house of feathers, if you take my drift."

"Be honest, Phillipe . . . you loved every last minute of it, didn't you?"

He slapped a moistly perfumed towel over Brett's face and shoved her head beneath a streaming wash of hot water. "I must admit I rather liked the line about the lady who knew it was time to have her buttocks lifted because her son was scheduled for cosmetic surgery. Or the one you quoted as saying 'Anyone who says money can't buy happiness doesn't know where to shop.'"

Phillipe shifted her abruptly into an upright position in front of the softly lit mirrors. Briskly he toweled her head. Then he began turning her this way and that as his scissors flashed and clippings of Brett's long hair fell to the floor.

"Actually, Phillipe, my sweet . . . I didn't come here today just to get cut and dried. What I need is some inside information, and who better to ask than you?"

Phillipe adjusted his blow dryer and began playing a hot rush of air over Brett's head. "Bite your tongue and forget it. Where you're concerned, loose lips sink ships. Self-immolation is simply not on my list of priorities."

"Whatever you tell me will be kept in the very strictest confidence," Brett assured him. "I always protect my sources."

"If I spill the beans to you I'll need an armored car and body guards," Phillipe quipped above the sound of the blow dryer. "Although, I must admit there is a certain morbid delight in seeing the ultra-rich suffer indignity."

"The story I'm working on is a lot better than that. Whether anyone wants to deal with it or not, the Casa Encantada murders involve far more than random violence by a boatload of Cuban refugees. I'm really onto something, Phillipe, and I'm going to get the information I need one way or another."

Phillipe switched off the blow dryer, and his long supple fingers began working a foaming mousse through her hair in preparation for styling. "Frankly, you disappoint me. I'm shocked that a Pulitzer Prize-winning journalist would stoop to tossing around cheap threats. I am only a humble hairdresser, after all. My lips are hermetically sealed by vows of self-preservation."

Brett sighed and examined her nails with casual disinterest. "Well, if you're that kind of friend, then you're not really a friend, I suppose."

"Oh, all right," he huffed. He went to the door, locked it, and pulled a stool up beside Brett's chair. He folded his arms, leaned close, and said, "Exactly who do you want me to destroy?"

Brett rewarded him with a reassuring smile and reached out to pat his knee. "Dear Phillipe . . . I was so hoping you'd help. Tell me everything you know about Dr. Florian Montes."

CHAPTER TWENTY-FIVE

"*L*ADIES and gentlemen, we are now on our landing approach to Great Inagua Island. We will be putting down at Seaview Airport in approximately ten minutes. Please extinguish your cigarettes and fasten your seat belts."

The passengers were looking out the windows, craning to see the island materializing upon the Grand Bahamian Banks. Great Inagua Island was very beautiful, peaceful and away from the tourist hustle of the larger islands of the archipelago. A sleepy island paradise forty-four miles from the northeastern tip of Cuba.

As Brett gazed out from her window seat, she wondered what she was going to find there. The message she had found on her telephone answering machine the day before certainly had not told her.

Santos's voice had spooled out, low and intense. Santos had instructed her to take a commercial helicopter flight from West Palm Beach Airport to Nassau on the following morning. There was a one-hour layover before catching the noon flight, which was the only flight to Great Inagua on Air Caribe. Upon her arrival on Great Inagua, Brett was to check in at the Hotel Tropicana in Matthew Town and await further instructions.

The flight from Nassau finally touched down upon the blistering macadam airstrip overgrown with tufts of withered grass.

It looks like just another poor hot tropical backwater, the ass-end of nowhere.

Brett had not the slightest idea of what to expect next. She was traveling light, with only a canvas carryall and her photographic equipment carried in a hanging leather case. The open-shed terminal building was lacking the hustle of the more popular tourist destinations, Brett discovered. There was no duty-free shop or much of anything else except a ticket counter, baggage claim, and fly-blown newstand offering a variety of out-of-date magazines.

She passed through customs and started walking briskly toward the exit with an almost overwhelming sense of expectation. Then, as she stepped outside into the sunlight she was greeted by a young black with native African features and a flashing white smile. "Welcome to Great Inagua," he beamed. "I promise you are going to love it here."

He firmly clasped her arm and she was propelled through the wilting heat toward a vintage pink Cadillac with *Hotel Tropicana* painted across the door. The ride into town from the airport was spectacular with magnificent vistas of sparkling sea and distant islands of lush verdant green. Yellow shower trees lined the road, and crimson poinsettia and splashes of pink and orange bougainvillea ran riot over ancient stone walls.

But if there was matchless natural beauty to the island setting, there was also an underlying poverty.

Tin-roofed shacks clustered together with pigs rooting in the yards. Ragged black children ran out to the road to watch their car speed past in a swirl of dust. She was back in the Third World, where poverty was always right next door to violence.

The driver talked throughout the journey, but Brett was scarcely listening. She remained lost in her thoughts until they finally skidded into the narrow rutted streets of Matthew Town, scattering chickens, starving dogs, and ragged street urchins before their blaring horn.

Hot Caribbean sunlight poured down over the ramshackle

collection of polyglot architecture with rusting corrugated tin roofs, iron-grilled balconies, and deeply shaded verandas.

The Hotel Tropicana was located about a mile outside of town and turned out to be surprisingly modern. There were a series of bungalows surrounded by tropical gardens. An aquamarine swimming pool shimmered in the center of a tiled patio with small tables scattered around beneath striped umbrellas. There were at least a dozen vacationers in residence, and at least half of them were sunning themselves at the outdoor bar where the ebony faced barman was rattling an ice-filled cocktail shaker like Spanish maracas.

Brett found that a reservation had been made in her name, but she was disappointed to discover that there were no messages.

She was feeling travel-worn and very hot with her clothes sticking to her body. She was in need of a shower and some time to get her bearings. The bungalow assigned to her was bright with brilliantly colored chintzes. There was a bedroom with air conditioning, a small living area with a utility kitchen, and a balcony overlooking the beach. The sea was pale as jade with snow white surf running up the sands. Palm trees rustled in the light off-shore breeze.

After ordering a late lunch and eating it outside on the balcony, she went into the bathroom, stripped off her clothes, and got under the shower. The cool water washed away the muggy heat, battered her face and shoulders and ran over her breasts in rivulets. Compared to the bronzed bodies she had seen sprawled about the pool and lounging at the bar, Brett noticed she had lost most of her tan.

The sense of her own nakedness brought thoughts of Raphael de Vargas to mind. Brett suddenly turned off the shower and wrapped herself in an oversized towel. The prospect of making love to Santos was the last thing she wanted to think about.

She was nothing to Santos. His obsession with Castro was

everything. She was merely an observer venturing into the dangerous pathology of terrorism; to forget the reality of her situation for even a single instant might very well prove to be fatal.

Brett dried herself and wandered into the bedroom to draw the blinds. She felt so tired that she dropped to the bed, covered herself with a sheet, and lay there allowing her thoughts to drift.

Brett knew she would have to perform an intricate balancing act in order to safely negotiate the dangerous terrain upon which she found herself. She realized only too well that journalists were always at risk; not only for what they might witness but also for what they might think and consequently for their interpretation of events and circumstances.

Had she become entangled in some madman's dream? She wondered. The entire Santos scenario was full of questions but without any real answers. What standards was she to use in judging how much brutality was legitimately necessary to achieve visionary ends? How far should she go in trying to balance the objective facts with her own subjective emotions?

Brett wondered drowsily what would happen next. When would Santos contact her? She then drifted off to sleep, lulled into submission by the whispered wash of the waves upon the beach.

When Brett awoke, the luminous hands of her bedside travel clock read one in the morning. She got up, put her bathing suit on beneath a robe, and went outside to sit by the pool. She listened to the sounds of the tropic night. She could hear the sea pounding on the beach and the shrill intermittent cry of night birds. The incessant and strangely comforting chirping of crickets and the low pitched humming of the outside air conditioners from the adjacent bungalows.

There was no one about. Brett sat alone in the darkness smoking quietly. She stared upward. The stars seemed like distant beacons as unattainable as some future century she would never live to see. The moon had been violated by the boots of men and her purity could never be regained. Nothing was forever. Everything changed. It was hopeless to resist change, yet there were those who did.

Santos was one of them.

Brett found bitter irony in the awareness that the children of revolutionary change had become the supreme reactionaries of the age. Violent, troubled and volatile young people, trying to turn back the clock to an earlier time.

Was Santos any different? Was she fooling herself? Had she become part of the insanity?

That despairing thought carried Brett into the water of the pool with a long graceful dive. She began swimming laps. It felt good to stretch her muscles, to feel the strength in her limbs expanding. To take deep even breaths and feel the oxygen filling her lungs.

It was good not to think, just to swim. . . .

And then she saw it. A shadowy form bulking up out of the darkness and moving quickly toward the pool along the graveled garden path. For a moment her heart raced, fearing it was Cujo.

"Evenin', missus," the black man called out in a deep West Indian voice. "This make a good night for a swim."

Brett paused at the deep end of the pool, clasping the tile edging with one hand and drawing back her wet hair with the other. She was treading water and staring at the looming figure that had now moved beneath the light hanging over the shuttered bar by the pool.

"Good evening," Brett said, willing her heart to stop pounding. The man was wearing a tan uniform which had the Hotel Tropicana security logo imprinted on the shirt. He was big, but not as big as Cujo. He seemed more reassuring than threatening. There was even a certain shyness to his smile.

"I'll bet you're the night watchman," Brett said.

"Yes, missus, just checkin'. Makin' sure everythin' okay out here." He doffed his cap and remained at a respectful distance.

"I couldn't sleep and thought a swim might help," she offered as explanation. "It's so warm and lovely tonight."

"Right balmy it is, missus. Tomorrow be a right fine day for goin' out to Coco Island. This man come here he say ole Captain Moses be waitin' on the town dock. You be there noon tomorrow."

So this was it. The beginning of a frightening but exhilarating flight into an uncertain future.

Would she look back later, Brett wondered, and wish she'd taken a different course at that moment?

No, probably not.

In the middle of the night Brett awoke drenched in sweat, her screaming echoing through the bungalow. She thrashed until she was free from the twisted sheet, then sat shakily on the edge of the bed and waited for the nightmare to leave her. Her nightshirt clung to her body. She dropped her face into her hands but the images wouldn't leave her.

She was cutting flowers in the garden at Marisol when there was a noise like a firecracker exploding or a car backfiring.

But that wasn't it. Something was terribly wrong. She ran along the winding garden path in the direction from which the sound had come. It seemed to take forever to reach the lake. Her eyes swept the scene but everything appeared idyllically peaceful. She heard a muffled sound to her right and turned to see her father slowly falling. He was inside the summerhouse.

He was grasping a wrought iron table with both hands. He was hunched over and retching. Then he fell face down on the flagstones with a dull dreadful thud.

She uttered a low moan and ran toward him.

She knelt beside him, and he managed to raise himself up. He wasn't ready to die. There was something he had to say.

"*Father!*" she cried.

She didn't think he could see her because his eyes had begun to glaze over and blood was spilling from his mouth.

His chest heaved and his lips soundlessly struggled to form the words: *forgive me*.

She put her arms around his shoulders and tried to embrace him but he slipped away from her and fell back against the stone floor. His muscles coiled and tensed before releasing the last breath of his life with a choking rasp.

Then his body went completely limp. She pulled away from it. Panicked, she screamed, rose to her feet and started to back away, shaking her head. She then hunched over and began pounding her thighs with her fists. "No . . . No . . . No . . ." she screamed again.

Seconds passed and yet she seemed to have aged a lifetime. Her father was a corpse and his blood was turning black upon the flagstones.

Brett sat on the edge of the bed sobbing silently. For the first time her father's death had become an emotional reality. Clutching herself tightly and rocking back and forth, Brett cried until there were no more tears.

CHAPTER TWENTY-SIX

"THERE she be, missus! Coco Island. Nothin' but jungle pirates and a tribe of bloodthirsty savages that would skin a man alive for the gold in his teeth."

Captain Moses offered Brett a toothless grin, a wink, and a cackling laugh as the fishing sloop *Blue Fin* plowed through the swells toward the island.

Brett stood leaning against the railing of the small, garishly blue-painted fishing sloop with the warm tropical wind whipping her hair about her face.

She had long since discovered that Captain Moses was among other things a spinner of tall tales. According to the desk clerk at the Hotel Tropicana, Coco Island was an old coconut plantation that had undergone a variety of incarnations since its early days as the haunt of pirates and savage Indians.

In the thirties the ramshackle plantation Great House had been turned into a tourist hotel. In the forties the American Navy had set up a loran station to monitor wartime merchant shipping in the Caribbean. In its latest guise, the island had been used for on-location filming of a series of grade "B" action/adventure movies.

It was currently owned by a rich Cuban living in Miami, the

desk clerk informed her. There was also a movie being shot there, he said.

As the sloop drew closer to the outer reef, Brett took out her 16mm camera and panned the shoreline. Coco Island was roughly shaped like a three-quarter moon and spanned several miles in length. The lagoon was crystal clear, and through the dense cover of vegetation, punctuated by strands of graceful palms, Brett could see the old Plantation Hotel with its sharply peaked slate roofs, circular turrets, and gingerbread facade.

The sloop *Blue Fin* was Coco Island's only link with the outside world, and she had gotten a lift on the weekly "milk run" carrying crates of supplies and foodstuffs for the several dozen people Captain Moses said were currently on the island filming a movie.

The sloop throttled down as they entered the lagoon and finally bumped alongside the wooden jetty extending out into the crystalline water. Brett had halfway been expecting to see the *Callisto* riding at anchor, but there was only a Chris-Craft cabin cruiser moored on the other side of the pier.

While Brett continued to scan the dense vegetation along the shore with her camera, Captain Moses jumped to the pier with surprising agility to secure the sloop. There was a well-worn path leading up to the hotel. Looking through the view-finder, Brett saw the figure of a woman come into focus.

It was Gabriella Marquez and she was accompanied by two commando types who had on khaki uniforms with rifles slung across their shoulders.

Brett quickly adjusted her camera's zoom lens close-up to the 200mm setting, seeing that there was far more to Gabriella Marquez than she had previously suspected. The heroin-addicted nightclub singer had quite clearly been transformed into someone else.

In place of the sequined G-string and tasseled pasties, Gabriella now wore faded khaki fatigues. And the weapon she carried beneath her arm with such casual familiarity was only too familiar: the deadly AK—47 with its distinctively curved magazine and brightly laminated woodwork.

Gabriella ordered the men to start unloading the boat and was standing there supervising their work when Brett jumped onto the dock, slinging her carryall over one shoulder.

"So you've come," Gabriella said. "I'm a little surprised."

"I was invited," Brett said briskly, slipping on a pair of dark glasses to shield against the glare. "Or weren't you told I was coming? Santos made all the arrangements."

Gabriella stared at her. "I was not consulted, nor do I care. However, I think it only fair to warn you that this is not some glamorous resort. Discipline is very strict here. Rules are followed by everyone."

Gabriella was full of surprises, Brett thought. Her sudden command of the English language was probably the least of them. "I'm perfectly willing to follow the rules," Brett assured her. "But one question: just what is your game?"

There was a flat hostile look in Gabriella's dark eyes. "Raphael de Vargas is my game, and it has begun to look like he has become your game, too. He has only to call and you come running like a bitch in heat.

"But," she continued, "you mean nothing to him. When he has gotten whatever he wants from you, he will throw you to the sharks. I share something with Santos that you never will. I share his passionate hatred of Fidel Castro. Together we will destroy the Communist pig."

"While we're on the subject," Brett said coolly, "how exactly was it that you planned to assassinate Castro for the CIA? I've heard all about the poison cigars, the exploding seashells, and the depilatory to make his beard fall out. What did they hire *you* to do, Gabriella—fuck him to death?"

The yellow cottage with its peaked roof, wide veranda, and creaking mahogany floors reminded Brett of an old Key West conch house. Captain Moses had shown her to her accommodations before quickly departing back to Matthew Town. The interior smelled strongly of insecticide. The furnishings were scarred and worn. A general air of decay and neglect permeated the entire premises.

The half-dozen cottages surrounding the old Plantation Hotel had been built in the thirties, and each of them was secluded by hedges of flowering hibiscus and densely overgrown tropical foliage. The central structure had been constructed in the 1800s with coral block foundations, deeply shaded verandas, and wrought iron grillwork shipped over from Spain. The hotel itself was no longer in use, and all the doors and windows were shuttered.

The cottages were in obvious disrepair. Years before each had been painted a different color in faded and peeling pastels. From the veranda of her cottage, Brett could see the water of the lagoon receding outward in ever widening bands. They darkened from azure to indigo blue. The jagged submarine patterns of the coral reef were clearly visible.

As soon as Brett had unpacked her things, she decided to go for a swim. The sand was hot against her bare feet as she hurried across the beach toward the water's edge. She slipped on her swim fins and face mask—snorkeling gear she had discovered stashed in the bedroom closet of her cottage. She wasted no time in launching herself into the shallows and striking out toward the reef with a speargun clutched in her hand.

Under water Brett could see browsing parrot fish, gently waving sea ferns, schools of brilliant neons jetting off through gardens of staghorn, brainhead, and delicately branched bluesponge coral. At certain points the coral arched up to form towering castle keeps and cathedral-like vaults swarming with brightly colored reef fish.

Her tension began to melt away as she breathed from the tank and swam down into the hazy underwater silence where the lagoon deepened into canyons.

On the sand below, a manta ray took hasty flight. Brett's

shadow passed over a sunken wreck whose skeletal remains were inhabited by several large groupers and a school of brightly patterned angel fish. Brett surfaced briefly before drawing in a deep breath, then paddled lazily down to skim along the sandy bottom through undulating gardens of delicately trailing sea fern.

Then, just as her air supply was beginning to dwindle, Brett spotted a large rainbow-hued pompano swimming languidly just off to her left. She quickly swung around, aimed the speargun, and in the next instant a silvery projectile was streaking off through the water to impale the big fish upon its steel shaft. The pompano writhed and twisted. Swiftly she thrust herself upward toward the light, coughing and gasping for breath with her prize catch securely in tow.

As she swam slowly toward shore, the sound of hoof beats attracted her attention. She glanced off down the beach and saw Raphael de Vargas cantering toward her on a Rhone stallion, leading a riderless chestnut mare. He soon reined to a halt and sat watching as she emerged from the water and walked up the beach toward him, the pompano still thrashing on the speargun's shaft.

Brett was aware of the way he was looking at her. A tingling anticipation went up her spine. Her skin glistened with tiny droplets of water and her brief two-piece bikini clung wetly to her hips and breasts.

Santos looked as he had the day they first met in the swamps of Nicaragua: brooding and bearded, in camouflage fatigues with a red bandanna tied around his forehead.

"I see you're as good with a spear gun as you are with a pistol," he smiled, flashing his strong white teeth. "We'll have the pompano for dinner tonight. Now go and put on some clothes. There's something I want to show you."

They were halfway across the island when the mare reared up and whinnied as a brightly banded coral snake slithered through the grass beneath its hooves. "Easy, girl," Brett said, gripping the reins with both hands and tightening her thighs against the saddle.

She calmed her mount with soothing words, skirted the snake's path, and rode up the hillside out into a clearing where there was a panoramic vista of pastel seas.

Santos had gone on ahead and was waiting for her as Brett reined in beside him. They both sat silently, watching a distant cormorant diving into the lagoon for its daily feeding ritual. The setting was peaceful and idyllic, but the long low line of mountains brooding upon the southern horizon appeared ominously disquieting.

"That is the coast of Oriente Province," Santos pointed out. "The American base at Guantánamo is just beyond those mountains. Soon . . . very soon now," he said, "we will get Castro."

Brett looked at him, silent and uncertain. "I won't betray you," she said finally. "Surely you must know that by now."

Santos smiled. "I never trust anyone completely—I can't afford to. Too much is at stake."

"Then why did you ask me to come here? Obviously this place—this island—has some important part in your plan."

"Your role in all this shouldn't be too hard to figure out," he said carefully. "A political terrorist's primary aim is to get the attention of large numbers of people . . . to have an impact worldwide. My most important objective is to deliver a message."

"And once you've captured the attention of a global audience," Brett said, "you need someone to give your actions clear symbolic significance. That's why I'm here, isn't it? You're counting on me to deliver the message that one side's bloody mindless terrorist can be transformed into the other side's hero, visionary, or perhaps even martyr."

"I always knew you were bright," Santos smiled. "So I'm going to hand you your next Pulitzer on a silver platter."

He flicked his reins to set his horse in motion, and Brett immediately followed suit, her curiosity aroused.

As they made their way down the trail through a deeply shaded grove of pale green banana trees, Brett thought about what Santos had said. It was true that journalists were important to the political terrorist because they not only relayed information but, like good drama critics, they interpreted it as well.

The slant they gave by deciding which events to report and which to ignore could make a crucial difference. By intentionally but subtly expressing approval or disapproval, the journalist could create a climate of public support, apathy, or anger. In fact, capturing the attention of the audience was the easy part.

Santos, like any successful political terrorist, had a definite flair for histrionics. But in order to sustain interest, either hers or that of the public at large, he would have to do exactly what he was doing. Changing acts, locations, and performers.

He had been notoriously successful in the past and had chosen his targets carefully. The most ingeniously staged terrorist action if repeated too often could cause the audience to turn away in boredom. To be effective, the revolutionary terrorist could not strike too often in the same place or in the same manner. And he could not risk improvisation.

Brett was beginning to suspect that Santos's ultimate scenario was a tightly scripted one. And that she herself was being introduced as one of the principal players in the drama, not just an observer.

Her feelings were compounded and supported when they rode out of the banana grove and onto a low bluff that gave view to a military encampment shielded from casual observation by the surrounding jungle. Directly ahead was a small sandbagged fort with machine gun embrasures and a raised firing platform surrounded by dugout trenches. Beyond that were orderly rows of thatched huts built around an open parade ground.

A double fence of barbed wire sandwiched a deep ditch encircling the entire encampment. The wire obstacles were ten feet high, and there was a guard tower at each corner of the stockade.

Sweating in the late afternoon sunlight, at least a dozen men wearing only khaki shorts were performing vigorous calisthenics to the shouts of a uniformed instructor. A short distance away a dozen more men were sitting in orderly rows on wooden benches with another instructor at a blackboard diagramming techniques for setting explosives.

It looked like a movie set, Brett thought. But there was a chilling reality to the scene that belied any celluloid fantasy. Amazing. Under the guise of making war movies, Coco Island had become the training ground for a true-life revolution. Clearly, Santos's plans went far beyond the assassination of Fidel Castro. The question was how far?

"Who are those men?" Brett asked.

"*Los Huelgos,*" he said. "The final strike force. They may look like actors on a movie set, but each one of them has been carefully chosen and is being trained for the job he will be required to perform. For the past five years groups like this have been training here before being infiltrated back into Cuba. There are now hundreds of *Los Huelgos* awaiting my signal to overthrow Castro's ruinous regime. Some of them are officers in the Cuban military, others are in key government positions, and a crucial handful have even infiltrated into Castro's own personal guard."

"*Los Huelgos* will set the trap," he said ominously. "But I alone will spring it when the time is right. Tomorrow you and your camera will have run of the camp. It will be the last day of training. Tomorrow at midnight a small fleet of fishing boats will anchor offshore to transport the strike force back to Cuba."

As they started riding back toward the cottages, the golden afternoon was swiftly drawing to a close. Lavender clouds marched across the sky as the firey orb approached the horizon.

There was a moment of breathtaking beauty as the sun abruptly dipped into the sea like a flaming disc.

Brett couldn't help but wonder what the coming night would bring.

Santos had built a fire in a clearing surrounded by wild sea grape. Brett had grilled the pompano she had speared earlier in the day, and they ate with their fingers from banana leaves, relishing every delicious bite.

Between them was a sense of shared intimacy. Santos had produced a surprisingly excellent bottle of vintage Pommard from the cellars of the old hotel, and that combined with the night and the stars only served to make Brett more aware of the compelling physical attraction she felt to Santos.

He fascinated her on so many levels. His intellect, his candor, and that brooding and deeply mysterious aura he carried about him. Ultimately brilliant, highly creative, and infinitely complex, he was very much the modern equivalent of the Renaissance man.

They sat drinking wine in the firelight and talked about everything. He knew astronomy and pointed out various patterns in the night sky that Brett had previously thought of only in the most abstract terms.

The constellation Orion hung low over the southern hemisphere while the Dog Star, *Tau Seti*, blazed directly overhead. At that latitude the brilliance of the distant galaxies was awesome, with the Milky Way wheeling across the heavens in a vast spiraling of starlit phosphorescence.

At last they both fell silent. Santos had been in a reflective mood throughout the evening but Brett was caught completely off guard when he asked about Julia DuShane.

"What is she like?" he asked softly. "Who is this incredible woman who through some bizarre twist of fate happens to be my mother?"

Brett replenished her wine, drew her legs beneath her, and leaned back against the weathered gray trunk of a palm tree. "I think you would have liked her. Julia had spirit, courage . . . and an almost obsessive passion for life. She went after everything she wanted with absolute determination. Yet, in the very midst of all the glamour, the celebrity and the power, she remained a strangely solitary woman.

"I used to think," Brett mused, "that Julia used it all just to fill the emptiness. She was the woman who had everything except what she really wanted."

"And what was that?"

"I'm not completely sure . . . but certainly she never got over what happened in Cuba. The loss of her children . . . the degrading humiliation she suffered at the hands of your father while you were still very young. Julia was nothing if not a great romantic, and Don Ramon de Vargas was her obsession. She never stopped loving him and she never stopped hating him either, right up to the end."

"You speak as if she were already dead."

Brett sipped her wine, and stared into the fire burning low on the sand before them. "I only wish she *were* dead. I went to see her a few nights ago at La Caraval. It was dreadful. Degrading. All those needles and tubes and machines. Your mother has become a living testament to the monstrous inhumanity of medical science. It's the last thing in the world she would have wanted."

Brett fell silent and the shadows closed in around them. A falling star blazed across the southern skies.

"That's how Julia would have wanted to go," Brett said in a gently wistful voice. "Just like that star . . . in a sudden spectacular blaze of glory."

Santos turned and regarded her closely. "So that's why you sought me out," he said. "I wasn't sure until now. That's the bargain you spoke of. If I want the jewels . . . I'll have to give my mother her freedom."

* * *

Brett lay in the dimness, listening to the sounds of the tropic night. There had been something wonderful and incredible about the evening—it was as if she had come to Coco Island obeying some long-awaited summons.

Was Santos right about why she had sought him out? She wasn't sure. Nor was she sure what it was that Santos represented or what she wanted him to be. All she knew was that the situation in which she found herself had become a duel of chemistry between a man and a woman.

Finally she slept and dreamed. Fitfully at first and then fearfully. She was back at Marisol and the walls were closing in on her. There was no ceiling. When she looked up she saw the face of Florian Montes leering at her. Gradually he transformed himself into a monstrous spider spinning a golden web.

There were sensual and luminous dreams as well: Brett found herself lying naked in Santos's arms high above the world on a towering pillar of rock. He sundered her with his sex and exploded inside her with powerful, wonderful thrusts. A wildly ecstatic sensation overcame her.

Then she awoke, thanks to the echo of footsteps pacing outside on the veranda. The figure of a man appeared in silhouette against the curtained windows. The pacing continued.

Brett got up on the daybed in the living room and sat there staring as the figure approached the outer door, and then paused in shadowy contemplation. She knew it was Santos. Brett felt anguished, expecting the door to suddenly open and then . . . they would be face to face in the darkness. And anguish turned to . . . anticipation.

The figure turned slowly away and she heard the footsteps moving off down the outer stairs to the garden path. Brett realized she had been holding her breath. As her lungs expanded she experienced a dizzying sensation of relief, a feeling she knew only too well.

CHAPTER TWENTY-SEVEN

JUST after daybreak the following morning, Brett and Santos set out for the encampment on horseback. They started off along the beach riding beneath the high blue sky. The trail turned inward and giant ferns, mango and breadfruit trees converged to overarch the narrow path. The morning air was already warm and moistly scented.

Birds of bright plumage chirped and flitted in and out of the pale green banana trees. Stands of coconut palms rose majestically against the sky to march off in stately procession across the island.

With Santos taking the lead, Brett lagged slightly, immersed in her own thoughts. She needed time to sort things out.

The most frightening aspect about being in a combat situation, she decided, was that you usually got hit when you least expected it. As long as you remained alert, even though advancing under fire, rarely did you receive a hit.

But, the moment you relaxed your guard or allowed yourself the luxury of feeling safe, the bullet with your name on it arrived. An apparently trifling wound would prove to be fatal because the bullet had cleanly severed an artery or neatly lodged itself too near the heart.

Santos's appearance on her veranda the night before had been the bullet that Brett had been expecting. But it was more than that. She had also been on guard against her own feelings.

This morning she thought the danger was well past, but there had been the brief pressure of Santos's shoulder pressing against hers as they mounted their horses, the slight touch of his hand on her arm as he adjusted her reins. Fleeting and unsettling contacts that had left her all too vulnerable. . . .

It was over ninety degrees in the shade when they finally reached the encampment. Santos wasted no time in taking full command of the strike force.

Throughout the morning he put *Los Huelgos* through their paces with vigorous calisthenics and automatic weapons training. There was a specialized unit of frogmen practicing underwater demolition tactics in the lagoon. Brett knew what their ultimate objective would be, but not the *when,* the *where,* and the *how.*

She followed the strike forces everywhere with her camera. They were eager young men with hard ruthless faces and a killing look in their eyes. *Los Huelgos* displayed an unswerving and almost worshipful dedication to Santos, and their every movement and action appeared to be calculated for his blessing.

Gabriella Marquez was very much in evidence at the encampment. When they finally broke for lunch, Brett felt the sullen lash of her eyes as she served up a stew of stringy meat and overcooked vegetables. Brett could only speculate on what additional duties she might be performing for the cause of revolution.

The men of the strike force lined up in silence before the mess tent. There were no smiles or horseplay. They displayed not the slightest curiosity about Brett's presence among them. They seemed like lean, hardened killing machines as they wolfed down their food in noisy gulps and used their fingers to wipe their bowls clean.

Immediately following lunch, an electric generator was switched on and Santos turned in the shortwave radio to pick up *Radio Marti* in Havana. The station was rebroadcasting a recent speech by Castro. Everyone sat smoking and listening, grimly intent upon the words of the man they had committed themselves to destroy.

Notably absent from Castro's speech was the kind of flamboyant improvisational rhetoric that he had introduced to the world some twenty years before. Instead, the graying revolutionary *Jefé* read from a prepared text for a mere forty-five minutes, compared with the five- and six-hour harangues he had so passionately delivered in the past.

As a youthful and charismatic guerrilla leader, Castro had descended like a savior from the island's rugged Sierra Maestra Mountains. But the revolution that had electrified the western world had by now gone from spontaneity to virtual stagnation. The signs of decay were everywhere. The Mariel boatlift only served to underscore the growing malaise of the Cuban people themselves.

With a population of only ten million, Castro had, however, converted his country into a significant global participant with some forty-five thousand troops and advisors operating as Soviet proxies in such far distant countries as Angola, Mozambique, and Ethiopia.

The speech continued in grandiloquently-phrased Spanish. In assessing the achievements of his prematurely middle-aged revolution, Castro took special pride in extolling its social benefits. Yet what he failed to mention was that strict food rationing was still an integral part of revolutionary Cuban life and disenchantment with his far flung global adventures had reached epidemic proportions at all levels of Cuban life.

The Cuban leader also failed to mention the country's vast foreign debt crisis or its almost total dependence on the Soviet Union for its ultimate survival. In effect, the Cuba military had become an international militia fighting for Communist supremacy throughout the Third World. In just twenty years, Fidel Castro's dream had become a one-party dictatorship backed by a wide-ranging and repressive political apparatus that the Cuban people had come to both hate and fear.

Perhaps, Brett thought, as Santos rose to switch off the radio, the time was ripe for a new leader to be swept into power.

Throughout the afternoon the strike force practiced guerrilla warfare under cover of the surrounding jungle. Brett concentrated on recording the action on film. Brett captured the dense greenery, bringing the lithe and stealthy figures briefly into focus as they melted in and out of dappled light and shadow.

Brett slid her body around the tripod she had set up and peered through the lens to capture Santos. He was stripped to the waist and his body glimmered with a sheen of sweat. He was crouching, dodging and twirling like a dancer while the muscles of his arms and shoulders rippled with every movement.

Through the camera's lens, she captured the way he ran among the trees with long elastic strides, the way he crouched low and sprung with a flashing dagger wrapped in his fingers. She captured his menace, his dominance, and his mystery in shot after shot.

In telephoto close-up, Brett scanned the enigmatic mask of Santos's bizarrely painted face. The camera induced a moment of clarity; of rare and intimate closeness.

Brett was exhausted by the time they started back to the cottages. The sky was turning mauve and smouldering on the horizon. She felt as if she had lived years in the past twenty-four hours, and she wouldn't have chosen to be anywhere else in the world.

Later, they rode out onto the beach to see the *Callisto* at anchor in the lagoon. The eggshell-white hull was reflected in the water like a fine Chinese porcelain. The masts and deck had been newly varnished and the polished brass work gleamed in the setting sun.

The tranquility of the moment was shattered when Brett saw Cujo rowing toward them across the water. She shuddered. There was something about the man that terrified her.

As Brett was drawn from sleep, she blinked her eyes and tried to focus in the dimness. The only light came through the bedroom door, illuminating the figure of a man moving slowly toward her bed. It was Santos. It was happening at last. . . .

When he touched her, it was more than she had previously imagined. A hoarse groan came from deep in his throat. There was a warmth emanating from his body; his strong arms reached out to sweep her from the bed and lock her into an iron embrace. His passionate mouth was on hers. And his eyes—those incredible eyes devoured her.

Then Santos was on his knees before her; his hands moved slowly upward to encompass her breasts. As he gently kneaded and stroked them with his fingers, he bent his head to kiss the silken juncture of her thighs. He made love to her with his lips, his teeth, and his tongue. Brett arched her back, gasped, and cradled his face in her hands.

It felt like heaven, and seemed like forever. Santos lifted her in his arms and placed her gently back on the bed. He stripped off his clothes, stretched out nude beside her, and drew her into his secure embrace.

They explored each other endlessly with their hands and their lips, touching, probing and caressing; searching out and defining.

Brett felt the urgency rising within her and reached down to grip the iron hardness of his erection. Santos was filled with tension. She shuddered against him, breathless with heady anticipation. He was penetrating the core of her inner being. They were becoming indivisible in body and soul; melting and blending together through miraculous osmosis. She felt overwhelmed by the heat of his passion. Their bodies were slick with sweat and moving in perfect synchronization in every possible way.

Brett murmured his name when Santos rose up to brace himself above her, his arms fully extended. Their eyes locked and he was staring into her.

Brett had never felt so close to another human being and wanted to make it last forever, but self-control was out of the question. She felt herself hurtling toward the brink. She was breathing deeply and rapidly, thrusting herself upward and then drawing away when the pleasure became ecstacy. Her body was quivering all over. Brett sensed his onrushing orgasm and swiftly rose to meet his stroke with her own ardor. Brett tossed her head and cried out deliriously. Again and again she came, swept by a swelling tide of passion, power, and aching need.

She knew now that she would never be able to let him go.

Afterward, exhausted, they lay side by side in the warm night smoking Santos's strong dark cigarettes.

"I must go," he finally said. "I'll try and get a couple of hours sleep aboard the *Callisto*. We sail for Miami at dawn."

Santos rose and started dressing. "Tomorrow morning I've instructed Gabriella to take you to Matthew Town. You're already booked on the noon flight to Nassau."

Brett smiled. "I don't want to say anything as trite as 'when will I see you again?' But plans do have to be made. . . ."

"I will contact you in five days," Santos answered. He leaned over the bed and kissed her again. For a brief sweet moment their tongues met.

Then he pulled back and looked down at her in the dimness. "You should be in Havana next week for Fidel's revolutionary celebration. I think you will find the occasion of special interest."

Santos stroked her face with his fingertips. His voice was low and serious. "I want you to be very careful of Castro, Brett. He cannot resist a beautiful journalist any more than you can resist a big story. Don't get too close to him."

After Santos had left, Brett thought about what he had said. What had he meant about not getting too close to Castro? Did he mean not getting close in the intimate sense? Or was he being altogether literal. Santos had indicated when the assassination was going to take place, yet the pieces didn't fit.

Brett badly needed sleep. Yet no sooner had she slipped into it than the yellow cottage was shaken by a powerful explosion.

Leaping from bed, her heart hammering wildly, she ran out onto the veranda to see the *Callisto* in flames. The sleek white schooner she had last seen riding serenely at anchor in the moonlight had become a roaring inferno with fiery shards of wreckage raining down upon the still, black waters of the lagoon.

Brett stared in dazed disbelief. Shivering uncontrollably in her light cotton robe, Brett caught sight of something moving just off to one side of the shore. A massive, ominous form was coming up out of the darkness, moving steadily toward her along the graveled path leading up from the beach.

Brett knew who it was.

She knew exactly what was going to happen.

Comprehension turned to horror. She wanted to scream, but fear silenced her.

CHAPTER TWENTY-EIGHT

S HE was frantically trying to lock the door of the yellow cottage when Cujo kicked it open. He was inside with the door securely bolted behind him and Brett was backing away.

"Where is Santos?" she demanded.

"Santos is dead," he leered. "You saw what happened to the *Callisto*, pretty lady. Now you belong to me. Your friend Santos is feeding the sharks."

"Bastard!" screamed Brett. "It was you who set us up for ambush in the Tortugas. You've sold Santos out, haven't you?"

He stood grinning at Brett. His huge black fists clenched and relaxed as he hungered to get his hands on her. Cujo took a step toward her. And then another, as she kept backing away. He was toying with her. Cat and mouse.

Brett noticed the knife. It was fastened to his belt in an open sheath. She knew it could be gripped in his hand in a matter of seconds, slashing at her flesh and stabbing her. He had cornered her now, pressing in close to roughly squeeze her breasts with one hand while the other shoved hard between her thighs.

The rough physical contact seemed to snap her out of the trance into which she had fallen. She twisted from his grasp and ran past him into the kitchen alcove, where she shielded herself behind the breakfast counter.

Cujo's laugh was maniacal. His demonic gaze glinted with macabre amusement. He had allowed her to easily slip away from him, Brett realized, because he was thoroughly enjoying the chase.

"Get the fuck out of here!" Brett screamed as he continued to advance toward her with slow, deliberate steps. Seizing a frying pan from the stove top, she brandished it overhead, trying to throw him off guard. Anger, fury, and hatred consumed her. He had killed Santos. The desire for vengeance burned within her like the fire on the *Callisto*.

Brett hissed at him and growled deep in her throat. She swung several times with the heavy iron skillet, causing Cujo to duck and weave. He was ponderously slow. Then with lightning speed and extraordinary strength, she hurled it at his head and struck him a glancing blow on the right temple.

Cujo staggered backward with blood running down his face. The pain from the blow transformed him. His expression was malevolent. There was sheer madness in his expression. His eyes glared monstrously.

In the moment it took him to regain his balance, Brett had begun hurling dishes at him, one after another, sending them crashing against the walls and floor. The hail of crockery didn't stop him. He came rushing toward her. He tore the breakfast counter from its moorings in one swift move.

Lifting it high overhead, Cujo sent it crashing down where Brett had been standing. Vaulting clumsily over the wreckage, he grabbed her by the shoulders, clearly expecting her to pull away. Instead, she turned toward him and drove one knee hard up into his crotch. Then she jabbed his eyes with her nails. He howled in pain and lost his grip. She pushed and writhed away, toppling him backward as he windmilled his arms and fell heavily to the floor.

"*Puta* bitch!" he wailed before doubling over and vomiting on the floor.

Brett knew she wouldn't have time to throw the cumbersome

bolt off the door. And there was nowhere to run if she should manage to get out of the cottage.

She heard him behind her, getting up. . . .

The speargun.

It was in the bedroom closet.

Slashing her bare feet on the broken dishes, Brett ran into the bedroom and slammed the door behind her. She fumbled with the key and finally engaged the lock. She was sobbing, and her breath, coming in hoarse gasps, filled the room in a symphony of pain and horror. She raced to the closet and frantically searched for the scuba diving gear on the floor.

The speargun wasn't there!

Cujo kicked at the door. It shook violently. There were only seconds left. Brett remembered where it was. She grabbed the weapon from the shelf just above her head.

She jammed the long steel shaft into firing position and turned to face the doorway from the far side of the bed. From where she stood a full length mirror opposite her on the back of the door captured the image of a total stranger, a wild-eyed harried creature whose ashen features were framed with a dark tangled mane.

Cujo kicked the door again, bursting it inward off its hinges. Panting and sweating, his massive shoulders were hunched forward. His head was lowered, ready to charge, to smash and destroy anything standing in his way. Then he saw her.

Cujo hesitated, unsure of the game. He was no longer even half rational. His glacial black eyes had turned hot and fevered with blood lust. Sweat streamed down his face, and his thick lips worked wordlessly as he slowly withdrew the knife from its sheath.

Brett clenched her teeth and cocked the speargun.

Cujo was moving and weaving the blade before her eyes. He took another step with only the bed separating them. Brett lined up the speargun dead center on his chest so she would be sure to hit something vital. He moved forward. She squeezed the trigger.

Nothing happened.

Incredibly, she had forgotten to throw off the safety catch.

Cujo circled the bed. Brett swore as she thumbed the tiny lever to release the safety mechanism. She fired the gun without pausing to take aim again.

Cujo howled as the shaft pierced his shoulder. The knife flashed away to clatter against the wall. He bellowed in pain and rage like a demon from hell. He lunged forward and struck out at Brett before dragging her screaming and flailing to the floor. They rolled over in a tangle of arms and legs.

Brett was snarling like a rabid dog and snapping at his jugular with bared teeth. Their bodies came up hard against the wall with a jarring impact, and Cujo managed to roll over on top of her, rough and heavy as he crushed her beneath him with that hideous face pressed close. His breath was hot and putrid.

Brett gagged with disgust and choked with horror and pain as he tore at her robe and shredded her silk panties. He shoved his thick blunt fingers up into her sex. The pain was excruciating. She scratched and clawed frantically at his eyes. He jerked his head upward just as the whipcrack of a pistol shot sounded above their heads.

It was Gabriella standing in the doorway with a .38 revolver clutched in her hand. She shrieked something in Spanish and moved closer, threatening Cujo with the weapon until it was pressed firmly against his temple.

"Leave the bitch for later," she snapped in a voice filled with outrage. "We don't have time to play games. We must get to the radio transmitter and send a message to Havana. Afterward, do whatever you want with her."

Cujo was only barely comprehending. His face was bleeding profusely where Brett had raked him with her nails. Brett managed to quickly disengage herself from him and scrambled away on all fours. Her abdominal muscles were painfully taut, her mouth was dry as dust.

Brett's breathing was convulsive, gasping. . . . She got to her knees, pulled herself up against the dresser, and then stood there swaying slightly, staring into the cold, venomous eyes of Gabrielle Marquez.

"Santos won't be back," Gabriella announced. "He's dead."

Brett tried pulling her torn robe close about her but one breast remained exposed. She could feel the warm, wet trickle of blood between her legs. "I don't believe you," she hissed. "He's not dead, you cunt. He's too smart to have gotten himself blown apart by you and your moronic compatriot!"

"He's dead!" shrieked Gabriella, slapping Brett hard across the face with the back of her hand. "You tried to take him away from me—and now you're going to pay. Cujo will see to that. Now get some clothes and put them on before I ruin that pussy face of yours."

With her hands on her head, Brett was led from the cottage and up the gravel path to the old hotel. It was just before dawn. Gabriella unlocked the heavy oak door beneath the veranda and it swung open with a rush of cool moist air. There was a wine cellar below which was totally dark.

The muzzle of Gabriella's gun jabbed into Brett's shoulder blades. Brett staggered downstairs, nearly falling on the old stone stairway. Lowering her hands to steady herself against the chill stone wall, she expected a shot in the back of her head. But, there was no shot. The door was slammed behind her, then locked. She was left alone to make her way unsteadily down the steps.

Brett's footsteps echoed on the stone flooring as she cautiously found a way through a maze of wooden wine racks with row upon row of dusty bottles. Finally, she sank down on the cold stone floor and sobbed, not for herself but for the man she had come to love in so very short a time. It was a long time before her crying stopped. Then, exhausted, she wiped her eyes and took stock of her surroundings as her vision gradually adjusted to the cellar.

A faint ray of light had begun to filter down through a vent high up on the wall where the dawn was beginning to turn steel into gold. Shock had deadened her fear. Agony for Santos overrode the terror in being at the mercy of Cujo and Gabriella. She had been tortured, almost raped, and could easily imagine what Cujo would do to her upon his return.

The fear of Cujo was a disease sapping Brett's will and distorting her judgment. Shuddering, panic overwhelmed her. She fought to stay calm and in control. Yes, that's it. Santos would expect her to remain calm. She thought hard about him . . . and gradually the threat of hysteria began to recede. She recalled his kisses of the night before. . . . She remembered the special magic of being held in his arms. . . . They had been as one. . . . It had been magical lovemaking. At least she had that to strengthen her courage. The end really didn't matter so much. What was important now was to be able to face it with dignity, to keep Santos alive in her mind as she went to meet him in the spirit of all they had known together.

The thought gave Brett peace. . . . She settled down to wait . . . and prayed. How strange it was, she thought. After living her life in the belief of a coldly cruel and indifferent universe, she could still find solace in prayer.

The sea hissed and murmured as the still-flaming *Callisto* sank beneath the black water of the lagoon. Then Santos began swimming slowly toward shore.

He was bleeding from facial cuts and his hair was matted with blood oozing from a deep scalp wound. Every part of him ached, and the pain in his side caused him to wince with every stroke.

He suspected he'd suffered a concussion because of the throbbing pain in his head and blurring vision. With every stroke he had to fight the nausea and the threatening loss of consciousness.

Santos knew he wouldn't be alive now had he not exercised caution and decided to sleep outside on the deck of the *Callisto*. The booming detonation of the explosion from below deck had quite literally propelled him into the sea and away from the ensuing fire. His underlying suspicion of Cujo had ultimately saved his life, and something was driving him that was sharper than the pain in his ribs and stronger than the ferocious pounding in his head. He knew that to stop and rest for even a moment might well condemn Brett to total torture and a hideous death.

There was no current in the lagoon and the sea was as smooth and quiescent as green bottle glass. Santos continued swimming toward the distant beach. He squeezed his eyes tightly together for moments at a time as waves of dizziness swept over him.

More than anything else, Santos believed in the power of the human will. Dedication and determination had always been the driving forces in his life. He was used to surviving under conditions that would have proven fatal to any ordinary man. But he had always known that he was not an ordinary man. Now there was an added dimension. A very new emotion kept him going. For the first time in his life, fear sent the adrenaline pumping through his bloodstream. The concern for Brett was strong enough to overcome his injuries, at least for the moment. Without him, Brett would surely be lost. He had to save her.

In spite of the wearing pain in his chest, his legs were powerful and they drove him steadily toward shore. The water was warm and buoyant. Upon reaching the shallows, Santos stretched out his arms and swam the final yards, grunting painfully with each stroke.

When he finally crawled up out of the water and lurched across the beach, the path leading up to the yellow cottage seemed to waver and dissolve before his eyes. When his legs wouldn't support his weight any longer, he collapsed to his knees and tried to crawl until the sand came up hard to meet him and everything started sliding away into a fathomless black infinity.

It was nearly light when Santos recovered consciousness. He blinked and slowly shook his head, woozy and confused by his surroundings. His clothes had begun to dry on his body. There was salt encrusted on his skin. He closed his eyes for a moment, trying desperately to orient himself.

His head ached tremendously, but eventually he felt strong enough to pull himself up against the trunk of a palm tree and stagger up the path to the yellow cottage.

The front door was open. Santos knew that Brett would not be found inside. If she were still alive, he knew exactly, instinctively, where they would have taken her.

If she's still alive, he thought to himself.

When Brett heard the oak door at the top of the stairs creaking open, she ducked down behind a wine rack, clasped a bottle by the neck, and broke the bottom off against the floor. It was probably a hopeless gesture, she realized, but she was determined to go down fighting to the death.

Brett listened intently to the feet slowly descending the stairs. Then, peering cautiously out between the dusty bottles, she could hardly believe her eyes.

Brett recognized Santos leaning against the wall, clutching his side. She cried out his name and ran into his arms, weeping hysterically.

"They said you were dead!"

Weary, wincing with pain and numb with relief at finding Brett alive, Santos found it difficult to speak. It had taken all the strength he had just to reach her and suddenly, that accomplished, there was nothing left. Groaning, he slumped groggily against her with everything spinning out of focus.

"Oh, god, you're hurt!"

Brett held him and gradually eased him down to the floor, where she cradled his head against her breast. His scalp wound had reopened. There was blood on her hands.

"You . . . must . . . listen," he rasped laboriously. "Tell me . . . tell me . . . where they . . . went."

"Gabriella said they had to use the radio to contact Havana. They went to the encampment in the cabin cruiser. I heard the engine as they left the lagoon. Santos . . . they're going to give everything away. They'll tell all your plans, all about *Los Huelgos*. They're going to destroy everything you've worked for!"

Santos's face was the color of paste. The wan smile on his lips was twisted with bitter derision. "I've already destroyed the radio. I had begun to suspect that one of them had gone over to the other side."

Santos managed to sit up, and with Brett's help, leaned back heavily against the wall. "How long ago did they leave?"

"Half an hour, perhaps . . . not much longer than that. They said they were coming back and they were well armed. What can we do? There's no way to get off this island now without the cruiser."

"We are going to wait for them to return," Santos said. "And then I am going to kill them both. Since they think I'm dead, they won't be expecting anything. Just help me up the stairs and onto the veranda."

Santos told Brett to open a long wooden box hidden among the wine racks. Inside was a Kalishnikov rifle, six clips of ammunition, and a single hand grenade.

"I always keep an insurance policy hidden away somewhere," Santos told her. "Like I said before . . . I never trust anyone completely."

It seemed to take them forever to climb the stairs. Several times he had to stop and rest until the weakness and dizziness passed. With one arm slung about Brett's shoulder and the other cradling the rifle, he was staggering like a drunken man when they finally reeled outside into the bright morning sunshine.

They could hear the cabin cruiser's engine approaching the entrance to the lagoon. The sound expedited their ascent up the broad veranda stairs, where they crouched down behind the railings, shielded by flowering oleander bushes. With the sound of the cruiser growing closer, Santos stretched out on the wood-planked floor with the Kalishnikov aimed through a slot in the gingerbread tracery decorating the railing.

"Now I want you to go," Santos ordered in a hoarse ragged voice. "Hide yourself until you hear shots fired. Then run to the boat and get the hell out of here. Don't argue. There's no time."

Brett was incredulous. "What happens if you black out? I can't go! Not now!"

Santos put his hand firmly over Brett's and looked her directly in the eye. "They have to die. Cujo and Gabriella cannot be allowed to leave this island or all is lost."

"This is crazy!" Brett said, shaking her head and wiping the sweat and tears from her face. "I'm not leaving you here alone."

"Please, Brett . . . just do as I tell you. Now . . . for christ's sake . . . go. I'll build a bonfire on the beach . . . when it's safe to come back."

Santos dismissed her with a scowling grimace and started loading a clip into the Kalishnikov. There was no point in arguing further. The cabin cruiser was at the dock now and the engine had fallen silent. Brett knew what she had to do. There were only minutes left.

The sun was well up by now. From where Brett had hidden herself crouched beneath a leafy green canopy of dense foliage, she could see the lagoon. The cruiser was moored at the dock and there was no one on the beach. Then she heard Cujo's and Gabriella's angry voices coming up the path leading to the hotel. It was time to make her move.

When Gabriella and Cujo reached the turn in the path they were completely stunned to see Brett running across the grassy quadrangle and up the veranda steps. Gabriella was so taken by surprise that she screamed out a stream of obscenities in Spanish and ran after Brett. Meanwhile, Cujo unleashed a wild barrage of gunfire that shattered the gingerbread trim high up among the eaves of the old hotel.

Gabriella was racing toward the stairs where Brett had vanished seconds earlier when Santos's Kalishnikov caught Gabriella head on with three shots in the chest. The impact threw her violently backward against Cujo, who did a double roll on the grass and disappeared into the undergrowth before Santos could get off a full clip in his direction.

Then everything was very still. Santos turned on Brett with anguished fury. His hands were shaking on the stock of the rifle, sweat shone on his face, and blood was running down his neck to stain his shirt.

"I'm not leaving here without you," Brett snapped. "You're not going to make it on your own, so just forget it! Cujo is out there and as soon as he figures out where we are he's going to blast us to never-never land."

"Okay," Santos agreed wearily. "You're right. I'm weak as hell. If I black out now, we're finished."

Brett stared at him. "Show me how to fire that gun. Just tell me what to do and I'll do it."

Gravely, Santos shook his head. "With an AK-47, he'll blow you away before you even have a chance to pull the trigger. That bastard Cujo is a pro. I'll never be able to take him by surprise the way I did Gabriella. Not now."

Santos blinked his eyes and Brett saw he was fighting off the slide into unconsciousness. Then he slumped back from the railing and the Kalishnikov slipped from his hands. "The grenade," he gasped. "If Cujo comes in shooting, pull the pin and count to three. Then throw it . . . and pray. That's our . . . only . . . chance."

With that, Santos collapsed in her arms and there was panic in Brett's eyes. She bent over him. Santos was breathing raggedly and his face filmed with beads of sweat. He had lost consciousness and the only sound was his harshly labored breathing.

Brett carefully set the Kalishnikov aside and took the grenade in her hand. It was egg-shaped, corrugated, with a ring on a pin attached to one side. She held it close against her breast, willing her hand to remain steady, while memorizing his instructions.

Brett repeated to herself. Pull the pin. Count one . . . two . . . three. . . . Throw it as hard as you can. She had seen enough of combat to know the kind of damage the blast could do, especially in a confined space.

The grenade was cold and obscenely heavy in her grasp. If Cujo sneaked up on them, she had to remember the sequence exactly. If she mistimed or dropped it . . . neither of them would have to worry about anything ever again. One way or another, Brett was determined that Cujo would never get his hands on her.

Brett looked at Santos lying now with his head in her lap. A wave of tenderness swept over her. She was so glad that she hadn't run away as he had ordered. Only she could save him now, and somehow that thought comforted her. She settled down to watch and wait, alert to the slightest sound or sign that might give advance warning of Cujo's approach.

It seemed to Brett that she remained crouched there for hours. The sun had begun to climb the arch of the pure blue sky, and birds were flitting through the trees. The body of Gabriella Marquez lay in full view with the arms outflung. A pool of blood had begun to congeal about her torso as flies crawled across her open sightless eyes staring upward at the sky.

Brett placed her hand on Santos's forehead. It was cold and clammy, while his ashen palor alarmed her. Somewhere out there in the garden fastness, Cujo was waiting to make his move. She figured that he must have guessed where they were hiding by now. She listened intently. Her senses were taut and straining to catch the slightest movement or sound.

A slight scraping noise pricked up her ears. Her fingers tightened around the grenade but she had no clue where to throw it. If Cujo managed to rush them suddenly from the front, the tremendous firepower of the AK-47 would certainly cut her down before she would have time to count and throw. The only advantage they had was that Cujo would have no idea that Santos was seriously injured. Cujo was clumsy and slow moving and it would be sheer madness for him to launch a direct attack.

Then Brett heard the scraping sound again. She suspected suddenly that it was caused by someone trying to open one of the window shutters of the blue cottage that stood no more than forty feet away from where she and Santos were hiding. She felt paralyzed with dread. She remained frozen and immobile, crouching down low behind the railing that was screened by flowering bushes. Her eyes were glued to the blue cottage and silent tears of desperation streamed down her face.

When the front door of the cottage began to open just a crack, Brett thought that perhaps it was just an optical illusion. She squeezed her eyes tight for just an instant. But then, when she opened them again the crack had widened.

Brett made a soft whimpering sound involuntarily deep in her throat. There was no longer any doubt about it. Cujo was inside the blue cottage. The door was slowly, soundlessly opening, and she could now see the short ugly snout of the AK-47 poking through the crack and taking deadly aim in their direction.

Drawing in a deep shuddery breath, Brett waited while the gap widened. She was now able to glimpse a shadowy form hulking just inside the doorway. She pulled the pin of the grenade and counted aloud. "One . . . two . . . three." Then, employing all her strength, she pitched the grenade with uncanny accuracy and fell heavily on top of Santos's inert form.

The explosion detonated inside the cottage with magnum force, collapsing the front wall outward in a walloping hot blast that swept Brett's breath away. There was a volcanic eruption of flames and a rain of shattering glass, splintering wood, and chunks of human remains. All of it showering down upon them. . . .

CHAPTER TWENTY-NINE

THE helicopter lifted into the bright and cloudless day over Nassau, then choppered across the Northwest Providence Channel, a silver glint in the sunlight.

Brett unfastened her seat belt and stared out over the seductive panorama spreading out below: sun-spangled waters and a chain of green islands stretching away to the south. She was on a direct flight to West Palm Beach Airport and would soon be passing directly over Bimini.

Brett had come to that place where she had never intended to go. The journey she had undertaken to Coco Island had changed her completely. She now had no choice but to confront herself. She must cross over to find that place where she would never again be afraid, not of age or loss or even death.

Brett thought she had never been so weary. Her eyes were grainy and ached from lack of sleep. The sunlight glaring in at the window was too strong, and she slipped on a pair of oversize sunglasses. Every muscle ached, every bone and sinew from head to toe.

Following the climactic events of the early morning, she and Santos had left Coco Island to the sun, sea, and timeless wash of the waves upon the beach. With Brett at the wheel of the cabin cruiser and Santos propped up on cushions, drifting in and out of consciousness, they had headed for Matthew Town.

From the docks, they had taken a taxi to the only hospital on Great Inagua Island, where Brett proceeded to pace the hallways waiting for word of Santos's condition.

Lying was rather like learning to ride a bicycle, she thought abstractly, pacing and smoking one cigarette after another. Deception was a little awkward at first but as easy as sin once you got the hang of it. The cover story they had concocted between themselves seemed to have satisfied everyone concerned.

They were tourists whose schooner had been wrecked upon the reef just off Coco Island, she told the admitting doctor. They had been rescued by a passing fishing boat. All their identification had been lost. She had to leave "her husband" in the hospital's care as it was imperative that she immediately return to Florida.

Brett was ultimately assured that Santos was resting comfortably and suffering nothing more serious than several fractured ribs, numerous abrasions, a deep scalp wound, and a mild concussion. What he needed was observation and a period of complete rest, the doctor informed her, before he would be well enough to travel.

The charade had gone off without a hitch. But now, halfway back to Palm Beach, Brett's bone-deep fatigue had left her entirely vulnerable to the roiling tide of emotions swirling through her mind. Laura would say that it was "love." Brett wasn't ready or willing to accept that. Love and pain had always been too closely linked together in her life. She dared not believe that she had fallen in love with Santos ... to do so would leave her without any defenses.

As the Bahama Air helicopter roared across the petal blue sky, Brett found she had no energy or desire to think about it. Deliberately, she relaxed, leaned her head back against the seat rest, and closed her eyes. The past was like quicksand and the future loomed ahead—uncertain. In less than two hours she would be back at Marisol.

* * *

It was late afternoon when Brett's taxi pulled up in front of the house at the end of Country Club Drive. She breathed a sigh of relief. It was good to be home, but she couldn't help wondering what awaited her.

After paying off the driver, she grabbed her bag and camera equipment and mounted the steps only to have the front door swing open abruptly just as she slipped her key into the lock. It was Consuelo, but her warmly welcoming smile was absent. Instead there were tears streaming down her seamless brown cheeks. Her expression was anguished.

"*Carrida!*" Consuelo cried. "Something terrible has happened! I was just going to call the police when I saw you drive up."

Brett and Consuelo entered the pool house through the partially open door. It was very dim inside. The drapes were drawn and the louvered shade had been closed over the skylight during Brett's absence. Consuelo hovered behind her in the doorway as Brett switched on the ceiling light, walked into the living room, and gave a startled cry.

The place had been systematically demolished. Table lamps had been smashed against the walls and the glass shelved etâgère containing her collection of rare porcelain figurines had been reduced to shattered fragments. The sofa and armchairs were slashed open, with chunks of foam and wads of cotton padding material scattered about the floor.

The wicker furniture had been reduced to kindling, and the lovely French provincial writing desk in the corner looked as though it had been attacked with an axe.

The paintings by Jasper Johns, Klee, and Rauschenberg still hung upon the walls, but each canvas had been slashed to ribbons. Ashes had been scooped out of the fireplace and ground into the marvelous Shiraz Persian carpet that was Brett's pride and joy. Even the plants and ferns that she had so lovingly nurtured had been torn from their ceramic pots and strewn about the room at random.

Consuelo was weeping softly while Brett herself was stunned into dazed silence until the first wave of shock gave way to anger.

"Christ. . . ." Brett said between clenched teeth.

It wasn't the cost of the furnishings that upset her, most of which were covered by insurance in any case. What disturbed her most was that her possessions had been so ruthlessly vandalized. The sentimental value of the belongings she had collected from all over the world was beyond price. Angry tears filled her eyes.

A brief glance inside her darkroom revealed that everything there was in shambles as well. All her photographic equipment had been demolished; a shelf full of bottles containing developing chemicals had been used to destroy all her negatives and prints.

Numb with disbelief, Brett slowly climbed the spiral staircase to discover that the bedroom was another disaster altogether. All of her clothing had been wrenched from the closet and spread out. Clothes were piled on the floor and bed, where most of them appeared to have been badly damaged. Lapels and pockets were torn from sportswear, parkas, and coats. The seams of skirts had been ripped open, and her favorite silk blouses were reduced to colorful rags.

Who could have done it? And why?

The door to the adjoining bathroom was closed. Brett threw it open. There was the foul stench of excrement. Brett gagged and staggered slightly. The first thing she saw inside was a decapitated white-feathered chicken hanging from the ceiling light fixture by one leg. The mosaic tiled flooring was puddled with its blood. Also, her platinum-flame fox fur coat was a sodden mass in the bottom of the shower stall. Someone had smeared it with what appeared to be human feces.

"Oh, god . . . I'm going to be sick. What in the hell happened here?"

The answer had been scrawled across the mirror above the wash basin with a tube of her own bright red lipstick.

"HOMBRES DEL MUERTO." A bloody handprint on the wall encircled with a blood-smeared drawing of a writhing snake provided further explanation. It was the same message she had seen at Casa Encantada.

Her life was in jeopardy, she realized. The terror hadn't ended on Coco Island, not by a long shot. . . .

Returning to the main house, Brett locked herself in the library, where a safe was located behind a tranquil and luminous landscape by Monet. She deftly whirled through the combination with her fingertips, swung the door to the safe open.

Brett's father's Colt .45 was there. It was the very gun with which he had taken his life. Something of far more value was missing, however.

Julia DuShane's diaries and her own tapes of their conversations had disappeared.

According to Consuelo, Charlotte was staying on board Florian Montes's yacht. The dinner party formally announcing their engagement was being held that evening and Charlotte had gone aboard earlier in the day to supervise the arrangements.

The El Condor was a sleek white yacht that dominated the Del Mar Marina. The streamlined superstructure was dazzling in the late afternoon sunshine. The polished teak decks gleamed and the brass work shined. The railings had been strung with swags of orchids and ferns in preparation for the evening's affair.

The guests invited to the engagement party were scheduled to arrive in less than an hour. As Brett walked up the gangplank she found white-coated stewards busily setting out china, silver, and crystal along a white linen table set up beneath the candy-striped awning over the aft deck.

A string quartet was already tuning up in the sumptuous main salon. According to the yacht's first officer, Charlotte was dressing for dinner in one of the cabins below deck.

Brett was just about to knock when the door swung open to disclose Phillipe dramatically poised in midflight, wearing a lavender sateen jumpsuit and a look of imperious hauteur. He was harried, with a blow dryer in one hand and his famous black cosmetic "beauty bag" clutched in the other.

"Well, shut mah mouth," Phillipe drawled, posing with arms akimbo. "If it ain't Miz Scarlett as ah live 'n' breathe." "Miz Scarlett" was Phillipe's pet name for Brett.

With a comic grimace, he stepped out into the companion-way, shutting the door noiselessly behind him. "Honey . . . ya'll know how ah detest bein' the harbinger of ill tidin's," Phillipe offered *sotto voce*. "But the wicked bitch of the West ain't zactly thrilled tah hear ya'll come aboard at this most inauspicious time what with her tryin' tah stay dry under the arms 'n' all."

"Probably just a case of very premature bridal nerves," Brett said tersely. She was not in the mood for humor. "I have every intention of putting a hex on this fiasco that would turn a voo-doo witch doctor green with envy."

Phillipe's expression was that of a debauched cherub in a Canaletto fresco. "Well, ah do declare, Miz Scarlett . . . ah tend tah detect ah general fuck ya'll attitude—wrathful, huffy, and pissed off."

"You just bet your sweet ass you do. And that's just for start-ers. I think my mother and I are about to have a screaming cat fight that's been brewing for the past twenty years."

Phillipe licked his lips lasciviously and glanced at his watch. "Well, ah'd just love tah hang 'round 'n' watch the feathers fly 'tween you 'n' yo' mama but duty calls." Phillipe made a sweeping bow, gesturing toward the stateroom door. "She's all yours, Miz Scarlett."

Brett's insides were churning as she stepped inside the state-room to find Charlotte in the process of dressing behind a tapestry screen. "So you're back," snapped Charlotte. "You might at *least* have informed me that you were going away. It would have been the *polite* thing to do after all."

"Something came up," Brett said airily. "I had to go to the Bahamas on assignment."

From behind the richly paneled screen there was a flutter of white arms thrusting upward through some lacy undergarment.

"You know, Mother, you and I have never wasted much time on politeness, have we? There's something I have to ask you and I prefer to do it face to face."

There was a long silence before Charlotte said, "You have a bad habit of asking far too many questions, Brett, and you always seem to ask the *wrong* ones. You couldn't have picked a more inconvenient time for this little chat of yours. Fix yourself a drink . . . I'll be finished shortly."

Brett moved to the bar and splashed a crystal balloon glass half full of Courvoisier. She then browsed restlessly about, wanting desperately to smoke but knowing that Charlotte would immediately object.

The stateroom was a spacious and luxurious boudoir furnished with eighteenth-century Venetian antiques. The decor was pure Renaissance with Torloni hangings, beautifully inlaid paneling, and a small illuminated Tintoretto of Madonna and Child.

Sipping her brandy, Brett paced back and forth, pausing here and there, reaching out to briefly touch a blue velvet jeweler's case, a sheer mauve silk scarf, and a jeweled belt. They were all her mother's possessions. Yet Brett couldn't seem to exorcise the sense that they belonged to a stranger. Charlotte's world had become a foreign place to her. Brett knew that she would never again be able to inhabit it.

Finally, Charlotte stepped out from behind the screen and, without giving Brett so much as a glance, crossed the room to regard her own reflection in the Cormandel pier-glass. She had long been considered the best dressed woman in Palm Beach and was a stickler for detail. Everything about Charlotte was tasteful from the polished soles of her satin pumps to the extra pair of white gloves she always carried in her purse.

Charlotte was gowned in a gauzy floral garden-party dress of soft pastels, and wore a matching Mandarin silk coat lined with flame-colored taffeta. Exquisite, Brett thought. Charlotte looked ageless if not young, while her figure was stately rather than voluptuous like Laura's. She had flawless skin for a woman her age, and the overall effect was stunning.

Charlotte turned from the pier-glass and came forward to brush Brett's cheek with a small cold kiss. "Well now," she said crisply, stepping back to regard her daughter with a look of frank distaste. "I can see that you're back to your old habits. Honestly, Brett, you look like someone that just fell off the back of a Goodwill truck. Naturally, you show up like this when I'm expecting guests."

"The hell with what I look like. I want you to tell me what happened to Julia DuShane's diaries and my tapes."

Charlotte stared coldly at Brett. "What? Really, Brett, you bore me when it comes to Julia DuShane. I gave everything to Florian. Good riddance to all that crap." Charlotte turned away, crossed the room to settle herself at the mirrored dressing table, and opened the velvet jeweler's case.

"Mother," Brett said, trying very hard to control her anger and frustration, "I think it's time that you became aware of some rather disturbing facts about Florian Montes. Did you know, for instance, that he had Luisa released from a mental institution into his personal care?

"The diaries prove he was giving Julia drug injections and that she received a shot of something only hours before her collapse. Who do you think was responsible for making Luisa Julia's legal guardian? And why, pray tell, is Montes so determined to keep her hooked up to all those machines when Julia herself had expressly forbidden it? Whether you choose to believe it or not, your fiancé is as slimy as the worst snakes in the Everglades."

Charlotte's face tightened. She continued to regard her own reflection with an air of icy composure while reaching up to attach a dangling sapphire pendant at each ear.

"Florian warned me that you might try something like this," Charlotte accused. "You know as well as I do that he has been giving those same shots to half the women in Palm Beach for a long time. He's a doctor, for God's sake. As for Luisa, I choose to believe that Julia had asked him to have her daughter released when she found out where she was. He's a *kind* and *caring* man. I simply cannot comprehend why you persist in pursuing this absurd vendetta against him."

Brett decided it was time to play her ace in the hole. "If Montes is such a good Samaritan, why don't you ask Laura why he set her up with Maurice Begelman? Or why Montes has been supplying Laura with cocaine and amphetamines ever since she arrived in Palm Beach?"

"I don't believe a word of it!" Charlotte cracked as she attached a gorgeous sapphire necklace around her throat. Then she picked up a silver-backed brush and proceeded to add the final touches to her hair.

Brett had witnessed her mother perform this same ritual a thousand times. Everything about Charlotte had a fixed and ordered pattern. Rigid. Inflexible. There was not the slightest crack in her composure.

Suddenly, it was all too much for her. She snatched the brush from Charlotte's hand. "You just don't get it, do you, Mother? Florian Montes is vile. He's using you . . . just like he's using Laura, Luisa, and Julia . . . for his own sleazy, malevolent purposes. God only knows what his ultimate objective is! I'm just trying to stop you from making the biggest mistake of your life."

"My dear girl," Charlotte said primly, "you really have gone off the deep end. Florian is absolutely right in saying that this entire Julia DuShane affair has unbalanced your ability to deal with reality. You've become totally paranoid."

Brett's laugh was short and abrasive. "Florian Montes is to reality, Mother dear, what mud wrestling is to the performing arts. He's a fraud . . . a charlatan . . . and worse. If you marry him, he's going to take you for all you're worth."

Clearly out of patience, Charlotte rose to confront Brett face to face. "Perhaps it's time you considered leaving Palm Beach," she said firmly. "God knows you've caused nothing but trouble ever since you've come home. Your shabby little affairs . . . those dreadful articles you've been writing . . . and your continual interference in other people's lives.

"Oh, I can see it all too clearly, Brett. You are determined to spoil this for me just the way you destroyed my marriage to your father. Don't think for a moment that I didn't know what was going on between you two. I always knew what a sly seductive little slut my daughter was."

With that, Charlotte stalked off across the stateroom to slam the bathroom door shut behind her.

Brett could hear water running as she stood staring out through one of the portholes. The sun was dying in the west.

For the first time Brett realized that her mother despised her. Charlotte had taken every possible opportunity to exhibit her thinly veiled contempt, and Brett herself had given it back in kind.

Now there was nothing she wanted from her. They had disliked each other for too long and nothing remotely resembling love was left. Not even the slightest shred of respect.

CHAPTER THIRTY

Brett circled the swimming pool and mounted a flight of steps to Laura's Garden Suite at the Royal Poinciana Hotel. It was nearly two A.M., and peering through the sliding glass doors, Brett could see a single lamp burning inside the living room. A Russian sable coat had been tossed across the back of a chair and a pair of sling-heel pumps appeared to have been kicked off just inside the threshold. From somewhere at the back of the suite came the sound of running water.

"Anyone home?" Brett called after sliding the door open.

The water ceased its flow and a figure appeared in silhouette at the end of the hallway. It was Laura. She seemed to float toward Brett in a filmy white caftan that flowed gracefully about her lithe and willowy figure.

"Brett, *darling*!" Laura cried in her husky drawling voice. She released her familiar bubbling laugh, swayed tipsily forward, and threw her arms about Brett in a fond embrace.

"Christ almighty, kiddo . . . I thought you'd run away with the circus since you did your latest disappearing act. No one seemed to know where you were."

They laughed easily together and hugged again. It had been several weeks since Brett had seen her last, and Laura looked noticeably thinner. Without benefit of makeup, her face appeared tightly drawn and pale beneath the tan.

"It's terrific to see you, Laura," Brett said, sliding the door closed behind her and taking off the scarf tied around her hair. "How did you know I'd been out of town?"

"I ran into Simon at the Bath and Tennis Club," Laura replied mischievously. "He looked very much the odd man out and said he was leaving for a medical convention in California."

"I'll have to call him." Brett frowned with a sudden twinge of guilt. She hadn't even thought of Simon from the moment she had received Santos's summons to Coco Island. Now he seemed to be part of another world completely.

Laura arched a finely penciled eyebrow. "So, tell your Auntie Laura all, sweetheart. Where did you go? Who were you with? And what was he like in the sack?"

Brett immediately and deliberately changed the subject. "I grabbed my bail-out bag and took off for the Bahamas for a couple of days where a friend was shooting a movie on a beautiful little island. There was lots of action and not all of it in the script but that particular story will have to wait for my memoirs. However, I expected to come back and find you in a state of nuptial bliss. What happened to your wedding in Nassau?"

"The three quintessential moments in a woman's life," Laura said with exaggerated seriousness, "are getting your first period, losing your virginity, and marrying a man richer than God. The first two are ancient history by now, my dear—no comment necessary—and the third keeps getting postponed because Maurice is always flying off to Las Vegas or someplace else on business."

"My, but the Gods do seem to work in strange and wondrous ways," Brett suggested wryly. "Take my word for it, no amount of kissing is going to turn your Mafia frog prince into anything but a toad. Now, why don't you fix me a drink while I collapse. It's been one hell of a day."

"Hell you say, sweetie? I can do better than that," Laura

tossed over her shoulder as she headed for the wheeled liquor cart. A half-empty bottle of Mezcal Con Guzzo was standing lone attendance surrounded by glasses, mineral water, lemon wedges, and a silver ice bucket.

"You know, Brett, I happen to loathe all things Mexican except, of course, their booze and the occasional Acapulco beach boy." Laura dropped ice cubes into crystal tumblers and splashed them half full of Mezcal. "Trust me, darling. A couple of these postmortem specials are guaranteed to resuscitate anyone this side of an autopsy table. *Viva la revolucion.*"

Brett had settled onto a large pile of cushions with her arms drawn loosely about her knees. She was wearing slacks, sweater, and tennis shoes, having walked all the way up the beach from Marisol. Laura brought their drinks on a tray along with the bottle of Mezcal.

Brett winced as she took her glass in hand. "I must admit I have certain aversion to drinking anything with an embalmed worm in it, but what the hell." Brett lifted her glass to Laura's. "What shall we drink to?"

"To life," Laura proposed. "You only live once but if you do it right . . . once should be enough." They clinked glasses and drink the fiery liquor down neat.

Brett coughed and choked while her eyes watered. "God that really hits the spot. Set 'em up again and tell me where you were all evening. I've been trying to get hold of you for hours."

"Well, let's see," Laura pondered as she refilled their tumblers. "I started out the evening with cocktails at Nando's . . . went on to a dinner party at La Monegasque . . . and ended up dancing my little tootsies off at Ta-boo. I had at least a dozen other invitations to this and that . . . but I decided to make an early night of it and get my beauty sleep."

Brett sipped her drink cautiously and lit a cigarette. "According to all available reports, your reputation appeared to have been lower than whale shit before I left town. To just what occurrence do you attribute this sudden upswing in social intercourse?"

"Just feast your eyes on this!" Laura exclaimed, picking up a glossy color booklet from the coffee table and handing it across to Brett. "Once again, the Palm Beach rumor mill seems to be in overdrive. Everyone is talking about *El Mirador.*"

The cover of the booklet depicted an artist's conception of Maurice Begelman's half-billion-dollar casino-resort extravaganza rising like a spectacular mirage from the dunes of Singers Island. It was a very expensively produced promotion piece. Brett had barely begun to scan the print when she recognized that expensive was what El Mirador was all about.

Upon completion, the exclusive resort would only be accessible by yacht, helicopter, or private plane in order to protect the privacy of those wealthy and privileged enough to be accepted for membership. The main complex of buildings was to be constructed in the opulent style of a Moorish palace. A dazzling composition of minaret towers, domes, and arches surrounded by acres of landscaped oasis-like gardens descending in terraces to a deep water yachting marina.

According to the promotional booklet, the Cabaret Sheherazade promised to provide the glitziest names in entertainment. And for those with a predilection for high-stakes gambling, there would be the Casablanca Casino, rivaling anything along the Las Vegas strip.

"I guess this proves that it doesn't matter what you do as long as it's done with style and megabucks," Brett said dryly. "I take it that *tout* Palm Beach has decided to adopt its very own Godfather as the price of admission. Am I to assume that your sudden surge in popularity has something to do with your unholy alliance with Begelman?"

Laura's smile was enigmatic as she reached up to remove the towel wrapped about her head, allowing her platinum hair to tumble loosely about her shoulders. "You know the old saying,

'What goes around comes around.' If you care to read the credits on the last page you'll see that darling Maurice has named me as Chairman of the Admissions Committee. Take my word for it, Brett, some famous facelifts are going to fall when they are refused acceptance!"

Their eyes met. "I get the feeling, Laura, that there's more to this arrangement than you're telling me."

"Who . . . *moi?*" Laura asked, holding Brett's penetrating gaze without the slightest flicker of an eyelash. "Why what on earth can you be talking about?"

"About Begelman. Why didn't you tell me that Florian Montes is behind the whole thing? He was the one who fixed you up with Begelman in the first place, wasn't he?"

Laura turned abruptly away and something seemed to settle between them. "Florian Montes is a piece of shit! No two people in the world truly deserve each other more than Montes and Charlotte."

Laura downed her drink and then poured herself another. "It must have been Phillipe who told you. He's the only one who knew. And I thought one's hairdresser was like a priest—sworn to secrecy. Silly me!"

"Never mind that now, Laura. Phillipe also told me that Montes has been supplying you with cocaine and enough other pharmaceuticals to keep you in permanent orbit around the planet. Are you going to tell me the whole story or shall I wait till the sheriff comes to haul you off to some maximum security twilight zone?"

"The idea of spending my golden years in prison simply does not tempt me, in spite of all those bondage movies about sex behind bars."

"In that case I think we'd better talk. I want the truth."

Laura paced the length of the living room, then paused before the sliding glass doors and stared out over the illuminated swimming pool. "You realize, of course, that Montes will have me put to sleep if he ever finds out that I told you. My *beauty* doesn't need that much rest."

"Try to look at it this way. If you're involved in what I suspect you are, you'll have to date your age with Carbon 14 by the time you're eligible for parole. Probably sometime near the turn of the century ... and I don't mean the year 2000. Come back to earth, Laura. This situation is like a roller coaster running out of control and you're in the front seat with no belt."

Laura looked anguished and stricken. "It looks like I'm caught between a rock and a hard place, kiddo. If I tell you what you want to know, I'm going to end up looking like chopped beef in a dumpster somewhere. I'm in this thing right up to my false eyelashes, and I don't see any way out."

"Laura," Brett assured her, expressing concern. "I can help you and I will. Please, *trust* me. This is your only chance. I'll do everything I can to cover your lovely *tush*, but you have to level with me. Otherwise, we're talking charges of conspiracy here, along with murder one and drug dealing on a monumental scale. This situation is ready to blow and I'd hate to see you left holding the bag."

With that, Brett withdrew the tape recorder from her purse, set it on the glass coffee table, and pressed the record button. "Okay now ... I want you to tell me everything you know about the Montes-Begelman connection ... from the beginning."

CHAPTER THIRTY-ONE

For the next four days, the weather matched Brett's mood. After months of balmy sunlit days with only occasional rain showers, the weather turned overcast and humid with a major tropical stormfront glowering upon the horizon. There were streaks of whip-crack lightning. The ominous booming of distant thunder. Then, finally, the worst storm of the season was upon them.

After several days of quixotic wandering to the south, Hurricane Wanda swept up out of the Caribbean to unleash a howling maelstrom all over the coast of Florida. Winds, tides, and torrential rains moved with sudden and frightening speed as the storm blew in over the shallow Bahama shelf to strike Palm Beach.

The waves swept in to explode against the beaches; tides rose to alarming heights, and when the storm finally reached its peak—with winds reaching over ninety miles per hour—great swaths of white sand beaches were torn away in the dark of night.

Hurricane Wanda had begun receding northward and out to sea when Brett received the message she'd been waiting for from Santos. An envelope arrived at Marisol by bonded messenger and contained only a matchbook cover emblazoned with the name *Davey Jones' Locker*. She recognized it as a popular swinging singles disco in Fort Lauderdale. The name *Enrique* was scrawled inside the flap.

Brett glanced down at the softly illumined speedometer and increased her speed to send the Porsche Silver Spyder rocketing down the highway in the dismal rain-wet night. The storm had passed on but the rain still streaked against the windows as the speedometer rose to eighty-five miles per hour and then continued its ascent.

Brett strained to see the highway through the sweeping windshield wipers. She was impatient to reach Fort Lauderdale and refused to let up on the speed even though visibility was greatly reduced.

The season, the intricate conundrum of Julia DuShane's life, and Brett's own agonizing period of indecision was drawing to a close. She was filled with a powerful sense of resolve.

She reached out to press "Play" on the tape recorder resting on the dashboard.

"Okay, kiddo . . ." Laura's voice said. "Here it is. Maurice Begelman is the head of the cocaine connection and Montes is his partner. Montes smuggles the stuff in aboard the twice weekly flights from his beauty spa in Santa Marta, Colombia. The local officials in these parts are not about to run a frisk on the wives of some of America's richest and most powerful men."

"How exactly does it work?" Brett's voice intervened.

"Begelman is the money man and Montes is the supplier. Montes flies the raw cocaine in from Colombia and has it processed in a laboratory set up in his private hangar at the West Palm Beach Airport."

"What happens then?"

"The processed coke is taken to La Caraval and distributed from there. I mean what could be safer? Julia DuShane is lying there at death's door with prayer vigils being held around the clock. Hardly the scene for a DEA drug bust, if you take my drift."

"How is it distributed?"

"The coke is bussed out of Palm Beach by drug runners posing as born-again converts to Jerusha's flock. Begelman launders the cash through banks in the Bahamas and, presto . . . chango . . . you have a half-billion-dollar casino resort complex suddenly going up on Singers Island."

"And what's your part in all this, Laura? How deeply are you actually involved?"

Laura's laughter became slightly sardonic and husky. "Let's put it this way, sweetie, even as we speak, suicide is not a totally unreasonable solution to my problem. Your Aunt Laura was the perfect front from the very beginning. What else do you think I was doing, traipsing around town in a bullet proof limousine with two humongous thugs riding shotgun like something out of Murder Incorporated. I hustled the coke in one direction and the money in the other.

"But I was also the courier between Montes and Begelman. They couldn't afford to be seen together and didn't dare transact business over the telephone. It was too dangerous, so I carried—back and forth between them—tape recorded messages disguised as gossipy comments about who was out partying and where, with all the names and places coded.

"At first I thought I had died and gone to heaven. Maurice was more than generous with stacks of thousand dollar bills, and Florian kept me well supplied with drugs."

"It was all strictly show biz in the beginning. I was the glitzy front for the operation and there were all those little gifties from Cartiers and Van Cleef & Arpels. Maurice never intended to marry me. That was just a smoke screen for popular consumption. With all those little forked tongues whispering away over my antics, nobody paid any attention to what was really going on."

"Tell me about Jerusha? What part did she play in all this?"

"In case you haven't noticed . . . the woman is off somewhere in cloud cuckoo-land. Jerusha actually believes she's going to raise Julia from the brain dead. But that isn't her wildest delusion. Not by a long shot. . . .

"Jerusha is convinced that she has been chosen to lead the Sodom and Gomorrah of beauty, wealth, and privilege down the garden path to spiritual salvation.

"Don't you just love it, dear heart? She has actually come here to save us from ourselves! The woman is bananas. However, I rather doubt that penitential chic will turn out to be all the rage next season. Somehow, I fail to envision the ladies of Palm Beach dressed in mauve nun's habits designed by Valentino, handing out religious tracts door to door."

Laura's voice started to take on a despairing echo. "Brett . . . I'm a victim of outrageous manipulation. This is no longer anything like I thought it would be. I mean playing Mata Hari in Palm Beach drag is one thing. But murder just never occurred to me."

"Oh, shit. You might as well know it all. I listened to one of the tapes that Maurice sent to Montes and it scared the hell out of me. He was the one who ordered the Casa Encantada killings. Montes got a crew of his drug runners to carry it out. They both wanted to get rid of Roberto Castillo and it couldn't have been a better setup with the boat lift going on and all these deranged Cubans swimming ashore to rape, pillage, and stock up on designer jeans. Something went terribly wrong at Casa Encantada. All those other people weren't supposed to die. They just happened to be there . . . innocent victims. It was a ghastly tragedy.

"The whole fucking fiasco has gotten beyond fun and games. I'm in a panic now. I can just imagine what Maurice will do to me when he discovers I sang like a platinum-plated canary. This whole scenario is starting to read like 'My Life' was written by Franz Kafka. You've simply got to help me."

"You always did have a definite flair for self-dramatization, Laura dear. To be sure, it's not a very pretty story but I think there is a way out for you. In fact . . . I'll make a deal with you.

What I want you to do is to continue playing your role in this as if nothing has changed. I think you've given me enough information to slip the noose around Montes's neck, but the timing isn't quite right just yet. Continue playing it to the hilt until the Diamond Tiara Ball tomorrow night. I think there's a way I can get you safely out of this."

Laura's voice, in response, was tremulous with hope. "What exactly do you have in mind that doesn't include feeding the fish? I may be a dumb broad but I'm not naive enough to think that Montes and Begelman would ever let me live to testify in court."

There was a prolonged silence on the tape. Then Brett's voice questioned, "Do you think you could be happy in Brazil with nine million dollars and no extradition treaty?"

Laura gasped audibly. "You have to be kidding! With nine million dollars and my essential bodily parts still intact, I could be happy in Tierra del Fuego."

Brett switched off the tape, smiling grimly to herself. The pieces of the puzzle had finally fallen into place. The sudden flood of superior-quality cocaine was being smuggled into Florida aboard Montes's private jets shuttling back and forth between South America and West Palm Beach. A closely guarded hangar was being maintained that was capable of processing hundreds of kilos of high-grade cocaine.

What safer distribution point could there be than La Caraval, where an aged social icon lingered in limbo with all Palm Beach looking on anticipating her imminent demise. Indeed who would have suspected some of Sister Jerusha's legions of highly disciplined black disciples of being drug runners—let alone killers? The cadre of militant religious fanatics who came and went daily from the estate could easily distribute the drugs beneath the guise of seeking converts to Jerusha's ever-growing flock of dedicated charismatics.

The massacre at Casa Encantada had been ruthlessly ordered to eliminate Robert Castillo from the competition.

Even Montes's proposed marriage into one of Palm Beach's oldest and most respected families had been carefully planned to place him above and beyond suspicion. Charlotte Farrell's unknowing involvement might very well have kept Brett from looking too deeply into the tangled web of deception and intrigue that Florian Montes had so clearly woven.

Laura had been easy prey. As Brett reached the outskirts of Fort Lauderdale, she couldn't help but think that the gods must indeed protect those of good heart who habitually fucked up in spite of themselves. In twenty-four hours, Laura would be on her way to Rio de Janeiro with the past behind her and the future bright with promise.

Everything about Davey Jones' Locker seemed to be garishly exaggerated. Flashing strobe lights ricocheted from the mirrored ball turning slowly above the dance floor, while the atmosphere was one of anonymous sexuality. The spring break had just begun for college students, and the air was close, smoky, and redolent with the smell of burning hashish.

From a tinted plastic bubble high above the shiny Plexiglas dance floor, a twentieth-century Pied Piper steadily increased the volume on the Dolby stereo system.

Brett was not sure what she had been expecting to find at Davey Jones' Locker, but certainly it was not the full-fledged bacchanal so uproariously in progress. Shadowy figures moved together in the dimness of pillowed nooks, and others openly kissed, fondled, and caressed amid a jungle of synthetic plants twinkling with colored lights. No one seemed to mind the heat or the close bodily contact.

The disco's cocktail lounge was a study in behavioral patterns. The most beautiful girls and best looking men sat perfectly composed at the circular tables surrounding the bar. Their bronzed bodies were displayed to languid perfection in the best of the current fad fashions as they watched and courted one another with studied disinterest.

Those who were less physically attractive but still in the running tended to sit or stand alone along the bar. They showed themselves to be less sure, yet still managed to convey the message that they were relatively unimpressed by the proceedings.

The third and largest group of hopefuls making the scene were composed of plain Janes and anxiously awkward males gossiping nervously among themselves and casting expectant glances of quiet desperation. No question about it, Brett thought, everyone seemed out to get laid. The place fairly reeked of sex on the prowl.

Brett managed to find a vacant stool at the bar and was immediately approached by a darkly tanned and bearded, blond bartender. He was impressively built and his body shirt was partially unbuttoned to display a sculpted chest matted with crisply curling hair. He wore a golden chain with a shark's tooth around his neck. He reminded her of an oversized "Ken" doll.

"I'm looking for Enrique," Brett said after ordering a Scotch mist. "I'm supposed to meet him here tonight."

The barman nodded, flashed a smile, and placed her drink on the bar top. "What happenin', journalista?" he asked. "I think you are supposed to have something for me. *I* am Enrique."

The Gucci portfolio containing a diagram of the grounds at La Caraval, instructions for gaining entrance to the library through the French windows opening onto the garden, and the all-important combination to the safe was lying on the bar beside her. Brett placed her hand upon it, took a sip of her drink and asked, "What have you got for me?"

Enrique reached into his shirt pocket and handed her a circular metal claim tag with a small key attached. "There's a briefcase waiting for you in the coatroom," he instructed, nodding toward the entrance of the lounge. "Pick it up on your way out. Your instructions are in the envelope inside."

* * *

The rain had stopped by the time Brett drove away from Davey Jones' Locker after midnight. She headed west along Everglades Road and then turned north on Highland Boulevard. The rain-slicked streets were nearly empty. By the time she reached the downtown section of Boca Raton, she noticed that she was being followed by a dark blue Camaro.

The traffic light was red at the intersection of Royal Palm and Lake Park. She gunned the Porsche with a scream of tortured rubber, skidding left onto the Dixie Highway and continued north at eighty-five miles per hour. Gripping the wheel tightly and glancing back to see the Camaro in the rearview mirror, Brett was soon cutting in and out of traffic and feeling thankful that there were relatively few cars on the road.

She was going much too fast and completely ignored the red lights when the signals went against her. The Camaro was still behind her as she passed through the outskirts of Del Ray Beach. Minutes later she was speeding northward along the Florida Turnpike with the swampy fringes of the Everglades stretching away into total darkness on her left.

Glancing apprehensively into the rearview mirror, she could see the Camaro moving up fast behind her in the outside lane. Within seconds the car had drawn abreast and the figure of a young black was turning to glare at her with a sawed-off shotgun leveled across his driving arm.

Brett suspected that it was one of Montes's *Hombres del Muerto*. She jammed her foot down hard on the accelerator, sending the Porch rocketing ahead just as bullets crashed through the rear window, missing her by no more than inches.

The highway had narrowed into two lanes with a diesel truck barreling toward her from the opposite direction. Brett's hands were moist on the steering wheel as the Camaro began moving up once again. There was only one possible option. Reaching into her bag, she withdrew her father's Colt .45 that had become her constant companion ever since her return from Coco Island.

As the driver of the Camaro started to draw abreast again, Brett was ready for him. Her window was already down. Gripping the wheel with one hand, she fired off three shots, exploding the Camaro's front right tire to send the car skidding directiy into the path of the oncoming truck.

There was a terrible wailing blare of the diesel's air horns, the blinding glare of headlights, and the scream of shredding rubber as the Camaro's driver swerved the wheel sharply to the left. Brett briefly glimpsed the look of blank terror on the man's face as he only narrowly missed the onrushing truck and went crashing through a wooden guard railing before plunging into the swamp.

CHAPTER THIRTY-TWO

ON the night of the Diamond Tiara Ball, the entire breadth and span of Palm Beach luxuriated beneath the aura of moonlit radiance. The moon was pale and immense above the sea, while the long drive leading up to the Breakers Hotel was illuminated by flaming torches and lined with expensive cars.

Upon arriving beneath the porte côchère of the hotel, the masked celebrants mounted the staircase between ranks of handsomely liveried footmen. A parade of rich and famous names with social pedigrees stepped into the brilliant glare of the arc lights where Daphne Shelldrake was holding forth in her television debut.

"*The foremost charity ball of the season is upon us at last,*" Daphne informed her viewers. "*Traditionally, the Diamond Tiara Ball marks the official ending of the Palm Beach season. As you can see, everyone of importance has come out tonight to celebrate themselves and the rarified world in which they live such charmed lives in this defiant stronghold of luxury and glamour.*

"*This is Palm Beach, after all, and the preparations for one of these lavish affairs begins well in advance. For the past two weeks, a veritable army of set designers has been hard at work transforming the grand ballroom of the Breakers Hotel into a fantasy version of the fabled Hall of Mirrors at Versailles.*

"The rich and the elegant are never happier than when they're whooping it up at a posh charity ball. The Diamond Tiara promises to be no exception under the whip of social lioness, Charlotte Farrell, who has taken over the chairmanship from the legendary Julia DuShane.

"Tonight, the principal luminaries of Palm Beach will all be 'en masque' and parading the colors of their own special breed. There will be beautiful people in abundance, although there is no longer any question that the most glamorous couple of the season are Charlotte Farrell, herself, and Dr. Florian Montes with his own special brand of gracious charm. Their engagement was announced only this week and at this very moment they are greeting over a thousand guests moving through the official receiving line like compliant courtiers before a reigning king and queen."

Inside the hotel the mirrored ballroom was decorated in silver and gold with swags of hothouse flowers encircling the fluted marble columns. The guests were all in formal attire and wearing an incredible fantasia of masks. Bejeweled, sequined, painted, feathered, and all marvelously crafted. Glittering iridescent masks. Traceries like ancient Venetian lace. Masks that were plumed like the wings of birds and others painted in a profusion of rainbow hews to approximate exotic animal faces. The overall effect was both unearthly and spectacular.

The grand ballroom took up one entire wing of the hotel and was reached by a dramatic sweep of marble stairs descending from the hotel lobby. At the far end of the ballroom, tall French doors opened out onto a broad terrace overlooking the sea.

Elaborate gowns shimmered and jeweled adornments glittered beneath the hanging crystal chandeliers. The orchestra played for dancing and uniformed white-gloved waiters moved decorously among the guests, bearing silver trays of gourmet delicacies.

Brett was at the right point of inebriation. The champagne she had been putting away had spread to her remotest extremities as she slowly circled the dance floor to pause before the buffet. Briefly, she sampled the braised pheasant with a tiny silver fork. She had scarcely eaten anything all day but had no appetite at all for the elaborate display of culinary marvels displayed between banks of floral arrangements and monumental ice sculptures.

She ultimately selected a secluded nook on the very edge of the dance floor, partially screened by potted palms. Here was a small pool of tranquility where she could quietly sip her champagne with an unobstructed view of the proceedings. She allowed her gaze to travel about the room to where Charlotte and Montes were holding court surrounded by a coteries of fawning admirers.

Imposing, arrogant, and brilliantly malign, Florian was clearly unnerved by Brett's presence. She had seen fear in his glittering black eyes as she had passed through the reception line. Charlotte had remained distantly imperious, dismissing her with an arctic glance. For the moment they reigned supreme.

Brett had already written Florian Montes's epitaph in her final article on Palm Beach. Brad Harraway had given his word that her report would be held in the strictest confidence until twelve midnight tonight. After that, he would present the DEA with an advance copy of Brett's revelations, and the authorities would take it from there.

The music played and the champagne flowed as Brett regarded the spectacle playing itself out before her eyes. She had dressed carefully for the occasion, and the overall effect was simple and to the point. A minimum of makeup, a modest assortment of simple jewelry, and a floor-length black-jet sheath with a black satin eye mask.

Black, she had decided, was the color of endings.

Soon she felt suffocated in the midst of all that well-bred revelry with its vague subtleties and subterranean tempos. What she needed was fresh air. After accepting another glass of champagne from a passing tray, she made her way outside onto the terrace to be alone with her thoughts.

She remembered how she had first returned to Palm Beach feeling disconnected, aimless, and very much alone. She had been haunted by dim perceptions of fatality and undefined dangers. But all that was in the past. No longer was she afraid to face whatever the future might hold. One long journey had ended. And another was about to begin.

It was now clear to Brett that she had seen a vision of the future. Reality had come with the smell of fire and death; with the echo of relentlessly marching feet and the defiant voices of the disposed. All was in jeopardy. On that final evening in Palm Beach, she now knew that Jerusha had spoken the truth.

Brett was destined always to feel herself a stranger. Always seeking . . . always traveling about the world in search of something that could not clearly be defined. Jerusha had also been right in predicting that she must be prepared to risk everything—even death—in her quest for ultimate truth.

Brett knew that she was on dangerous terrain. Taking the next step would alienate her forever from the rich heritage that had nurtured and protected her throughout her life.

From this night onward, Brett would be one with the revolutionaries of the world. Those beyond the rules of *acceptable* behavior, clamoring to be heard with bombs and guns and political assassinations. No longer would she merely be a voyeur—an observer safely documenting the carnage through a camera's lens.

She glanced at her watch and saw that time was slipping away. Simon would be returning from his medical convention in California that evening. He had promised to meet her at the ball sometime before midnight. By then, however, she knew she would have already passed beyond the point of no return.

Anxiously, she scanned the dance floor. Then from somewhere nearby, Brett heard Laura's laughter rising above the convivial mix of music and voices drifting out through the open terrace doors. Brett caught a glimpse of her aunt's restless blond mane and diamond-braceleted arms entwined about the neck of a handsome admirer.

Clearly, Laura was enjoying herself. An extravagant vision in gold lamé, slit to the thigh with plenty of cleavage and a gilded mask. She was dancing as if she hadn't a care in the world, and wearing every jewel she owned.

After a few minutes, Brett was able to catch Laura's eye and tugged briefly at her own right earlobe. It was a prearranged signal between them. Laura winked in response. Her bodyguards were obviously keeping a low profile near the service bar, looking bored and uncomfortable in their ill-fitting tuxedos.

Leaving the ball through the hotel grounds, Brett made her way to where she had parked the Porsche along the outer drive. The arrangements had already been made. At precisely eleven P.M., a helicopter would be waiting near the nineteenth hole of the Palm Beach Golf Course. From there Laura would be whisked away to Miami where she would board an eleven-forty-five flight for South America.

As Brett cruised up before the hotel entrance, Laura came trippingly down the stairs trailing her sable coat and radiantly smiling. Then she was inside the Porsche and they were speeding away from the Breakers Hotel, heading northward on Ocean Boulevard.

Laura drew in a deep breath and sighed with relief. *"Sic

transit gloria," she said. "Get me the fuck out of here before the shit hits the fan."

"That should be shortly after midnight," Brett informed her. "I think you've given me enough on Montes to take him out of circulation forever."

"And what about Begelman?" Laura asked. "He's one bridge I'd like to burn before I come to it."

Brett kept her eyes fixed upon the road, shaking her head in response. "Montes is bound to squeal like a stuck pig. But it's doubtful that the feds can actually pin anything on Begelman. He's been far too careful about keeping in the clear. As of now, there isn't any real proof for them to nail him with."

"I suspected as much," Laura acknowledged. "Quite frankly, the thought of Begelman still on the loose is enough to give me delirium tremens. The man is slime. I want to see him put away for good."

With that, Laura produced a small cassette tape from her bountiful cleavage and handed it to Brett. "This is a message from Begelman to Montes about a drug shipment they have coming in. I was supposed to deliver it tonight but decided to take out a life insurance policy, if you take my drift. I think this tape might go a long way toward putting a lock on the entire Montes-Begelman connection."

Brett laughed. "Whoever said that you were a dumb broad? This is a stroke of pure genius, Laura. Mata Hari strikes again."

"Just get me aboard that helicopter, *toute suite*. This burg has become about as much fun as a barrel of dead monkeys. Rio de Janeiro, here I come! Talk about living out one's wildest fantasies. All those hot-blooded Latinos on the beach at Ipanema and nine million bucks to boot. It's beyond Nirvana!"

Brett could not help smiling as she checked the rearview mirror to make sure that they hadn't been followed. In spite of the tension gripping her, she carefully kept their speed under thirty miles per hour, not daring to chance getting stopped by a prowling patrol car.

"I've never really understood your obsession with cold cash," Brett said seriously. "It's hardly the holy grail, at least in my estimation."

Laura cast her a withering, sidelong glance. "I'll tell you what money is. Money is the ultimate enhancement. If a woman's beautiful, money can raise her attraction to dazzling candle-power. Exquisite grooming . . . glamourous clothes . . . jewels . . . and fabulous surroundings. Money is every woman's birthright. In every fiber of her being, a lot of loot can expand and magnify the excitement of being a woman. It's known as pussy-power, kiddo. The most intoxicating feeling on earth."

"You sound like a cross between the *Wall Street Journal* and Dr. Ruth. What are we talking about—economics or sex?"

"Brett . . . *cher enfant*," Laura chided. "We are most certainly talking *love*. Enough money can give a woman the right to turn her fantasies into reality. No matter where she goes, chic parties, luxurious hotels, the very best clubs . . . even walking along the street . . . or hanging out in sleazy bars, there's always the chance of meeting the man of her dreams. The thrilling adventure of falling in love with love. Fake love, cheap love, or even love by the numbers . . . it doesn't really make any difference. All cats are gray in the dark!"

"Not even if it ends in pain?" Brett asked.

Laura's expression turned somber, her voice suddenly serious in tone. "All of life's most important lessons are learned in pain, kiddo . . . at least then you know that you're alive."

"The way you spend money, you could be broke in six months. What then?"

"Bite your tongue," Laura said, crossing her heart for emphasis. "With nine million dollars, I have every intention of going to my grave without ever again having to hear the word *poverty*."

Brett sat watching Laura's helicopter lift off and clatter away across the night sky with a deep sense of loss. Tough, vulnerable, magnetic, and terminally oversexed, Laura Gentry was an original in a world of carbon copies. Brett felt that her brother, Laddie, would have wanted Laura to have his share of the inheritance. For Brett it was blood money but to Laura it would mean freedom.

She was going to miss Laura.

The Palm Beach electrical power relay station was located just one mile from the Breakers Hotel in a sheltering grove of palmetto palms. It was a small, Spanish-style building of white stucco with a red tile roof. As chain link fences were against the local building ordinance and since the main power station was located across Lake Worth in West Palm Beach, the relay station was unprotected and unmanned.

Brett parked the car some distance away and set the automatic timer on the explosive-rigged briefcase she had picked up at Davey Jones' Locker. Then, the deadly device clasped firmly in hand, she made her way on foot to the power relay station, keeping carefully under cover of the trees and shrubs.

The briefcase was placed in position according to Santos's instructions, and then Brett was speeding back to the ball.

The plan to retrieve Julia's jewels from La Caraval was simple: at that moment, Santos was lying in wait aboard a powerful Riva speedboat, cruising stealthily toward shore.

Brett had provided him with everything he would need to penetrate the estate without detection, recover the jewels from the library safe, and make his escape. The explosion at the power relay station would be the perfect diversion. One that was guaranteed to throw the entire island into chaos.

As she drove along back to the hotel, Brett recalled the day that Julia had shown her the rarest of all her treasures, the Manchu jewel collection. Brett had been awestruck when Julia had opened the safe. They were all perfectly flawless stones and none of them weighed in at less than twenty carats.

Never could Brett have imagined the diversity of diamonds resting within the tray of black velvet. A translucent shimmer of lemon, amber, blue, and pink with others as crystal clear as snowmelt in mountain streams. There were pigeon egg rubies with fiery depths. Emeralds that glowed and blazed like hot green coals and star sapphires of dazzling depth and brilliant clarity.

Julia had estimated their collective worth at somewhere approaching twenty-five million dollars. Santos had already made arrangements for the sale of the jewels in Miami. And even at half their market value, he had assured Brett, the amount was sufficient to launch the assault against Fidel Castro and his ruthless communist regime.

It was nearly midnight. Brett felt as if she were riding the crest of a great wave just before it crashes. Simon held her closely in his arms as they danced. He seemed to sense that something had ended between them. They didn't speak because there just didn't seem to be anything to say.

There was, of course, no possible basis for comparison between the two men who had become the stark polarities of her life. All Brett knew with certainty was that with Simon she had felt loved and deeply cherished, while her relationship with Santos filled her with a sense of dangerous ecstasy. There was an almost mystical attraction between them, an affinity so deep and so powerful that it stirred something wild and fierce and primitive within her, touching the essence of her being.

With her head resting against Simon's shoulder, Brett tried to take some comfort from the knowledge that she had never intended for any of this to happen. She still loved Simon and always would—but, she was being drawn toward Santos with a passionate commitment that was awesome in its intensity. Her choice had already been made.

The orchestra played on as Brett and Simon continued to

move about the floor in each other's arms, surrounded by the masked celebrants, wheeling and turning beneath the crystal chandeliers. They reminded Brett of painted marionettes dancing in a palace of mirrors. Light merged into shadow. Substance into illusion. And reality into fantasy. The mirrors reflected only the surface appearance of things, giving nothing back but fleeting quicksilver images. Eternal visions of youth and beauty replicated to infinity.

At the stroke of midnight Sister Jerusha arrived at the ball. She wore a red gown that accentuated the ivory pallor of her features. She stood poised at the top of the white marble staircase leading down in the ballroom. Her eyes were huge, and her mouth was a startling slash of bright baroque red.

Word of Jerusha's arrival began to flash through the ballroom. Heads turned while bodies twisted and rotated for a better view of the woman whose mysterious presence in Palm Beach that season had come to hold them all in thrall. The dancing stopped and the orchestra fell silent.

Out on the terrace the shadows had gathered into human forms. The moon was pale and hanging low above the sea. The solemn black faces of Jerusha's followers shone in the torchlight. There was something threatening in their sudden appearance. They had materialized like an ominous vanguard, standing sentinel and watching impassively.

As the hush lengthened and deepened, an unseen hand swung one of the powerful spotlights away from the bandstand to the staircase where Jerusha stood. The light was so powerful that it surrounded her with a ghostly brilliance, endowing her features with an exhaulted mystical expression. Everything about her conveyed the impression of burning internal fervor.

Jerusha lifted one hand in supplication. "The hour of atonement is drawing near," she cried out in a full commanding voice that echoed against the walls. "And who of you here tonight is without stain of sin? Beware. Beware the apocalypse!"

In the moment there was an explosion like the sound of distant thunder. The chandeliers swayed above their heads. People cried out in alarm. Then, suddenly, all Palm Beach went black.

CHAPTER THIRTY-THREE

BRETT was the only person in the Mermaid Snack Bar at the Miami International Airport. She was standing at the counter drinking a mug of steaming hot black coffee and smoking a cigarette.

It was five A.M. and the human tide that perpetually ebbed and flowed through airports around the world had slackened to a mere trickle. Simon had offered to drive her down from Palm Beach but Brett had refused. The last thing she wanted was a poignant farewell played out in some cavernously impersonal departure lounge.

Upon checking in earlier for her Aero Cubaña charter flight to Havana, Brett had found a cablegram awaiting her. It was from the Cuban Ministry of Information, notifying her that Fidel Castro had granted her request for a personal interview. The following morning, she would be picked up at her hotel in Havana in order to accompany *El Jefé* to the dedication of a massive new hydroelectric dam project in the Sierra Maestra Mountains.

Castro's dedication of the dam was to be the keynote event of the Cuban Independence Day celebration. Over one hundred journalists were flying to Havana aboard a government-arranged press junket in order to document the twentieth anniversary of the Cuban revolution for the world press.

Brett was only slightly surprised at being singled out to be Castro's personal guest for the occasion. He was known to select important journalists of international reputation whenever he wanted to reveal some dramatic new aspect of his revolutionary dogma or unleash a scathing new barrage of accusations against the United States.

Yet, the fact that she had been chosen to accompany him to the Sierra Maestra on that particular occasion seemed nothing short of ironic to her. She would be interviewing the most vocal and vehemently rabid foe of Western capitalism on her own thirty-fifth birthday anniversary. The very day that she herself was to inherit a large fortune by accident of birth into a world of wealth and privilege.

Brett wondered about Santos's threat to blow Castro halfway to South America. She had thought that he was joking at the time. But what about the underwater demolition team she had seen training on Coco Island? Or Santos's final enigmatic warning about Castro—that she was not to get too close?

It could happen, Brett acknowledged. Yet the possibility of Castro being assassinated in the Sierra Maestra, while potently symbolic, was only that . . . *a possibility.* Nothing was going to stop her now.

Brett had almost finished her coffee when her attention was drawn to the television screen on the far wall where a meticulously groomed talking head had just begun to deliver the morning news.

"This is News Center Four in Miami bringing you the fastest breaking story of the day.

"Following the annual Diamond Tiara Ball last night in Palm Beach, officials of the U.S. Drug Enforcement Agency moved in to arrest one of the resort colony's most prominent citizens. According to a spokesman for the DEA, Dr. Florian Montes is believed to be the mastermind behind the biggest cocaine smuggling operation in Florida history.

"In related events, a search of Dr. Montes's closely guarded private hangar at the West Palm Beach Airport uncovered a drug processing laboratory along with quantities of ether, acetone, and hydrochloric acid. All commonly used in processing cocaine for sale on the street.

"As part of an expanding investigation, a raid of the Cristo Redentor Society during the early morning hours netted suspects in the Casa Encantada killings. A large amount of high-grade cocaine was also discovered on the premises with an estimated street value of ten million dollars.

"Charismatic cult figure Sister Jerusha is presently being held for psychiatric evaluation. Although authorities maintain that she and her congregation of born-again charismatics are believed to have been no more than innocent dupes of the powerful drug mafioso who have turned Palm Beach into the main distribution point for the Columbian drug trade.

"Also arrested in the drug conspiracy case was multi-millionaire financier Maurice Begelman, reputed to have wide-ranging connections with organized crime.

"In another development, authorities are searching for Begelman's beautiful blond mistress who mysteriously disappeared only hours before the arrests.

"Laura Gentry, long known to the tabloids as the 'platinum playgirl,' is one of the most glamorous and highly publicized ornaments of Palm Beach society. Her sudden disappearance has mystified the authorities who are not ruling out the possibility of foul play."

"Foul play, indeed," Brett uttered aloud. She couldn't resist smiling as she gathered her things and left the snack bar. With her camera case slung across one shoulder and her carryall gripped in one hand, she crossed the nearly empty terminal to a nearby newsstand and purchased the early morning edition of the *Miami Herald*.

"DRUG KINGPIN UNMASKED BY PULITZER JOURNALIST." They had given Brett's syndicated story front page coverage. Yet she quickly scanned through the pages looking for another headline that would serve to confirm what she already knew.

Finally, Brett found it on page six. It read: "JULIA DUSHANE DIES AFTER LONG ILLNESS." The story went on to relate that Julia had passed away at the stroke of midnight after the Palm Beach power failure had rendered her mechanical life-support system useless in the attempt to prolong her life.

According to the report, the authorities were still investigating the mysterious explosion that had totally destroyed the Palm Beach power relay station. As yet, they had no suspects.

For several long lingering moments, Brett stood staring as the print blurred and swam before her eyes. Then, blaring out over the loudspeaker system, the last call for her Aero Cubaña charter flight was announced and she was once again in motion. The final chapter of Julia's story had yet to be written.

Brett passed through the security check station without incident and reached the departure lounge just as the last of her colleagues were disappearing through the far door. A light rain had fallen sometime after midnight and, as Brett presented her ticket to the Aero Cubaña purser awaiting her at Gate Twelve, the air was fresh with the dawn. There was a gray luminous streak of light giving birth to the day upon the eastern horizon.

"You're the last to go on board," the purser informed her. "I knew you weren't about to miss the show."

At the sound of his voice, Brett turned to stare into the all too familiar eyes of Raphael de Vargas. Eyes that were the coloration of pale summer seas and infinite distance. A knowing smile flashed across his face, which had been dramatically transformed by the addition of long dark sideburns and a heavy moustache. He inscribed her name on the passenger manifest and removed the initial portion of her airline ticket.

"Will we meet again?"

"I don't know the answer to that," he said softly. "Perhaps . . . with enough luck."

Their fingers touched as Brett took the ticket he placed in her hand. She managed a smile. Then, without another word, she hurried through the departure gate and out onto the glistening tarmac toward the waiting plane.

The world was still in darkness, but for Brett there was only light.

DON'T MISS READING
▲ PaperJacks
OUTSTANDING BESTSELLERS

FREE!!
BOOKS BY MAIL
CATALOGUE

BOOKS BY MAIL will share with you our current bestselling books as well as hard to find specialty titles in areas that will match your interests. You will be updated on what's new in books at no cost to you. Just fill in the coupon below and discover the convenience of having books delivered to your home.

PLEASE ADD $1.00 TO COVER THE COST OF POSTAGE & HANDLING.

- -

BOOKS BY MAIL

320 Steelcase Road E.,
Markham, Ontario L3R 2M1

IN THE U.S. -
210 5th Ave., 7th Floor
New York, N.Y., 10010

Please send Books By Mail catalogue to:

Name _____
(please print)

Address _____

City _____

Prov./State _____ P.C./Zip _____

(BBM1)